ISBN 978-1-330-51922-6
PIBN 10072912

This book is a reproduction of an important historical work. Forgotten Books uses state-of-the-art technology to digitally reconstruct the work, preserving the original format whilst repairing imperfections present in the aged copy. In rare cases, an imperfection in the original, such as a blemish or missing page, may be replicated in our edition. We do, however, repair the vast majority of imperfections successfully; any imperfections that remain are intentionally left to preserve the state of such historical works.

1 MONTH OF
FREE
READING

at

www.ForgottenBooks.com

By purchasing this book you are eligible for one month membership to ForgottenBooks.com, giving you unlimited access to our entire collection of over 700,000 titles via our web site and mobile apps.

To claim your free month visit:

www.forgottenbooks.com/free72912

Similar Books Are Available from
www.forgottenbooks.com

SCENES
AND MEMORIES

BY

WALBURGA LADY PAGET

WITH A PORTRAIT

LONDON
SMITH, ELDER & CO., 15 WATERLOO PLACE
1912

E V.

M

A363665

PREFACE

My dear Children,

The impressions gathered together in this book, though written most of them in this last decade, are all of them taken from very voluminous recollections jotted down at a much earlier period. If one day any of you think it worth while to publish these wider recollections, they will give a true picture of the world as it has appeared to me ; for it has, throughout, been my aim to give an exact representation of my impressions of events, things, and people. That will be their only merit. I must explain, however, that the last chapter of this book, ' The Mysterious City,' which has never been published, is a fantasy written to please a friend long since passed away, by collating records about some very interesting but unknown villas around Florence of which he had taken the photographs. The events I allude to are all true, and most of them I witnessed myself during my frequent and long sojourns in the Mysterious City ; it will, however, be readily understood that names could not be given, though many of them will easily be guessed by those who knew the Florence of that day.

I wish to thank the Editor of the *Nineteenth Century and After* for so courteously allowing articles to be reproduced ; and I should like to add a word of grateful remembrance to his predecessor, Sir James Knowles, a man of singular charm and perspicacity, who accorded me the hospitality of the Review he. founded for thirty years.

I have nothing more to say except that my life has been lived very much in chapters. I gratefully record that in each chapter, in many different countries, I have found true and faithful friends, whose affection has followed me into many climes until the thread became invisible to mortal eyes, though I feel that it is tightly held by those ' gone before to the unknown and silent shore.'

Perhaps this little book, which speaks of more restful days, when charm and romance had not yet been throttled in the turmoil of our present era, may open a small window in the minds of some younger generation to what life held fifty years ago. So little in comparison with to-day, and yet so much more !

Ever, my dear children,
Your loving
MOTHER.

UNLAWATER HOUSE,
October 1912.

CONTENTS

SCENES AND MEMORIES

CHAPTER I

A CHILD'S RECOLLECTIONS

IT may not be uninteresting in these days, when life is such a rush and all that happens is so soon forgotten, to retrace the manners, habits, and customs, half a century ago, of a society and a country which then was, as a whole, hardly in the throes of its birth. The Germany of to-day was at that time only the barely conceived ideal of a few elect minds. The great masses never dreamt of such possibilities. My first recollections go back to the early forties; and though I was a very small child then, they are quite clear, and I am certain that they are not second-hand, as after the death of my parents, which occurred before I was grown up, the whole tenor of my life was changed, and those I lived with knew nothing of these early associations.

I passed the first years of my life in an ancient castle built by Henry the Fowler, Emperor of Germany. It dated back to some time in the ninth century; but I suppose it must have been a strong place even before that, as the Romans called it 'Bicheni,' which the Wends, on whose frontier it was built, changed later on to 'Puechau.'

The Emperor Henry had placed it there to protect the rich bishopric of Wurzen against the incursions of the heathen, whom it was his policy to push more and more eastwards.

The part built by the Emperor, and which still bears his name, is almost untouched, and stands beyond the moat. The castle itself is a great and picturesque irregular pile, romantic and mysterious, with inner court and many terraces on different levels all around it.

It stands on an eminence and looks out far over the land, over great oak-forests, rich pastures, and winding rivers, to a range of blue, once volcanic, hills. Some small towns and many villages with glowing red roofs and shimmering church spires gleam in the distance, and towers built by Romans, Goths, or Markomanns command many of the important places.

We were there in the heart of a very old country, which was the centre of Saxony, before some of its best provinces were lost by its rulers' weak and francophile policy during the Napoleonic wars.

A deep ravine, spanned by a narrow bridge, almost a viaduct, divided the church from the castle, and I used on Sundays to stand with my nurse under the great horse-chestnuts and watch the castle people walk across, two and two ; for there was not room for more abreast. They all carried great black hymn-books and nosegays, and the women were bareheaded.

Up the winding road from the village came the peasants with their families. The married women still wore the richly embroidered caps with flowing ribands and the stiff wide Elizabethan ruff. Flowered silk handkerchiefs were crossed over their breasts, and the large satin aprons trimmed with lace nearly covered the whole of their skirts. The girls often wore little wreaths of artificial flowers.

All of them, men and women, young and old, brought their posies of bright garden flowers mixed with pungent herbs, to keep themselves awake in the drowsy summer heat during the long hours of the sermon.

When first I was admitted to church and seated on a very high-backed leather-covered chair, all my attention was absorbed by the monuments of armoured knights and farthingaled dames below, and the tremendons cheeks of puffing seraphs on the bright blue *cassettone* ceiling above. Whatever there was left, was devoted to an interminable row of hour-glasses which I longed to turn, and which were ranged on a bracket against the whitewashed wall.

Near the church stood the manse, a fine sixteenth century building, grey and severe, with a tall steep roof and low rounded porch with stone seats. A trellised walk led from the church to this porch, and on each side of it there were great tangles of bright flowers, tall hollyhocks and flaming poppies, lilies and roses, with borders of mignonette and stocks.

I remember, as if it were yesterday, seeing for the first time our parson's newly married young wife standing in that garden. She was a lovely English girl, quite voung, of the Book of Beauty type. She wore a pale green dress, rather transparent, and a fine long gold chain round her neck, with glittering rings on her fingers.

The peasants who lived in the village below were all very happy and well off. They had great well-built houses, cool in summer, warm in winter, under their high-tiled roofs, and many maids and serving-men, though they themselves and their sons also laboured in the fields. They had much cattle in their stables, and the wives and daughters and maids looked after that, and cooked and baked and washed. During the long winter evenings the women all sat together in the great warm room, spinning ; whilst the men sang or smoked their pipes, sitting on the bench that ran round the monumental stoves.

Behind their houses were great shady orchards with tarns and clear wells and rippling rivulets into which the sun only shone in the early spring before the leaves had come out. I often gazed down from the castle into these mysterious shadows ; for out of one of the tarns a cry came at times, so strange, so sad and hopeless that my imagination was enthralled by it and filled by vague and wondrous thoughts, for I was told it was the 'Unke' which called there, a creature never seen and which never dies. I believed, like every German child, that if undetected at midnight on St. John's Eve, I could slip out and spread a blue kerchief on the side of the tarn, I should find a little golden crown upon it in the morning.

The castle was, as I have said, very large and rambling, with inner and outer courts and towers, and long passages filled with armour and pictures of my ancestors, which rather frightened me in winter, for houses were neither lit nor warmed in those days, and that is conducive to fear.

There was on one side a wide moat without water, in which fruit-trees grew. It was carpeted with the greenest turf, and the kennels were there.

We were kept, like most children of that time, under strict discipline, and not allowed to roam beyond the sight of nurses or governesses ; and when one day my mother, sitting on a terrace close to a court which led to the kitchen, told my brother, aged nine or ten, to deliver a message to the cook, he said : 'But where is the kitchen ? '

We children had a wing of the castle set apart for us, and no stranger ever penetrated there. We were never allowed to speak German, except on the rare occasions when we were out of hearing of our governesses, of which we always had one English and one French. Only the babies had German nurses. As we got older the staff of pedagogues was increased by my brothers' tutors, and drawing and music masters, and German was allowed at meals. There were always many guests, especially in summer, and nobody thought it extraordinary that some of them should remain for months together. One of them was Mr. Evelyn, an Irishman and a great fisherman. He lived with us for the best part of the year since I can remember, until my father's death.

One day a Prince and Princess Poniatowski arrived for a short visit. She was a very beautiful Irishwoman, *née* Laura Temple. My parents had known them at Dresden, which was at that time full of exiled Poles. They remained six or seven months, because they had no money to travel with. Mr. Evelyn admired his lovely countrywoman, who used to sit beside him when he was fishing, as she had nothing else in the world to do. I sometimes accompanied them, and though only four or five, quite took in the situation and was extremely annoyed, as I disliked Princess Poniatowska for always wearing my mother's clothes; and what exasperated me beyond expression was her using a white *moiré* parasol, with a very long fringe and lined with sunset colour, which had come straight from Paris. In my baby mind I docketed the Princess as what I now know to mean an adventuress.

My mother had a girl friend, a Countess S——, who, married to a Russian diplomat at Berlin, did not know how to dispose of her summer, so she came with a number of children and Russian servants and settled at Puechau for six months, till my little brother spoke more Russian than German.

The shootings in those days before the Revolution of 1848 were very extensive, for they were not broken up, as now, by the peasant properties. The peasants owned the land, but had not the right to shoot over it. My father, like nearly all Germans of his class, was a devoted sportsman, and in autumn and winter we saw very little of him, as he used to go off alone or with a friend for several weeks together to some of his other places to shoot.

I remember seeing him start for these expeditions in what was called a *Pirsch-Droschke*—a carriage which, I suppose, exists no more. It was very light, made to go over the worst roads. Always painted and lined with green, it had a narrow seat which joined the back seat to the box. Astride on this seat one could comfortably take rights and lefts without stopping the carriage. On the box beside the coachman, in green, sat the *Leibjäger*, liveried in the same colour. These men, who exist in every great German or Austrian house, are not the usual keepers who live in cottages in or near the woods. They live in their master's house and attend to his personal wants, accompanying him wherever he goes. They are often in a confidential position, having enjoyed a good education and knowing everything about forestry, which in Germany is a recognised career. As they grow older they are generally provided with a good situation as head keeper at one of their master's places.

My mother also moved about a good deal. Brought up amongst the mountains of Silesia, she longed for the hills when the great heats of summer came. There were hardly any railways in Germany then, and we travelled in a huge *Berline*, to which (I heard my mother's maid say) there were twenty-nine boxes attached. They each of them had their separate place into which they fitted. On the best of roads this enormous machine required four horses to pull it, and in hilly countries we always had six. There was room for six inside, but I never remember going more than four, for we often posted all night, and my brother and I regularly went to bed, whilst my mother and Miss Page, the nursery governess, sat on the other seat. The maid and footman sat in the dickey. We travelled all over Germany in this way, and to Belgium, Holland, and even to Poland.

My father went every summer, as most people in society did in those days, to Carlsbad or Marienbad, and sometimes we accompanied him. These places were at that time very select, and the resort of crowned heads, ministers, and diplomatists, and all that was best in European society. Everybody knew who everybody else was, and all consorted together on a footing of dignified intimacy unknown to our days. French was the language which was generally spoken, and all wrote it fluently and correctly. Good manners, ease, and gaiety were the prevailing features.

Thus it happened that, even as a small child, I was quite familiar with the great names of England, France, Russia, and Austria, as I heard them continually mentioned in conversation, and knew many of their bearers by sight as friends of my parents.

Diplomats, in those days, could not go home every year as they do now, and many of them visited us in the summer and autumn. The Court of Dresden was then a much-coveted post, and Puechau was in easy reach, as the first railway that was built in Germany went from Dresden to Leipzig, and passed within five miles of us.

I remember especially the Marquis d'Éragues, Louis Philippe's envoy. A sympathetic interest was attached to his pretty wife, who had been the heroine of a tragic *cause célèbre* in which she had shown a courage and devotion which might have ruined her whole life. She used to wear long Book of Beauty ringlets, and her two little daughters were my bosom friends. Then there was Mr. Forbes, who remained as H.B.M.'s Minister at Dresden for nearly forty years. He used to come accompanied by his two sisters. The elder, Lady Adelaide, a fat and jolly red-faced old lady, had been Byron's Ianthe when his years ' nearly doubled ' hers. No trace was left of Ianthe ; but to my childish imagination the admiration of the great poet surrounded her for ever with a halo of beauty.

We were at a very early age initiated to the classic literature of England and France, and knew it better than the German, because this—Schiller excepted—was too abstruse, and Goethe was not allowed. There were only few children's books then, except fairy tales ; and illustrated papers, the ruin of the children of to-day, did not exist. Before I was seven, I fell rapaciously on *Télémaque,* and repeated pages of Racine and Corneille by heart. A little later on Walter Scott and Dickens, Cooper, Mrs. Beecher Stowe, which were all in easy reach as they were published by Tauchnitz at Leipzig, excited my deepest interest; and before I was fifteen I had read all the English classics, nor was that exceptional, as all the girls who were fond of reading did the same.

Things are quite changed now that the national feeling is so strong. German children do not speak French and English with the fluency and ease so common in former days, nor are they so much at home in the literature of foreign countries. They are also less cosmopolitan and polished than we were, though they may know more in other special lines, and will probably develop into much cleverer men and women than we have become.

Ancient history, especially that of Greece, always so attractive to the German mind, we knew thoroughly, and the wars of the Greeks and Trojans appeared to us as occurrences of yesterday. We were thus enabled to understand and enter into the spirit of the *Iliad* and the *Odyssey,* and to see their heroes as living characters.

Young as we were, the politics of the day, which my father frequently discussed before us, aroused our lively interest. My father sat in the first or hereditary chamber, and was an eloquent speaker with a profound and intuitive insight into coming events. He predicted in speeches still remembered—and at the time of Germany's greatest disruption, feebleness, and humiliation—its gradual development, its coming power, and glorious future.

He was a Conservative with liberal ideas, and also deeply interested in social questions, and used among other things often to refer to the Malthusian theories which made such a stir in Europe. He little thought that there was a small mite of seven listening with all her ears, and whose hair actually stood on end at the idea that the world was becoming so over-populated that there would soon be no room to lie down, and everybody would have to stand up.

The decay of the Church in Germany also pre-occupied my father much. He had been a good deal in England, and was persuaded that the reason why the religious question there was so alive and actual, was because the clergy were mainly gentlemen, highly educated, who were socially on a par with the best in the land, and thus were able to influence all the classes. I often heard him say that if another son were born to him he should go into the Church. This would have been an unheard-of thing in Germany, and showed how much he had this question at heart.

The German clergy were, however, as a rule, well educated as far as science and learning went. In all great houses the tutors of the boys, before they went to public schools, were *Candidaten*—young men who had been ordained and were waiting for livings.

My father, who had between twenty and thirty livings in his gift, often assembled the most learned of his clergymen around him, and the conversation was frequently carried on in Latin, which they as well as my father spoke quite fluently. My father also resorted to Latin when speaking to his friends of things I was not to understand, quite forgetting that the smattering I had acquired in the Latin lessons I shared with my brother enabled me to gather the sense of all that he said.

I think people never remember sufficiently how much small children really do understand and notice. Few remember now the famous *procès* of the Duc de Praslin, who murdered his wife a year or two before the Revolution of 1848. The account of it was published in a French pamphlet, which my mother read out to her sister whilst she was painting. I was sitting on the floor cutting out pictures. I did not lose a single word ; I was deeply interested, and remember most of the details to this day.

The aunt just referred to was my mother's eldest sister, an old maid full of character and with a good deal of cleverness. She remembered all about the Napoleonic wars, and inspired me with a fine hatred of the ' Corsican brigand.' My mother's father was one of the men best hated by Napoleon, because he had held the only Prussian fortress which never surrendered. I remember on great occasions a set of fine damask tablecloths being used, with an inscription woven into them from ' The grateful citizens of Colberg ' for having preserved their town from the invader. It was he also who later on planned the junction of the Prussians with Wellington at Waterloo, and who, not only as a soldier but as a politician, had always opposed the French influence which had for 200 years crippled German development, and which, during the first years of the nineteenth century, exercised so baneful an influence over the weak and vacillating king, and through him on the fortunes of Prussia.

I did not wonder that nearly all the conversation was carried on in French in deference to our many foreign guests, and also I vaguely realised that it was *la langue diplomatique*, which had to be kept up at any cost ; but when the village people, especially the old men and women, interlarded their remarks with French words, it roused my indignation. They had been young during the French occupation, and the two places we lived at most were on the very edge of the great battle-fields around Leipzig. Many of the villagers had seen Napoleon and his generals : the Emperor had passed through the place and dined at the castle, Marshal Ney had slept for six weeks in my room, and Marmont was quartered close by. I knew that the country had suffered inexpressibly during those wars, though I did not then realise that the reason why the trees of all the avenues were so small was because they had been cut down, and the houses were so bare because they had all been plundered and robbed.

My paternal grandfather owned large tracts of the country around Leipzig and many houses in the town, and my father remembered, when he was quite small, Napoleon visiting his young and pretty mother, who had fled into the town and was the great lady there. He said the Emperor wore a black coat with frogs, and was not unamiable, for at that moment, just after the battle of Jena, the Saxons were his allies. My grandfather, however, was a patriot and loathed this unnatural alliance; and before the battle of Leipzig he retired to his country place, ordering his agent, whom he left in town, to make a *feu de joie* in case of success of a copse of very fine old oaks which grew upon a knoll and could be seen for many miles over the flat country. However, when the battle was won, the agent thought it a pity to set fire to the old oaks, and there they stand to this day.

Before my days of lessons began I used to accompany my parents to some of their other places, and delightful pictures of them still float in my mind. I remember especially a big sort of palace where there were many functions. It stood on the margin of a lake, on marshy ground. The rooms were large and bare, with stuccoed ceilings; but what endeared it particularly to me was that my English nurse on Sunday morning took me into the kitchen, a place I had never seen, and taught me to make a plum pudding.

Then we went to a great castle high up in the mountains. It was situated on the watershed between Saxony and Bohemia, and a small town clustered round its giant walls. It had been partially abandoned, but the arched ceilings and great halls beautifully carved with rich ornament excited my mother's admiration, and she wished to restore it as an ideal summer residence, for it was in the midst of immense fir-woods and 2500 feet above the sea. We visited various other places; but the one I loved best was not far from Dresden, beyond the valley of Tharand. My mother took us children there sometimes for a few days in May. It was a little whitewashed castle, with round towers and pointed red-brick roofs. It stood on the side of a valley overhung by lovely woods. All around it was a carpet of the greenest finest grass, intersected with small rivulets bubbling over silvery sand and enamelled with buttercups, daisies, forget-me-nots, primroses, and violets in such luxuriance as I have never seen since.

In the autumn we nearly always moved to a place not far distant from Puechau, but where the shooting was particularly good. The house had been built by a favourite of Augustus the Strong, Elector of Saxony, and later King of Poland. The Elector eventually beheaded the favourite, who is supposed to walk about with his head under his arm. The house, which was only inhabited for a few weeks every year, had big halls and staircases, and was hung with many pictures of the royal Saxon family. It was very cold, for the walls were not six or seven feet thick as at Puechau, and I trembled with fear and cold if after dark I had to go to a distant part. The country around was flat, with a river winding through meadows, and dark fir-woods which stretched as far as one could see gave it a melancholy beauty. Here my father's woods marched with Crown property, all forest, which extends to a distance of more than forty miles. This is what is called the 'Wittenberger Heide,' and it takes two days to ride through it. Only one little inn stands in the middle of the forest; besides that, there are no other habitations of any sort.

As the year '48 approached, and signs of unrest began among the people, we moved about less, and Puechau, which in itself was a strong place, was further fortified with iron doors and shutters, for hordes of rabble led by agitators roamed about the country, burning and sacking the houses of the aristocracy. Not far from us Prince Schoenburg's fine place was burnt to the ground and several others. My father had the peasants drilled so as to be able to defend the village, and our walks were limited to the gardens, for the country was overrun by vagabonds.

My parents were much beloved by all around them,

yet there were many acts of petty spite, and the thing which hurt my father most was the maiming of the splendid white stag and hinds (red deer, and very rare) which the King had given him. I used often from my tower window to watch, in the summer evenings, a herd of deer swimming through the lake below : the stately white stag with his two hinds, always a little apart from the others, shimmered golden in the setting sun.

We used every other year to spend the winter in Dresden. When we returned there after the Revolution, we found all our cots riddled with bullets, for in front of our house there had been a barricade and the hottest fighting, as the ' *Turnerhaus*,' a students' club, was just opposite. My father, who had returned to Dresden when the fighting began, said the dead lay in piles of six and seven before our door. Our house was a fine old one, with a large garden at the back, which joined on to the ' Promenade ' that extends to the far-famed Bruehlsche Terrasse, the rendezvous of the best society. We were taken there daily by our governesses, and walked two and two very smartly dressed, like well brought up children. One day, when I was only four or five, my father said he would take me out. I was somewhat frightened at the unwonted honour, and just before reaching the Bruehlsche Terrasse, at a place where there were some arches in the wall, he stopped, and pointing to a tall lady who, accompanied by a gentleman, was coming towards us, said : ' Let us hide and surprise mamma.' The lady wore a lilac bonnet and dress with a green cloak—a costume I had often seen my mother in.

We squeezed back into the arch, and at the moment the lady came up we rushed out upon her—I with a shrill scream of delight. What, however, was my dismay when, clinging to the lady's knees, I looked up into the face of a stranger, and I saw my father, hat in hand, making profound bows and uttering a string of excuses. The lady laughed and kissed me and picked up my glove, which in my fright I had dropped on the snow, and put it on for me. Both the gentlemen and lady seemed to be much amused. My father told me afterwards that they were the King and Queen.

My father was on a very good and intimate footing with the King, and when the troublous times came he supported him with moral influence and material help. He was therefore deeply disappointed when the King weakly fled from Dresden, leaving it a prey to disorder and dissension. From this time my father inclined more and more to Prussia, where he also had large estates, for he saw in Prussia's ascendancy the only chance of saving Germany.

I often went to Court in my infantine days, for Prince John, the King's brother, had a number of children.

There were six princesses, but a melancholy destiny seemed to brood over their fates. They were all good-looking, and some of them beautiful. The eldest, born an idiot, died as a girl of typhus. The second and only surviving daughter is the Duchess of Genoa, the mother of Queen Margaret of Italy. I remember her, a tall, fair, distinguished-looking girl, on the eve of her marriage bending over a sofa on which were seated her mother, the Princess John of Saxony, together with her twin sister, Elisabeth, Queen of Prussia, and kissing their hands. Then came Sidonie, very handsome and an angel of goodness ; she refused the Emperor Napoleon the Third, as her aunt, another Sidonie, whom I remember as a little crippled old lady, refused Napoleon the First. She also died of typhoid. Anne, the fourth and loveliest, with a throat like a swan, passed a year or two of sad married life in Tuscany, and died, it is said, of neglect after her child was born. Her mother-in-law, the reigning Grand Duchess, did not care for her. After her came Margaret, my friend. We were of the same age and devoted to each other. She married quite young the Archduke Charles Louis, and a few months afterwards she died of typhoid at Monza, whilst on a visit to her brother-in-law, the unfortunate Archduke Maximilian, who at that time was Viceroy of Lombardy. Sophia, the youngest daughter, also succumbed to typhoid, as well as her young sister-in-law, an Infanta of Portugal.

Dresden was a merry place for children, and we had many balls, at which we acquitted ourselves well, for most of us had been taught dancing by the great Taglioni. She was then a little old lady, in a shortish black silk dress with a white fichu, very thin and wizen' and with extremely neat and agile feet. A child's ball then was not a disorderly or aimless affair. We were under strict discipline the whole time, and knew exactly what to do. I was terrified one day at committing the unpardonable breach of etiquette of having given the same dance to two boys. They were much older than myself, and I nearly fainted with fright when they intimated that they would go and fight it out at once. It had, however, no more tragic consequence than a bleeding nose.

Talking of Taglioni puts me in mind of the great interest everybody, children included, took in great dancers. The ballets were then poems or fairy tales expressed by dance and pantomime. They had a definite story with a hero and heroine, and grace and beauty was what was sought, not effect. Lucile Graan danced for one winter at Dresden, and we children were enthusiastic at the spirituality (I can find no other word) of her interpretation, and amongst our elders she was a constant topic of conversation.

My father always had a team of golden chestnut mares, which were called by the names of celebrated dancers. Cerrito, Taglioni, Fanny Elssler, Carlotta Grisi, and so on.

Odd as it may seem, our French nursery governess was an intimate friend of Térèse Elssler, the sister of the famous Fanny, the friend of Frederic von Gentz, and the greatest dancer of her day. Térèse had been a dancer also, but highly respectable. I can now see her and Susette Blanc eating cakes together and drinking coffee, Térèse in a grey silk dress and a neat white cap with frills all around her face.

Passionately fond as I always was of fresh air and the open country, the long dark winters of Central Germany were a penance to me, shut up in a town where an hour's walk, if the weather was propitious, was all we got. My pleasantest recollections are of our walks in early spring through the fields, to the Grosse Garten, a royal palace about two miles from the town. During these walks the air appeared to me nectar, soft and balmy. Underfoot the anemones and primroses peeped out of the mossy grass. Overhead I saw the pinkish buds of shrubs and trees, and all around I felt the subtle intoxicating scent of the moist earth awakening to the warmth of returning spring. My French governess kept on chattering about Paris clothes and Paris theatres, but I was with the lovely women and stately cavaliers who had sat in the outdoor theatres cut out of hornbeam, in which we were standing, listening to a French play, or going through the mazes of a minuet in yonder attractive and rather frivolous-looking palace erected by the magnificent but incorrect Augustus the Strong.

Dresden was always full of foreigners, especially Poles, who were attracted to it by former ties. Many of the great Polish ladies were very beautiful, and they all wore their country's mourning—a black dress with a wide white band at the edge of the skirt. When quite small I was taught to say *tous les Ski sont des braves et toutes les Ska sont des belles*, and I religiously believed it.

Dresden was famous for its shops, especially china, linen, jewellery, and laces. The King and Queen, the Princesses, and any foreign potentates who might be there, spent a good deal of time shopping, just like any other mortals, and I remember, when accompanying my mother, frequently meeting some of them there.

Dresden was not a healthy place in those days : it was badly drained, like all German towns, or not drained at all. My mother had, however, very advanced ideas of hygiene, and put us under the care of Dr. Wolff, the most eminent homœopath of that day and the favourite pupil of Hahnemann. Dr. Wolff was not only a great physician, but a charming man and a great philosopher. He paid my mother frequent visits in the country, and encouraged her to bring us up under what we should now call the Kneipp system. We ran about without shoes or stockings in the grass, we wore a minimum of clothes ; in summer we were plunged into the river, a wide and rushing mountain stream ; in winter we had to break the ice in our tubs, and our nurses dashed basins of icy water over our backs. I can still feel the thin bits of ice mixed with the water slithering down over me. A fire in our bedrooms was never thought of, and the schoolroom was never more than nine degrees Réaumur (fifty-two Fahrenheit).

I was fourteen or fifteen before I knew what it was

to have something to drink at breakfast, as I did not like milk. Bread, with a little butter, was all I ever had. An egg for a child, if it was not ill, was considered quite absurd. Between meals we were given abundance of fruit—even during the years the cholera devastated Germany this allowance was not curtailed. We seemed all to do very well on this *régime*; but I wonder what a child of the present day would think of it !

When we were at Puechau it was usually the village barber, Berthold, who attended to any of our little ills. This man, from seeing people being born and dying continually, had acquired the most wonderful insight, and, aided by natural intuition, he rarely made a mistake. He cured generally with what are called old women's remedies. He belonged to a race now almost extinct, for too much science kills instinct, and curing is an art and not a science, so Professor Schwenninger, Prince Bismarck's famous doctor and friend, assured us only the other day in his profound and witty book ' The Physician.' It was not the fashion in those days for people who had large houses of their own to pay visits, but once in two years we were taken to see our cousins, a pleasure which was looked forward to for many weeks before, for excepting these two or three days we never had a holiday all the year round except Sundays, and Christmas, and Easter Day.

Before my lessons began I was sometimes taken to the great Easter Fair at Leipzig. It lasted, I believe, three weeks, and was world famous : the great mart of exchange for all countries. We used to start in the dark, for it was a twenty-mile drive, and got for breakfast to my grandmother who had a house at Leipzig. The whole picturesque old town was filled with booths, and the narrow thoroughfares seethed with a motley crowd shimmering in every colour of the rainbow. There were Russians and Poles with their furs, Turks with carpets, Armenians, Chinese, Arabs, Japanese, Negroes, Italians, and Greeks, all in their national costumes. The booths were piled with foreign wares ; panoramas, tight-rope dancers, merry-go-rounds, and musicians took up every other available space.

There were circuses for the children in the daytime and theatres for the grown-up people at night, and celebrated actors and even stars like Rachel and Dejaset came from Paris. People flocked into town from country houses to hear them, for the generation of that day still had the French tradition.

Christmas is, however, for every German child the pinnacle of the year. It is not only a time full of the intensest expectation and excitement, but it is very holy and mystical. The *Kristkindchen* sheds its halo over every child. If on Christmas Eve you look through the curtainless windows of the poorest labourer's cottage, you will see a little Christmas-tree lit up and adorned for the children.

For weeks beforehand my mother, our governesses, and any lady guests there might be, were employed in mysterious work shut up in jealously closed rooms. We children passed the long winter evenings in gilding apples and nuts, and cutting out ornaments in many-tinted papers for the Christmas-tree. Everything was made at home, and therefore more precious. My mother, who was the moving spirit in all these preparations, observed absolute silence ; but she went to town for two or three days and returned with a carriage piled with parcels. It was, I believe, on one of these expeditions that the coachman, as it got dark, lost his way in the snow. My mother, perceiving a signpost at some little distance, sent the footman to read the directions. This man, very stalwart and rather illiterate, did not succeed in doing so, and uprooting the signpost carried it to the carriage door for my mother to read.

The village people and the servants had their trees before we had ours, and everybody received a present adapted to their wants and their wishes ; not the least of them was forgotten. The guests, too, had each a remembrance, pretty or useful as the case might be. I remember one year when my mother's ingenuity was particularly taxed to find the right things, as the Prussian army had been mobilised, and we, being at one of my father's Prussian places, had for five or six weeks over thirty officers quartered in the house. The great ball-room was made into a wood of fir-trees with one very large one in the middle. They were all covered with glittering fruit and coloured devices, and lit with hundreds of wax tapers. This was the last Christmas in one of our beloved homes, so soon and so sadly to be broken up.

As I look back it seems to me that life in those days was so simple, so ample, so dignified. There was breathing time and space, and people grasped events ; whilst now they seem to slip through their fingers and their thoughts. There were no telegrams, no telephones, no electricity, no bicycles or motors—such things had never been thought of ; and when an old woman in the village prophesied just before her death that carriages would run on the roads without horses, and people fly along on a wheel as fast as trains went (in those days), everybody said she was mad.

I hear people now talking of communicating with Mars. Are they so very mad as we think ?

My only excuse for recalling these childish, and I fear too personal, memories is that they refer to a time already so far distant that very few remember it, and a younger generation may be amused and astonished that once there were those who lived with so little excitement and yet were quite happy and contented.

CHAPTER II

IT was soon after the death of the Emperor Nicholas the First, on the 2nd of March 1855, that I first went to live at Berlin.

The Court, the Army, and a great section of Prussian society were still under the impression of this event, rendered more tragic by the belief that the great White Czar's end had been hastened by the Russian reverses in the Crimea—reverses which had broken his heart.

The Emperor Nicholas had married a Prussian Princess, the beautiful daughter of the beautiful and unhappy Queen Louise. She was the sister of the King (Frederick William the Fourth), and the brother she resembled most was the chivalrous Prince of Prussia.

This Prince, who later became the Emperor William the First, and his Consort, a Princess of Saxe-Weimar and own niece to the Czar, were very liberal-minded. They alone sympathised with what were called in

27

those days the 'Western Powers,' and I remember Lady Bloomfield, whose husband was at that time British Minister at Berlin, telling me that hardly anybody would speak to them at that time except the Prince and Princess of Prussia.

As this Royal couple were not popular in Berlin, they only rarely inhabited their palace 'Unter den Linden.' The Prince moved about a good deal, and the Princess divided her time between Coblentz, where she was much beloved, and Baden-Baden, where she assembled around her a literary, artistic, and cosmopolitan society.

The King and Queen lived much at their favourite palace of Sans-Souci, near Potsdam. Built by Frederick the Great in a most ornate Louis the Fifteenth style, it was with its terraces, fountains, and avenues of noble trees an ideal summer residence. During the coldest winter months their Majesties inhabited the ancient and stately Schloss at Berlin, which was, and many say still is, haunted by the white lady, an ancestress of the Hohenzollerns.

King Frederick William the Fourth had been a very charming and witty man, but his brilliant intellect was then already beginning to wane under the influence of the long and insidious malady to which he eventually succumbed.

The fears of those who surrounded the King were hardly whispered ; but I remember that one day, when I had gone to an exhibition of modern pictures with my governess, he approached me, making some remarks about the paintings; but his tongue did not obey his will, and I was quite unable to understand what he meant.

In contrast to the King's sedate and somewhat severe *entourage*, his second brother, Prince Charles, held a brilliant Court. Married to the handsome elder sister of the Princess of Prussia, who was fond of splendour and amusements, they both took care to surround themselves with men whó were dandies and sportsmen and ladies who were pretty, lively, and fashionable. The Princess was an inveterate theatre-goer, and accomplished the wonderful feat of seeing during one winter the then famous ballet, 'Flick and Flock,' 123 times consecutively.

A fourth brother of the King, Prince Albrecht, also lived at Berlin; he was separated from his wife, a Princess of the Netherlands, and besides him there were only two or three unmarried Princes, distant cousins of the Sovereign, who led retired lives in their palaces, devoting themselves to art or science. Berlin at that time was a very small and simple town compared with its present splendour and expansion. Now it is perhaps the best-cared-for capital in the world; then, it had open gutters which were often very unsavoury. Few great families had houses of their own, and still fewer ever opened them.

Two Princes Radziwill inhabited a dignified palace, *entre cour et jardin*, in the Wilhelmsstrasse, one of the most aristocratic streets. Over the door was written up ' Hôtel de Radziwill.' The family was Polish, but the mother of the two brothers had been a Princess of Prussia and sister of the chivalrous Prince Ferdinand, and therefore related to the Royal Family.

They had married two sisters, daughters of Prince Clary, a Bohemian noble, and they each lived in a wing of the Palace, filling it with innumerable children. Their *train de maison* was patriarchal and simple, and they received only in a quiet and unobtrusive way.

Amongst the really Prussian families the Arnims were perhaps the most typical. They had a fine house, in which they lived in a kind of ascetic state. Tall, fair, stiff, aristocratic-looking, and caustic, they were a little difficult of approach, but upright and honourable in the extreme ; they were excellent when one knew them well.

Not being a Prussian myself, and living with my guardian, who was a diplomat, and also being too young to be out, I never saw but one Prussian *salon* from the inside, and that was a very remarkable one. The mistress of it was the still very beautiful Countess Lottum. She was well past fifty in those days, but I think I never saw such extraordinary outward refinement. She attached the greatest importance to dress, and succeeded in turning herself out in the most finished and attractive way. Her apartment was as perfect as herself, in the Parisian Louis the Fifteenth taste, and at a time when the average house was decked out, to its mistress's entire satisfaction, in mahogany and blue Utrecht velvet with a gum-tree in the corner, that meant a good deal of initiative.

Only a very few ladies and all the most brilliant men frequented Countess Lottum's *salon*. She never asked girls ; and the reason why I was taken there was because her lovely niece Wanda, who married a little later on Prince Putbus, her cousin, was my only and very intimate friend.

My guardian, who was also my uncle, being my father's youngest brother, was married to a lady who held at that time one of the greatest positions at Berlin, and though I was still in the schoolroom I was allowed to sit behind the tea-table (after dinner) when my aunt received every evening in what was called the *avant soirée* from nine o'clock till eleven.

The whole of the Diplomatic Corps, distinguished foreigners, and many of the gentlemen and ladies attached to the different Courts used to drop in, and I cannot remember an evening when somebody did not come. In spring the ladies often appeared in smart bonnets after a drive in the Thiergarten, for the latest dinner-hour was half-past six.

My aunt was a beautiful needlewoman, and whoever came she never quitted her embroidery-frame. I, too, had my work, to which I was supposed to attend if nobody spoke to me. Mlle. de W——, a former lady-in-waiting of my aunt, who lived on in her house, dispensed the tea.

My aunt when she married my uncle was the widow of one of the last Prince Electors of Germany. Her husband, who was old, had surrounded his young and pretty wife with great splendour and luxury. She had great taste in dress and in arranging her house, and had many beautiful and costly things about her. She kept up a semi-royal state and habits and knew the whole of the cosmopolitan world of that day.

It was a wonder that, though my aunt never made any calls, except on the very greatest personages, and rarely appeared anywhere except at Court, her *salon* should have been so popular and sought after, but she had created for herself quite an exceptional position.

Though there were in those days no Ambassadors at Berlin, the diplomats formed the chief feature of society. The foreign Ministers were expected to receive a great deal, and they gave many balls and dinners. Many of them were still comparatively young men and glad to amuse themselves. Just opposite to us was the French Legation, filled at that time by the Marquis de Moustier. He had a great position, chiefly owing to the anxiety his master inspired. I shall never forget the agitation and excitement of the Court and society during a short visit of Prince Napoleon (Plon-Plon) to Berlin. He lived at the Legation, and I saw him out of my window, driving up and down the *perron* of the house, fat, dark, and scowling. It was amusing to hear of the trouble everybody was taking to be sufficiently civil, without dropping too much of their conscience and dignity.

To the French Legation belonged a lady, the Marquise de Malaret, one of the Empress Eugénie's ladies. She was even in Paris a *grande élégante*, and besides she was clever, witty, and a thorough woman of the world. Some years later King Victor Emmanuel saw her, and was so pleased with her conversation that he insisted upon her husband being named as Minister to Turin. I had only been a few days at Berlin when my aunt sent for me one morning to present me to this lady. She was for those days very tall and had a Calmuck face. She talked loud and incessantly, but was natural and amusing. She wore the lately invented monster, a very large crinoline, and over it was stretched an extremely tight black silk skirt.

One had to be very beautiful indeed to hold one's own dressed in the ugly fashions of those days. They might perhaps have been made a little more palatable by clever Parisian dressmakers, but on the ordinary person they were truly ghastly. There is a curious tendency amongst young painters of the present day to revive the crinoline in their pictures, as something poetic and mysterious, but in reality, and in everyday life, it was a very ugly thing.

The Russian Legation, which played a great part, was housed in the fine palace 'Unter den Linden.' It belonged to the Russian Government, and was in reality an hotel for Russian Grand Dukes, who were always passing forwards and backwards through Berlin.

Baron Budberg, the Russian Minister, was a clever but somewhat sarcastic man. Some of the ladies belonging to the Legation were very beautiful, like Countess Shouvalow and Baroness Mohrenheim; but the one who had the greatest position and whom I frequently saw at my aunt's receptions was Countess Adlerberg, the wife of the Military Attaché. Though no more young she was still very handsome and extremely witty. I heard her say one evening of a lady's dress, who was proud of her feet and shoulders and showed them a little too much: ' Cela commence trop tard et cela finit trop tôt.' She was much *choyée* by the Prussian Court, for she was supposed to be a daughter of a sister of Queen Louise; and though this relationship was not officially recognised, it was tacitly admitted— indeed, the likeness between Countess Adlerberg and some of the Prussian Princes could leave but little doubt. The thing which interested me most in this lady was that she had been first married to M. de Kruedener, the son of the famous Madame de Kruedener, whose psychic and occult powers and great influence on the Emperor Alexander the First made her name so celebrated at the beginning of the last century.

The Comte de Launay, who was for thirty years at first Sardinian and then Italian Minister at Berlin, was married to a lady much older than himself; but she had a most beautiful and gifted daughter by her first marriage, Mlle. de Seigneux, who was immensely admired. To me she appeared, with her Grecian profile, long waved golden hair, and enchanting ways, a very ' Lorelei.'

It was during those evenings in my aunt's drawing-room that I made some lifelong friendships, now alas ! ended, at least for this world. One of the fastest and most uninterrupted ones was that with Count Kalnoky, later on Austrian Ambassador in Rome and Petersburg, and for a long time Minister for Foreign Affairs at Vienna. Another was Count Ferdinand Trauttmanns-dorff, who after a short and brilliant diplomatic career became Great Chamberlain to the Emperor of Austria. He was even in those early days a most magnificent and dignified personage, whose rather pompous ways were tempered by the kindest heart.

Some of the young princes, such as Prince William of Baden, who were quartered at Berlin or Potsdam, also frequently came to pass an hour before a ball or gay supper party; but as my uncle was ' Westmächtlich gesinnt ' (a sympathiser with the Western Powers), it was natural that he and my aunt should have seen but little of the purely Prussian society.

I had when first I arrived been much struck with the very military aspect of the city. Whether one drove ' Unter den Linden ' or rode in the Thiergarten, there were uniforms everywhere. Half the population seemed to consist of tall, flat-backed, square-shouldered officers, with light-blue eyes and sweeping blonde moustaches. They wore the large-topped cap affected by the Russian Army, and their big sabres clanked by their sides.

In the spring the Thiergarten, though far less well kept than it is now, was a great resource, and the *beau monde* used to drive there after dinner. At the beginning of June, however, the great heat drove everybody into the country. Our summers were generally spent at my uncle's place in Saxony, and the early autumns at Pisely, in Bohemia, which belonged to my aunt.

I don't think I cared much for the latter place, as, on account of the wildness of the surroundings, my usual walks, which were my only pleasure, were much circumscribed.

Knauthayn, my uncle's place in Saxony, had more charms for me than Bohemia. The country, though flat, was all meadow, river, and oak woods. The house, which had been built for a bet by a M. de Dieskau in the seventeenth century, had I don't know how many stories, and looked like the beginning of a tower of Babel, the object of the builder having been to make it as high as possible.

Unfortunately my uncle had in his bachelor days filled up the moat, which detracted from the originality of the design ; but the house had in spite of that a good deal of style, and was pretty and comfortable inside, with open fireplaces, large windows, beautiful parquet floors, fine pictures, and many articles of *vertu*.

My aunt and I spent nearly all our day at our embroidery-frames, and in the evening I read out some historical novel to her, whilst she still went on working. It was a lonely life, for my uncle, who did not like the country till the shooting began, generally lingered on at Berlin till he went to his yearly cure at some watering-place. My only amusement was driving a four-in-hand of little Polish piebald ponies when I was sent to Leipzig, our nearest town, with Mlle. de W—— to do some commissions.

We had on our way there to pass a wood where there had been a sharp encounter during the Napoleonic wars, and at the corner of this wood and close to the road a French officer had been buried under a great oak-tree. Every year, on the anniversary of the Battle of Leipzig, a wreath of flowers was laid upon the grave by an unknown lady dressed in deep mourning, but nobody knew who she was. At the time I am speaking of more than forty years had gone by, but on the 18th of October the flowers were always fresh on the grave.

This reminds me of another historical link of some interest. We sometimes used to visit my father's second brother at his place Dölkau, which was about ten miles distant from us. The road lay right across the battlefields of Leipzig and of Lützen, where Gustavus Adolphus, King of Sweden, fell pierced by a shot in his back. Nothing but flat cornfields stretched along on both sides of the road. At sunset these great plains look almost like the sea, with mirages of little red-roofed villages floating in the heated air. About half-way we drove through the little old-world town of Altranstädt, which belongs to our family, and where Charles the Twelfth of Sweden lived for two years previous to signing the peace which bears the name of this town, and by which he ended his German campaigns. An old groom of my grandfather, who was a native of Altranstädt, told my father and my uncles that he had often seen the King of Sweden walking over the market-place there.

As the peace was signed in 1707 it takes one a good way back. At Dölkau the chair was still preserved on which Charles the Twelfth sat when he signed the treaty. The house, which had been built by my grandfather in a good Empire style, was situated on a lake amongst great oak woods. It contained many interesting heirlooms ; but the thing which fascinated me most was a picture of Catharine the Second seated on a sofa and drinking tea with her sister, a Princess of Anhalt Zerbst, whilst her husband, Duke Peter of Holstein Gotthorb, leaned over the back of the sofa in a coat of silver cloth, with a red ribbon across his breast.

The figures were about one-third of life-size, and the faces showed by their varied expressions that careful attention had been paid to likeness. The Empress

Catharine, debonair and smiling, in a dress of pale-blue satin, with an immense pannier, took no notice whatever of her husband, who appeared somewhat embarrassed and rather scowling. To the Empress's left sat her sister in rose pink, a slight and sentimental-looking lady. She was the grandmother of my aunt Ida, my uncle's wife, and it was through her the picture came to Dölkau.

My parents, and quite especially my mother, had been on terms of great friendship with the Court of Weimar. The Grand Duchess Sophy after my mother's death transferred her affection to me, and I was in constant correspondence with her, and was therefore allowed to go and spend part of the summer with her at a lovely place in the Thuringian Forest, called Wilhelmsthal.

The Grand Duchess was the daughter of the King of the Netherlands, and she was one of the best, noblest, and cleverest women I ever knew. She was plain as far as features go, but she had so much grace and distinction that one hardly remembered it when speaking to her.

The Grand Duke was the son of the eldest daughter of the Emperor Paul of Russia. He was kind, benevolent, and chivalrous, devoted to art and literature ; he gave encouragement and active help to those artists who needed it. He was tall and slight, very upright and distinguished-looking, and his oddities of manner and rather eccentric way of expressing himself were extremely amusing and added to the pleasure of intercourse with him.

The hills which embosom the valley in which Wilhelmsthal lies are not very high, but have soft swelling outlines, and the whole country is most idyllic in character. The four or five white houses connected by colonnades which form this summer pleasance of the Dukes of Saxony stand half hidden by flowering shrubs and trees on the margin of a lake. Everything was simple and fresh there.

After breakfast the Grand Duke and Duchess used to go for a walk with their children, and I always accompanied them. The Grand Duke, who had travelled a great deal, was often interesting and always amusing, as he had made a point of knowing all the celebrated and clever people who came within his reach. As for the Grand Duchess, she was the spring of wise and good sayings, which seemed to flow without effort or hardly any thought from her lips.

We dined in the middle of the day and went for a drive afterwards, generally accompanied by the Grand Duke, or one of the gentlemen who was staying on a visit. We supped in a charming room, half library and half conservatory, and afterwards we had music.

Liszt, not yet an abbé and perfectly delightful in conversation, would, though he certainly remained a fortnight, never touch the piano. Instead of this he used to read out to the Grand Duchess when I sat with her in her room by the hour, galloping on at a most frantic pace. It was generally out of Sainte-Beuve's *Causeries du Lundi* that he selected passages. These hours in the Grand Duchess's 'boudoir à nous trois' enchanted me, for she and Liszt discussed the questions mooted by the readings, and they both of them spoke exquisite French. Liszt always wore lemon-coloured kid gloves, a frock coat and top hat; and one day when we had got out of the carriage and were walking on the brink of a precipice, I spied a rare flower growing on the rocks half-way down. No sooner had the exclamation of delight passed my lips, than to my horror I saw frock coat and top hat clambering nimbly down a place which was like the side of a quarry and victoriously flourish the little flower in the lemon-coloured hands. I thought of the odium which would attach to me had anything happened to this great genius, who was then at the culminating point of his celebrity. Gustav Freytag, already famous as the best modern German novelist, was one of the visitors, as well as Hans Andersen. The latter used to amuse us by his funny German and his boundless vanity. He was very tall and badly put together ; his body appeared to be a succession of knots and ropes, and he had never physically grown out of the 'ugly green duckling,' but he was full of geniality, and the slightest incident furnished him with food for a story. M. de Schwindt, the painter of the charming cycle 'Die schöne Melusine,' was frequently present, as he was employed upon the frescoes at the Wartburg which the Grand Duke was restoring.

We also had the historian M. de Reumont, who used to enliven us with his wit and knowledge. In appearance he was like the missing link, only in those days it had never been heard of.

The Grand Duchess had the most splendid jewels of almost any German Princess. She was always beautifully dressed, and on great occasions she used to dispose the stones herself on the dress and remain there whilst the dressers sewed them on, so that they should not have any responsibility if any of them were lost. On one of our walks she told me the curious story of her mother's pearls, which had been those of Marie Antoinette. The Queen of Holland kept all her magnificent jewels in a glass case in her bedroom—as is, I believe, the habit in Russia—for she was one of the Emperor Paul's daughters. One fine morning they were all gone, and the search for them was vain ; but it was generally believed that somebody very nearly related to her had taken them to pay debts. They were never traced, excepting the pearls, which many years afterwards were found hidden in a walking-stick in America, where they had evidently been all the time, for they had become quite brown and encrusted with a kind of growth. The Grand Duchess herself cleaned them and wore them continually, until they became quite white again.

The Grand Duchess was a very practical woman, and she told me that when her husband had first succeeded, the different palaces were entirely wanting in common necessaries, though the walls were covered with the most costly silks and velvets, so she and the Grand Duke for many years, on birthdays and at Christmas, presented each other with dozens of beds and other furniture. The Grand Duke was immensely interested in the restoration of the Wartburg, where his ancestress St. Elisabeth had lived, and he sometimes took me to pass some hours there, knowing how much I cared for all medieval art. I spent two very happy months at Wilhelmsthal.

Nearly all Germans and Austrians go in the course of the summer to some water cure ; my uncle and aunt were no exception, and I accompanied them to Kissingen on one of these occasions. After drinking the waters, and the early morning walk, there is nothing to be done except to amuse oneself, for every kind of exertion is forbidden, and the whole day is spent in social intercourse. We lived entirely with the Austrian set, and I was happy with my dear friends, the four tall and handsome daughters of a tall and beautiful mother, Princess Liechtenstein. Besides the Liechtensteins, there was Prince Schwarzenberg, the husband of the famous Princess Lory. He was beloved by all for his kindliness and intelligence. Countess Clothilde Clam Gallas, later on the Lady Jersey of Vienna, a slight and graceful woman, was chaperoning her sister, Countess Aline Dietrichstein, who married a year or two later Count Alexander Mensdorff, a clever, charming, and pleasant man related to Queen Victoria. There were many others whom in the course of those quiet humdrum weeks one learnt to know far better than one might have done in many years of town life.

From Kissingen we went to Baden-Baden, and there we lived mainly with the Russian colony. There was a ladies' club there which was a terrible trial to me. All the rank and fashion congregated in it. Madame Kalergis, with her wonderful flax-coloured hair, which nearly swept the floor when she let it down, and her cousin, Madame de Seebach, *née* Nesselrode, were great supporters of this establishment. Princess Lise Troubetskoi and Countess Lili Nesselrode, who used to walk *en négligé* with immense rows of pearls in the Lichtenthaler Allée, were also constant frequenters, besides charming Princess Hélène Biron and many others. All the fastest men were invited ; everybody talked a ' jargon de salon ' which at that time was fashionable, but which I only half understood. I was the only girl there, and happy to be allowed to dispense the tea, which was at least an occupation.

It was at Baden that I first saw the Prince of Prussia, an event which changed the whole tenor of my life, for he made my aunt promise that I should be one of the ladies of his future daughter-in-law, the Princess Royal, though, she being so young, the marriage was to take place only a year or two later.

I was sometimes allowed to pay short visits to my

brother and sister-in-law, and it was during one of these that I first met Prince and Princess Metternich, who were great friends of theirs. Prince Richard Metternich was at that time Minister at Dresden, and extremely popular there. Princess Pauline was not yet then, what she called herself a few years later at Paris, ' le singe à la mode,' but she had all the necessary qualities to become the fashion. Her face was plain, but her figure perfect. She had lively black velvety eyes and dark curly hair. Her rather thick lips in a colourless face gave her a very southern look. She was wonderfully quick and witty. The Prince was a good musician and played with taste and art, and we used to give him some theme which he had to express in music, and which the Princess had to guess. She never failed to do this, however difficult it might have been. One day she said she wanted to shoot something. We wandered out, my brother taking his gun. It was after dinner, and the Princess wore a much beflounced white Organdi dress edged with lilac. Her bare shoulders were covered by a Brussels lace fichu. She had many strings of large pearls around her neck. We were skirting the lake in the deer-park, when a wild duck got up at a considerable distance. She seized the gun and shot it stone dead. It was the first time I had ever seen a woman shoot, for at that time it was not yet the fashion.

Princess Metternich was the daughter of the eccentric Count Szandor, well known for his mad daring and wild feats in horsemanship. She had always a circle of admirers around her, but never in her long life in the great world has a breath of suspicion tarnished the shining mirror of her reputation.

One evening, late in the autumn of 1857, my aunt sent for me and told me she had just received a letter from Prince Frederick William, saying he was going to be married in January and recalling to her mind the promise made to his father, the Prince of Prussia, a year or two ago.

I was at first a little taken aback at this sudden change in my life, but though I was very young, and had never been out, I longed for independence; and the idea of being attached to a young and charming Princess, and especially an English one, attracted me very much.

I was to go under the care of Countess Perponcher, the future Princess Frederick William's Mistress of the Robes, to England, and assist at the marriage; and the weeks that elapsed before starting were so filled with preparations for this event that I don't think I ever did anything but try on various garments. My aunt, who was quite in her element, sat surrounded by rich stuffs, laces, flowers, and feathers, ordering about the French and German artists who had been convened, like a general on a battlefield.

I had before leaving for England to be presented to the King and Queen, who lived very quietly at Charlottenburg. The King's illness, which was softening of the brain, had made much progress, and he never appeared in public. Owing to the stringent laws about the reception of diplomates in Berlin, dating from the time of Frederick the Great, when one of them had committed some indiscretion, my aunt was not invited, and I had to drive to Charlottenburg all by myself.

It was in the evening about eight o'clock, after dinner, for the Court still dined at four o'clock. I felt rather nervous, but the King and Queen were both most kind and gracious ; and being the granddaughter of one of Prussia's most illustrious soldiers and patriots, it made up for my not being a Prussian by birth.

At last the day of my departure arrived, and having taken leave of my relatives the previous evening, I started in the morning at a very early hour in icy cold and pouring rain. It was quite dark still, and my heart was sore, but my imagination full of delightful pictures.

At the station I met the rest of the Princess Royal's household. The journey from Berlin to London was not as easy in 1858 as it is now. At Cologne, where we arrived in the middle of the night, we had to walk in torrential rain and a furious gale to a small open boat, in which, amongst huge floes of ice, we crossed the Rhine. The following night we crossed over from Calais to Dover in a frantic gale in one of the small cockleshells which carried the mail in those days. The day after, we got to London in the early afternoon , but there was a black fog and it was pitch dark, and all the fireplaces smoked at Fenton's Hotel, which was then one of the best. The rooms were small and unspeakably dingy ; neither doors nor windows shut properly. Accustomed to the large, spacious, well lit and warmed rooms in Germany, these arrangements might well have depressed me ; but I was determined to think everything perfect, as young ladies did then when they had just escaped from the schoolroom.

I shall never forget the impression Windsor Castle made upon me when, after a day or two's rest, we went on there. It was a clear and frosty afternoon, and the splendid pile rose like a fairy palace out of the plain, bathed in the soft light of a January full moon.

We had hardly arrived at the Castle when the Queen sent for us. We were ushered into a very small boudoir furnished in light greys and blues. The Queen stood there with Prince Albert by her side and the Princess Royal a little behind them. I was at once struck by the commanding look in the Queen's eyes ; they were very clear, blue and full, and when she spoke they became kind and gentle. Her ladies, as I noticed later on, stood in awe of these eyes, which saw everything.

Prince Albert, tall, calm, and good-looking, was exactly like the pictures Winterhalter painted of him at that date.

The Princess Royal, only just seventeen, was in

appearance almost a child. Her radiant eyes and
bewitching smile won every heart at once. She
was naturally a little shy when the Queen motioned
her to come forward and speak to us, but she
did it with great composure and gentleness. The
Prince Consort looked at her with pride and affection,
for her bright intellect and quick grasp of things had
responded brilliantly to the care he had bestowed on
the development of his gifted child.

At dinner I sat next to Lord Palmerston, of whom
I had heard from my infancy as the disturber of
European peace, and he amused himself by trying to
disturb mine, asking me a number of puzzling and
embarrassing questions. As, however, he appeared
to me to be very much advanced in years, and I had
been taught to respect old age, I bore them with
equanimity and answered as politely as I could. As
soon as the foreign Royalties began to arrive, the Court
removed to Buckingham Palace, and State dinners,
balls, concerts, and operas succeeded each other.
King Leopold, with the Duke and Duchess of Brabant
and the Count of Flanders, was one of the first to come.
He was benign, discreet, and dignified, and glided
about distributing advice in soft low tones and peculiar
inflections of voice. His daughter-in-law, the Duchess
of Brabant, was an Austrian Arch-duchess, with a
beautiful figure and brilliant complexion. The Prince
and Princess of Prussia were radiant at the realisation
of their long-cherished project, as also was Duke

Ernest of Coburg, bluff and enthusiastic, talking loud, and gesticulating much, quite different from his brother, Prince Albert. Besides these there were many other minor Royalties. A day or two before the wedding, Prince Frederick William arrived. He had for three years been in love with his young and charming fiancée, and it would perhaps be more correct to say that he adored her, for he respected her character and admired her cleverness.

The Prince was then not the splendid apparition he became ten years later. He was slender and only wore a slight moustache; but his kind blue eyes and charming address made him popular wherever he went.

The Prince was accompanied by a brilliant suite, amongst which was General Moltke, at that time quite unknown to the greater public. He was a most silent and taciturn man; and not knowing what mighty thoughts were working in that weighty brain, I teased and chaffed him constantly on the journey home to Germany. The experience I suppose was so new to him that we became fast friends.

The parting of the Princess from her beloved parents, from her brothers and sisters, and the adored land of her birth, was most affecting, indeed painful, for there was a passion in all her feelings which often made her suffer much.

The journey to Berlin was full of incident. At Brussels, where we arrived only just in time for a late dinner, it was found that much of the luggage had been left behind. I philosophically retired to bed, but was roused by my maid after midnight to say the boxes had come, and the Princess expected me in the ball-room. In ten minutes I had joined her and was dancing a quadrille with the Duke of Brabant.

We started again the next morning, and there were receptions all along the road. This compelled us to wear very smart light-coloured *moiré* dresses without any cloaks over them. At Hanover a great Court banquet awaited us. The reception was very splendid, but the long table groaned under the famous golden dinner-service which for so many years had, with other heirlooms, been the object of a great lawsuit between Queen Victoria and the King of Hanover, and which the English Crown lawyers gave in his favour. The Princess recognised it at once, and was much hurt; but she was there, as through the whole journey, gentle, charming, and affable : not for one moment relaxing her endeavour to make the best impression. There was in her appearance a childlike dignity and goodness which was most captivating. That night we stopped at Magdeburg, and our quarters looked so uninviting that Lady Churchill, who accompanied the Princess to Berlin, and I sat up all night in chairs, as we could not face our beds.

In the beautiful Cathedral the next morning the crowd was so anxious to catch a glimpse of the Princess that her clothes, a dress of tartan velvet, were torn off her back.

Some time before arriving at Potsdam, old Field-Marshal Wrangel, the most daredevil and original of Prussian generals, got into the train to compliment the Royal couple. After having done this he sat down plump into the middle of a succulent apple tart, which had been presented to the Princess at Wittenberg, a town renowned for this delicacy, and which the Princess of Prussia had put away on a seat. The tart clung to its position tenaciously whilst the Princesses, shrieking with laughter, tried with pocket-handkerchiefs and napkins to disengage the old hero from its sweet embrace.

It was General Wrangel who, when the rebels during the Revolution of 1848 threatened to hang his wife if he forced an entrance into Berlin, philosophically remarked, as he was leisurely riding down ' Unter den Linden ' : ' Ob sie ihr wohl gehängt haben ? ' (I wonder whether they have hanged her ?). This speech was all the funnier for the atrocious dialect in which he always spoke.

At Potsdam all the Prussian Princes and Princesses were assembled to receive their new relative, and the next morning we moved to a small palace called Bellevue, close to Berlin, where we changed our dresses for the State entrance into the capital.

It was a bitter cold though bright January day, and the Princess and all her ladies had to wear low dresses and keep the windows of the golden coaches down. Such a thing as a boa or a fur cape was quite unknown; but though the drive at a foot's pace took nearly two hours, nobody even got a cold.

That night there was the *Fackeltanz* in the Weisser Saal. It consists of a Polonaise danced by the bride and bridegroom, preceded by pages carrying torches, with all the Princes and Princesses present in succession. For a whole month festivities followed each other; but then Berlin relapsed into its former quiet, for the King's illness increased every day, and it was not deemed right that the town should amuse itself.

I was, however, very happy. I loved the Princess, and it is rather a pleasant thing to be eighteen and have good spirits; to be quite independent, go alone wherever one likes, receive whomsoever one wishes to see, have a carriage and riding-horses, and a box at all the Royal theatres, and nobody in the world to interfere with one.

That winter we lived in the Old Schloss, which had not been inhabited for a long time. It was badly heated and hardly lit. Endless dark corridors connected huge mysterious-looking rooms, hung with large pictures of long-forgotten Royal personages; the wind whistled down through the large chimneys, and the unspoken terror of the ' Weisse Dame ' brooded over all.

The Princess did not like being left alone in the vast apartments, and the Prince, who had been exonerated from his military duties for a time, hardly ever left her during these early days; but there was one thing she could not bear, that was his habit of taking every evening an hour's walk by himself in the streets. I often heard her imploring him not to go ; but much as he gave way in everything else, he never would make that sacrifice to her.

In the spring the Prince and Princess made a tour amongst some of the smaller German Courts. It was a wonderful experience, for it meant seeing life as it was a hundred years ago with all its restrictions and discomforts. The rooms were generally large and sufficiently warmed, but the beds were wonderful to behold and fearful to sleep or rather to lie awake in, for huge feather beds insisted upon either suffocating one or tumbling upon the floor. Baths there were none, but the exiguous washing-stand was garnished with slop-basins of precious china and ruby glass picked out with gold. Carpets and writing-tables were ignored, and so were bells, and shutters to the windows. The Princess, who was accustomed to English comforts, was much astonished, though from temperament she had very simple habits. The life she really loved, and which she began to lead very soon after her marriage, was getting up very early and going to bed almost by daylight. At Berlin she and the Prince generally lunched and dined alone, and they also drove out together without any attendance. When the Prince resumed his military duties it happened that sometimes for several weeks he had to be away all day long. On those occasions I breakfasted with the Princess at 8.30

o'clock, and never left her all day long. I often read out the whole morning whilst she was painting. She had great talent and much imagination, and had been very well taught.

The first summer was passed at Babelsberg—a modern castle in a picturesque situation on the river Havel, not far from Potsdam. It was a pretty but most inconvenient place. It was there that the Queen and Prince Consort came to pay a fortnight's visit to their daughter. How it became possible to make room for them in the castle seemed a miracle. All the ladies and gentlemen of both Courts were lodged in the palace at Potsdam ; only Lady Macdonald and I remained in attendance on our Royal mistresses at Babelsberg, where we lived in a tiny cottage on the roadside quite alone with our maids. It was a ten minutes' walk to the castle, and we had to go there for all our meals in all weathers.

It was a very gay fortnight. Most of the ladies and gentlemen used to take long rides through the lovely parks or row about on the river, and every evening there were large dinner-parties, to which all the Prussian Princes and Princesses, the Ministers and high dignitaries, the British Legation, and many distinguished foreigners were bidden.

Lord Bloomfield was at that time British Minister at Berlin. He was a charming man, urbane and courteous, and quite a diplomat of the old school. He was naturally somewhat punctilious about outward forms, and was very much distressed that Lord Malmesbury, who, in his capacity of Foreign Minister, had accompanied the Queen, would come to dinner in an alpaca tail-coat which he insisted upon wearing on account of the heat. Also one of his secretaries appeared on those occasions with a billycock hat, which he, being an enthusiastic fisherman, had liberally ornamented with flies. Lord Malmesbury was passionately fond of deerstalking, and begged the Queen's permission to precede her by a day or two so as to get a little sooner to his place in the Highlands. Her Majesty was much amused to hear that, finding the bridge of boats at Cologne opening to let a steamer pass, Lord Malmesbury, with both of his secretaries, leaving their servants and luggage behind, had all three vaulted over the ever-widening chasm and caught the train for Calais.

On the Princess's birthday, the 2nd of November, we went to live in the Palace, which became her permanent abode, and there, in the following January, the Emperor William was born.

For some hours the Princess's life was in great danger, and I never saw anything more touching than the Princess of Prussia's happiness when all was safely over. This lady, generally so dignified, actually danced with joy and embraced everybody she met.

The Empress Augusta, as she became later, has often been very much misunderstood. Her manners were perhaps a little stiff and affected ; but that she was a very clever woman nobody contested, however many thought that she had little heart and was not sincere.   Those who knew her well, knew that this was not the case, and that her nature was a very noble one. I had many opportunities of seeing her, as she often sent for me to accompany her in her long walks, and sometimes even in her journeys.   In those days there were no special saloons, and we travelled in ordinary carriages, badly lit and often very cold.   The Princess said : ' You must not strain your young eyes, dear child ; I will read out to you ' ; and, seating herself on the arm of the seat and holding up the paper to the wretched oil lamp to get a better light, she would read out to me for hours.

It was on such a journey to Weimar, where the Princess of Prussia frequently went to visit her mother, the venerable Grand Duchess Marie, eldest daughter of the Emperor Paul, that I first made the acquaintance of the good and charming Princess Stéphanie of Hohenzollern, who was then engaged to Dom Pedro of Portugal, and whose gentle life was to be cut off so suddenly and mysteriously the following year.   The Princess of Prussia was very fond of the lovely young girl, and had her constantly to stay with her.   There was something angelic in the childlike contour and expression of her face.   She had been brought up in Spartan simplicity, nevertheless she made a beautiful young Queen when she stood arrayed in Royal robes and covered with splendid jewels sent by her future husband, in the Hedwigskirche at Berlin, where she was married by proxy to him. Her death, so soon followed by that of the young and gifted King and his two brothers, was a tragedy which saddened the hearts of all who knew them.

The Princess Royal had wished to live in the Neue Palais, and it was now made over entirely to the young Royal couple as their abode when they did not live at Berlin. It was a magnificent edifice erected by Frederick the Great to show his enemies that his wars had not exhausted his exchequer. To further annoy ' les trois cotillons,' as he called Catharine the Second, Maria Theresa, and Madame de Pompadour, he put their dancing figures on the top of the cupola. Conceive the feelings of the two Empresses at seeing themselves in such company !

Long shady avenues stretched out from the Palace in every direction. The Princess and I used to walk there in the moonlit summer evenings when everybody had gone to bed, and lie in wait behind a hedge or a tree to try and frighten the Prince, who still would continue his nocturnal perambulations.

Early that summer the danger of war became imminent, and the Prince told me one day that on the next it was to be officially declared that Prussia would join Austria against France and Italy. On that day there was a great military dinner at the Neue Palais. The only ladies present were the Princess and her ladies.

The generals all knew what the next morning was to bring, and the great though suppressed enthusiasm was shown by the emotion on every face. A telegram was suddenly brought to the Regent, who stood up and said : ' Gentlemen, a peace has been signed at Villafranca between the Emperor of Austria and the Emperor of the French.' These words were received in dead silence.

It is difficult to imagine in these days the fear and distrust the name of Louis Napoleon inspired in Germany then. There were many still alive who remembered the ravages of the French, under the first Napoleon, and the thought that more terrible times might be in store for the Fatherland lay like a stone on the heart of every good German, for none but mediocrities had for many years guided the fortunes of the State, and the country had not yet awakened to its power.

Even the common people talked of nothing but Louis Napoleon, and I remember hearing an old washer-woman as she was wringing out the linen saying to her crony : ' Oh, if only something human would happen to him ! ' This was a curiously significative expression, as wishing for his death, and yet attributing something supernatural to him.

During this summer the Empress Dowager of Russia, the widow of the Emperor Nicholas, came to live at the Neue Palais for several weeks. A vast apartment had been prepared for her, as she came with an enormous suite. There were four maids of honour, who were dressed in black cashmere on work-days, and in French grey on birth- and feast-days. These young ladies had each of them several maids, who all slept on the floor, as did nearly all the other servants. There was a tradition that after these Imperial visits all the rooms had to be gutted and entirely renewed.

The Empress Dowager was the sister of the Regent (later Emperor William the First), and had been very beautiful. She still looked most distinguished and dignified. She was extraordinarily thin, but tall and erect, with deep-set eyes and very delicate straight features not unlike her mother, Queen Louise. She generally wore a plain black dress and a black lace scarf over her head, and loose light-brown Swedish leather gloves on her long narrow hands. On birth-days, however, she appeared in white, as splendid an apparition as a woman of her advanced age could be. Folds of costly lace enveloped her head and descended low down upon the rich white silk of her dress. Large pearls were fastened in her hair, and priceless pearl drops hung in her ears. Ropes of pearls encircled her neck, her arms, her waist. The only bit of colour was the pale-brown Swedish gloves, without which no well-bred woman of that day would have thought herself dressed. White was very little worn then, and never by old ladies ; the Empress's appearance was therefore most surprisingly fascinating to the unaccustomed eye.

When we returned to Berlin the Princess continued

to live her quiet, retired, and yet so well-filled life. Her mornings were passed in painting and attending to her correspondence, for she wrote almost daily to her parents. Just before luncheon she took a short drive with the Prince, and another in the afternoon. She seldom went to the theatre or opera, and always retired very early. Though almost a child still in years, she was even then a very remarkable character. She had great decision and a wonderful grasp of the situation, also a great power of adaptation. Her disposition was a very affectionate one, and has perhaps in later years been misused by those in whom she reposed too much confidence. She loved England and everything English with a fervour which at times roused contradiction in her Prussian surroundings. I was, perhaps, the only one who entirely sympathised in her patriotic feelings, but I was too young and inexperienced to reflect that it would be unwise to give them too much scope.

It was a great sorrow to me when I had to part from a Princess to whom I was so deeply attached, and I always remembered the two years I spent in her constant vicinity and intimacy as some of the happiest in my life.

CHAPTER III

THE EMPRESS FREDERICK IN YOUTH

THE day I first set eyes on the Princess Royal was late in December 1857. It was after tea in a small boudoir at Windsor Castle. The Princess was standing between the Queen and the Prince Consort, and as I advanced to kiss her hand I felt the flower-like touch of her fresh face on my cheek and saw her bright eyes smile into mine.

Though barely out of the schoolroom myself, the Princess appeared to me extraordinarily young. All the childish roundness still clung to her and made her look shorter than she really was. She was dressed in a fashion long disused on the Continent, in a plum-coloured silk dress fastened at the back. Her hair was drawn off her forehead. Her eyes were what struck me most ; the iris was green, like the sea on a sunny day, and the white had a peculiar shimmer which gave them the fascination that, together with a smile showing her small and beautiful teeth, bewitched those who approached her. The nose was unusually small and turned up slightly, and the complexion was decidedly ruddy, perhaps too much so for one so young, but it gave the idea of perfect health and strength. The fault of the face lay in the squareness of the lower features, and there was even then a look of determination about the chin ; but the very gentle and almost timid manner prevented one realising this at first. The voice was very delightful, never going up to high tones, but lending a peculiar charm to the slightly foreign accent with which the Princess spoke, both English and German.

Though all who knew the Princess at that epoch recognised the promise of some of the great and remarkable qualities which went to form the character of the Empress Frederick, nobody could foresee the circumstances and tragic events which shaped them in a peculiar mould. During those last weeks before her marriage the Princess appeared to cling with passion to all her family, especially to her father, whom she worshipped and admired with all her soul. She was highly cultured, and she felt she owed this to his incessant care of her. He, on his part, was proud of this lavishly endowed child and always said that it was of her and Don Pedro of Portugal, his cousin, that he had the highest expectations and felt himself best understood. Don Pedro died in the flower of his youth, and the Prince scarcely lived to see the development of his beloved daughter.

The Princess had a great feeling for fun and innocent humour, and was full of stories about her brothers and sisters. She adored the baby Princess Beatrice, who was only a few months old, and when fondling her the motherly instinct came out strongly. She was in fits of laughter about Prince Affy, who, having discovered that one of the gentlemen of the Court wore false calves, planted pins with flags into his silk stockings, and also much amused at Prince Leopold, who, aged four, always picked out the prettiest ladies and insisted upon helping them to do their hair.

It was not entirely a spirit of contradiction which, later on, made her depreciate her German surroundings, for even before she left England I never saw anybody so entirely attached to her home and her belongings and consciously appreciating them—a thing very rare in one so young. From the moment, however, that Prince Frederick William arrived, a few days before the marriage, his presence seemed to fill the whole picture out for her.

Anybody who ever approached Prince Frederick William knows how great his kindness, charm, and geniality were ; but he was undeveloped for his age, and, though ten years older than the Princess, it was easy to see who would take the lead. Her surroundings had been large, splendid, and liberal, whilst he had been brought up in a narrow, old-fashioned, and reactionary way, which had kept him back and subdued him. Nobody was more aware of this than himself or spoke more openly about it with his friends. The Princess, often from no particular reason, took violent fancies to people. She used at first to think them quite perfect and then came the bitter disillusion. She also took first-sight dislikes to persons, based often only on a trick of manner, or an idle word dropped about them in her presence, and thus she often lost useful friends and supporters. She was no judge of character, and never became one, because her own point of view was the only one she could see. This is a frequent defect in strong characters endowed with much initiative.

When I first knew the Princess Royal it was the Empress Eugénie who filled her young mind with admiration. She was never tired of extolling her grace and her beauty. She still treasured a piece of tulle torn off the Empress's dress at some ball in Paris when she accompanied the Queen there in 1854, and spoke of her in raptures. When she worked herself up to these enthusiasms, or, as the French would call it, *engouements*, she praised the fancy of the moment so excessively that it was difficult to agree entirely with her, thus often raising opposition and even contradiction, which, however, only fanned her enthusiasm to a brighter flame. She was in the habit of praising places and countries in the same exaggerated way, and her constant admiring references to England and everything English was what hurt the susceptibility of the Prussians and made them turn against her.

I am, however, bound to say that, referring to the letters I wrote to my family at that time (they were not Prussians, but living at Berlin), I gather that there was a party with whom the marriage was very unpopular long before the Princess arrived there, and the centre of discontent was the Court of the King. Frederick William the Fourth was a witty and amiable man, but at the time we are speaking of already very ill and suffering from softening of the brain, from which he died three years later. The Queen, a severely good woman, was exceedingly stiff and strait-laced, and had always been a devoted partisan of Russia, and in consequence she abhorred everything English, for the Crimean war was still fresh in all people's memories. I express in those letters (which were those of a child, and therefore speak the truth) my astonishment at all the unkind reports I had heard at Berlin, and I insist constantly on the indescribable charm of the Princess, the great dignity of the Queen, and the good looks of the Prince of Wales, all so contrary to the impression which had been given me beforehand.

The homeward journey of Prince and Princess Frederick William after their marriage was a series of triumphs, and the bright but icily cold January day on which they made their State entry into Berlin in a gilt coach with the windows let down, so that the people might see them better, witnessed a reception of unequalled enthusiasm in the annals of Prussia. When, after several freezing hours, the Royal pair arrived at the Old Schloss, where all the Princes and

Princesses of the House of Hohenzollern and many other Royal and illustrious guests were assembled to receive them, the Queen Elisabeth, as she somewhat frigidly embraced her new niece, remarked : ' Are you not frozen to death ? ' upon which the Princess promptly responded, ' Yes, I am ; I have only one warm place, and that is my heart ! '

All during the festivities which followed, the Princess won hearts by the thousand.   She was always at her best when amused and excited ; her shyness then had not time to show itself, and she was far more at her ease and spoke better when making that trying Continental institution, a *cercle*, during those first months of her married life, than she ever did afterwards, brilliant though she always was in intimate conversation, especially when she was alone with a person she liked.

The old King and his Queen lived at Charlottenburg and never appeared in public, a small circle of select friends only being invited in the evening.   The Prince of Prussia, who, soon after the Princess Royal's marriage, became Regent, and was later on the beloved and revered ' Kaiser Wilhelm,' was not in those days popular with the masses.   He had taken part with England and France against Russia in the Crimean war, and so did his wife, an intellectual and highly cultivated woman, who, however, amongst the Prussians proper had another title to unpopularity, which was her leaning to Roman Catholicism.

It was not to be wondered at, therefore, that all the affection of the people and the sympathies of at least all the young and brilliant section of society should go out to that young Court, presided over by a Prince whose kind nature and noble aspirations were known to all who came near him **and** by a Princess of seventeen, whose cleverness and charm enslaved even those who had been most opposed to what was termed ' the English marriage.'

There can be no doubt that the Princess from the first compared life at Berlin disadvantageously with her English homes, but at that time certainly without any bitterness. To the Prince, who adored her, England also seemed perfection, so there was no warning note sounded in that direction, and I, who had been brought up by English nurses and governesses, with English ideas and English prejudices, thought her quite in the right, and only wondered when some of those surrounding her took umbrage at what appeared to me to be only natural.

Nor do I think that many knew the difficulties and discomforts that the young Princess had to encounter. The first year of her married life was passed at the picturesque but highly inconvenient Old Schloss. She had a vast but gloomy apartment, where the windows rattled and the chimneys smoked. Of the heating of the huge stone staircases and passages there was no trace, and everything that had to do with hygiene was sadly neglected. The Princess, who was practical by nature and well up in all new inventions, and by temperament a Liberal and Progressive, was at first astonished and then shocked at the elementary installation. She took the greatest trouble and interest in arranging the Palace, which was to be her abiding home, with every English comfort and improvement. But even in that palace she had not quite a free hand, for it had been that of King Frederick William the Third, the Prince's grandfather, who had died in it, and his room had by his pious sons been preserved in exactly the same state as it was on the day of his death. This room was situated between the Princess's boudoir and library, and every time she went to her bed or dressing-room she was obliged to pass through it. The Princess was not superstitious, but the associations of the room, with its sparse and Spartan furniture, and the icy cold which always pervaded it, were enough to shake older nerves than hers. But there was more.

The door between the boudoir and the ' deathroom,' as it was always called, would sometimes open by itself. The first time it happened was on a winter's evening shortly before the present Emperor was born, and the Princess had only been a few weeks in the Palace. She was sitting on a light blue damask sofa next to the door, but with her back to it, and I was sitting opposite her, reading out aloud, close under the lamp, when, raising my eyes, I saw the door— which was a single one, and covered, like the walls, with blue silk—open noiselessly, and, as if pushed by an invisible hand, swing back gently on its hinges till it reached the wall. I was very much afraid of apparitions in those days, and I stopped reading and stared spellbound. The Princess cried, ' What do you see ? ' I said, ' Nothing, Ma'am,' and got up to close the door; but it will be conceded that it was very creepy and not agreeable for a young married woman in a delicate state of health to have so depressing a neighbourhood. The cause of the door opening in that way was discovered later to be quite natural; it was not set straight on its hinges, and the wall of the room extended as an arch over the street, so that the reverberation of any heavy waggon passing under it shook the doorposts and made the lock give way and the door swing back.

The first summer the Princess passed in her new country, the Royal couple resided at Babelsberg, a modern Gothic creation, with nothing to recommend it but a rather pretty situation on the river Havel. It was there the Prince Consort visited his beloved daughter in the month of May, 1858, for the first time after her marriage. He was just recovering from a sharp attack of typhoid fever, which left him weak and aged, and the Princess's happiness at having her adored father under her own roof-tree was much tempered by her anxiety about his health.

It was at Babelsberg also that the Queen, later on in the summer, paid a visit of a fortnight. There was only just room for the Royalties in the Castle, and all the Court removed to the Palace at Potsdam, at about half an hour's distance, with the exception of the Queen's lady-in-waiting and myself, who lived in a cottage about ten minutes' walk from the Castle. The cottage was such that I was in the habit of sleeping during the frequent thunderstorms of a German summer with my umbrella open and fastened to the head of my bed.

The next summer the splendid and roomy Neue Palais was, at the Princess's request, put at her disposal, and she made it in the course of years an abode as comfortable as it was beautiful.

There is no doubt that the very liberal tendencies the Princess had imbibed in England appeared utterly subversive to many of the reactionary Prussians of that day. Such men as Disraeli and Lord Salisbury were still in the dim future, and all her sympathies were with Lord Palmerston and his Ministry, especially such men as Lords Clarendon and Granville, who both came to pay her a visit at Babelsberg. There was nobody who showed more than the Princess, by the play of her mobile features and the vivacity or restraint of her gestures, whether she liked the person she was speaking to or not, and at that period the very approach of a Tory or a reactionary seemed to freeze her up.

The thing that often struck me about her was the tragic note in her thoughts, so little in harmony with the rest of her personality. It was curious in one so young and apparently so happy, and it seemed to spring from a want of confidence in the future and a passionate clinging to the present, if it was what pleased her. Later on it was the same with her children ; she desired with unutterable longing to keep them always in babyhood. She loved them as long as they were quite small with a violence as if she feared they would be taken from her. I was too young to make inductions in those days, but I always felt that the fear of the future, which so often seemed to loom over her, had something to do with her dislike to abstract thought and any spiritual problem. Everything seemed to approach her through the senses and not through intuition. She was a clever artist, and drew correctly and with decision, though with more adaptiveness than imagination. The drawing of hers that had most of the latter quality was done when she was fourteen. It represented a young woman bending over a dead soldier on one of the Crimean battlefields ; it was a dark picture well composed, with a lurid sky and the tragic element very strong in it. In art she preferred Rubens to any other painter, and everything she admired was always abundant and strong. It was not the fashion in the fifties to admire women of the gigantic latter-day pattern, but she always praised those of ample proportions, even if they were not good-looking.

In science, too, she only believed in the palpable

and positive, and she looked upon the beginnings of magnetism and hypnotism, often called spiritualism, at that time as absurd superstition. In medicine, for instance, she only saw salvation in the large doses of the allopath, and laughed at the homœopath as a harmless lunatic.

On the other hand, her grasp of events and facts was astounding in one so young, and only equalled by her capacity for adapting anything she might gather from others to her wants. Her memory was retentive for anything that interested her. She was not a great reader, but liked being read to whilst she drew ; she loved music, but was not so good a musician as the Queen. She was never idle and an early riser, but sometimes went to bed almost by daylight. Physically, she was indolent in those days, at least for walking, but she could ride for hours in scorching sun or cutting wind without ever feeling tired. She was not indifferent to dress, but could have done herself more justice had she understood what suited her. She was too often guided by what suited others, or what she thought pretty in a picture, or by sentiment. She was not twenty when I left her, and yet her character then was more formed than that of most women of thirty. I always noticed that men, especially clever men, understood her better than women ; and if she had not had a constitutional timidity which made it quite impossible for her to carry things through when she was opposed by a determined will, she would have accomplished a great deal more than she did. She was unable to tell those who surrounded her if anything in their behaviour displeased her, but she felt acutely the want of harmony produced by this state of things, and from this arose the many misunderstandings which darkened so much of her life. It was this timidity and want of *élan* which prevented her gaining the influence over the Regent, through which she might have fulfilled all her wishes instead of having to resort to the expedient of a ' go-between.' The Regent, chivalrous, very open to the influence of women, and proud of this young English daughter-in-law, would have been wax in her hands if she could have treated him with affectionate and familiar pleasantry, and behaved like a loving child with a doting father. Instead of this, she froze up with him, and especially with his wife, the future Empress Augusta, into a shy reserve which made intimate conversation impossible. Perhaps these two first years were the happiest of her married life. She had not then matured, in fact hardly conceived, the plans which made her later years a life of longing and unfulfilled wishes. She felt her powers seething in her, but she did not consciously adapt them. She loved the Prince, and he looked up to her as the perfection of womanhood. There was one thing alone in which he never gave way to her wishes : he steadfastly refused giving up his solitary evening walk in the streets of Berlin, after the Princess had gone to bed, though she was terrified, and entreated him over and over again to make this sacrifice for her. But those were still days of great security, and Prince Frederick William was beloved by high and low, so he only laughed at these fears.

During these years the Princess was not yet troubled with the thought of inadequate means to carry out her conceptions. It was not unnatural that, having been brought up amongst the riches and luxury of England, she thought herself very poor in her new life, and, like many people who have no clear idea of the value of money, she imagined herself sometimes on the brink of ruin.

At that time she saw none but bright and cheerful faces about her, and she was sure of the devotion of her surroundings ; the world lay at her feet—the daughter of a mighty Queen, and the future Queen of a great people. Nobody in those days then thought the day could be far distant on which she would ascend the throne. The first terrible blow was the death of the Prince Consort. I saw her some months later, still utterly crushed and listless ; and how many other blows have followed this first one ! and what a sad and tragic fate has been that of this remarkable and highly endowed Princess !

But my intimate association with her ended in the third year of her marriage, before the dark shadows of the wings of fate had lowered on her path. She arises in my memory in all her freshness and childlike simplicity, the eldest and most brilliant daughter of proud parents, the loving and admired sister, the adored girl-wife of a chivalrous husband, the affectionate friend, and the young and happy mother. There seemed to be sunshine everywhere. The future was mercifully hidden from all eyes, and she alone, though unconsciously, felt the gathering clouds with which an inscrutable Providence darkened the high hopes sprung from so radiant a beginning.

CHAPTER IV

A ROYAL MARRIAGE

IN ending the chapter of my recollections of Berlin and my Court life I do not think I laid sufficient stress upon the grief it was to me to part from a charming and highly gifted young Princess who during the two years I had been with her had showed me nothing but the most gracious affection and friendship.

The Princess Royal, then Princess Frederic William of Prussia, and later Empress Frederic, was at that time not yet twenty, but it was easy to see what great capacities she might develop. She always had a passionate love for her native country, and when I married she said she could only forgive me because I married an Englishman.

Our marriage took place at the English Legation at Berlin, of which Lord Bloomfield, one of the most amiable and polished men of that day, was then the incumbent. All the Princes and Princesses of the Royal House assisted. Princess Frederic William, whom I will in future mention only as ' the Princess,' insisted upon giving the breakfast, though she was in deep mourning for her grandmother, the Dowager Duchess of Coburg. After changing my dress at the Palace I took leave of the Prince and Princess with few words but many tears, and started with my husband for my brother's place, which had been lent to us. We spent a fortnight or three weeks at Hohenpriessnitz, walking or driving for hours through those enchanted woods which stretch away for forty miles in ' an endless contiguity of shade.' It was October, and the great beeches shone like gold in the mellow autumn sun against the background of tall silver-stemmed firs.

In the first week of November we left for England, and were almost immediately invited to Windsor. We arrived there on the Prince of Wales's birthday, at that anxious time when, returning from the United States, his ship was already ten days overdue. There had been frightful storms on the Atlantic, and the Prince Consort looked pale and worn.

A silent anxiety seemed to brood over the whole Court. The Queen alone kept up her spirits, her blue eyes shining as bright as ever. She did not admit that this delay could be due to anything but the usual November fogs and storms.

At dinner I sat next to the Prince Consort. The conversation naturally reverted to the Prince of Wales. I knew that both he and the Queen were very anxious to secure his future happiness by a marriage as desirable as possible, on private as well as on public grounds.

About a year before the time I am speaking of, the Princess (Princess Royal) had, after spending some weeks with her parents in England, gone on a private mission to make the acquaintance of some of the most eligible Princesses in Germany. There was, however, just then a great dearth of young ladies of high degree, and none of those she saw seemed to respond to the wished-for ideal. I alone accompanied the Princess on this secret tour of inspection, of which no one else knew. I never mentioned it to anybody till the following summer, when I was engaged to be married. My future husband being an Englishman and a diplomat, I knew he would be discreet, and I confided to him the dilemma of ' no Princess ' for the Prince of Wales. ' But I know the prettiest, the nicest, the most charming Princess,' he exclaimed ; ' Princess Alix, the eldest daughter of Prince Christian the future King of Denmark. She is only sixteen, and as good as she is pretty ! ' Armed with this knowledge, I went at once to the Princess and told her all about it. ' You must tell the Queen at once as soon as you get to England, and find out all you can in the meantime,' she said. My husband, who had for two years already been Minister at Copenhagen, often had opportunities of seeing the young Princess, and in his letters to me during the time we were engaged always spoke of her in the most admiring terms.

I now saw my opportunity, and when the Prince Consort spoke of his son I ventured to beg him to forgive me if I alluded to a subject that had been kept secret, but that perhaps he might remember that I accompanied the Princess the year before on a fruitless expedition to Germany ; but I now thought that the Princess so much searched for had been found, and I told him all I knew about Princess Alix.   I heard him repeating it to the Queen, who was on his other side.

After dinner her Majesty asked me many questions about the Princess Alix, and told me as soon as I had made her acquaintance to write to Princess Alice (then engaged to the future Grand Duke of Hesse) and send as many photographs as I. could find.

The journey to Copenhagen was not the easy and luxurious progress which it now is, especially in midwinter.   The trains were not heated nor were there any sleeping-carriages.   The hour and a half from Altona to Kiel had to be accomplished at night in a wretched carriage over rough ground.   Then came a six hours' crossing from Kiel to Korsoer, the boats frequently having to saw their way through the ice. At Korsoer there was a three hours' wait in a bare room at the station, and a slow train, starting at nine o'clock, landed us about noon at Copenhagen.

The cold was intense and everything covered with snow, and I knew absolutely nobody, and did not for several days summon courage to go out.

I was, however, cheered by receiving several delightful and affectionate letters from the Princess, of which I will give a few extracts, as they show her charming nature, which has not been sufficiently appreciated, and the happy, playful spirit of her younger years :—

BERLIN, *December* 10, 1860.

You cannot think what a disappointment it has been for me not to see you here. It was a happiness to which I looked forward with the greatest impatience, and now I am deprived of it. That is really hard. I suppose Stockmar [Baron Stockmar, the Princess's secretary] has sent you the album. I wished to add something of mine to Marie's souvenir. [Countess Marie Lynar, the Princess's other maid of honour, had married three months before me, and gave me as a wedding present a book with drawings of my rooms at the New Palace. The Princess had added a charming allegorical drawing of our two weddings.]

We three suited so well and were so happy together, like three friends only can be who love each other truly. I can't at all get over the separation from you two. My thoughts are constantly occupied with you, and I miss you dreadfully.

. . . It was with greatest pleasure that I painted the picture which is to be a remembrance of both your weddings and of the time we lived together. I had long promised to paint something nice for you, and never had been able to settle down to it, so I made use of the long evenings here at Berlin, as on account of the mourning we go nowhere, to finish this drawing.

. . . I have never thanked you for your two dear letters, one from Windsor and the other one for my birthday ; we have envied you with all our souls for being able to be in England. You happy one ! . . . Fritz goes shooting to-day to Letzlingen and returns on Thursday. On the 28th we expect Alfred, but I am sorry to say only for two days ; the dear boy ! I tremble with impatience at the thought of at last seeing him once more. I wonder what you think of Alice's engagement ? We are all so pleased, and she swims in a sea of bliss. . . . When you see Anne [Princess Frederic of Hesse and daughter of Prince Charles of Prussia, and a much-loved friend and cousin of the Prince and Princess] please give her a thousand loves. . . .

I should so much like to have a glimpse of your home at Copenhagen. . . . It is extraordinary what things do happen. If only that one thing would happen, which is to see Countess D—— safe with her belongings, I would build at least one pyramid from gratitude. [The lady alluded to was an excellent but incapable person, attached to the Princess's household. Both she and the Prince were too kind to put an end to an impossible position.] How is Snowy ? Does this unfortunate little beast still live, or can he no more be teased by you ? Or has he been gathered to his forefathers in a strange land because the family burying place in the summer theatre no more belongs to you ?

My love of animals always was a joke against me, especially in those days when pets were not as common as they now are. The summer theatre was a place near the New Palace where I used to bury my mice, bats, birds, kittens, etc., when they came to grief. The Princess's letters were generally written in a mixture of German and English, as she chose the most telling expressions in each language, and this is lost in the translation.

A few days later the Princess wrote again :—

I am sure you are furious with me that I have not yet answered your dear, long, amusing, and interesting letter, for which I thank you a thousand times. But Christmas is before the door, and you know how much there is always to do at this time. I cannot write you a long letter to-day, but wish you with all my heart a merry Christmas and a happy new year ; may the latter bring you many blessings. I shall think so much of you and Mary on the dear Christmas Eve, and I shall miss your dear face dreadfully. Countess D—— is now really gone over the hills and far away —that is, to Dresden—never to return. ' Johanna geht und nimmer kehrt sie wieder.' God bless the goody. At a distance I have the greatest respect for her sterling qualities. Please inform Mary of this great event or send her my letter.

As soon as I had recovered from my journey I began my audiences with the Dowager Queen and the Princesses. The King, Frederic the Seventh, was married morganatically to Countess Danner. He was divorced from his wife, who since had married the Duke of Holstein Gluecksburg. His Majesty led a very retired life, and I only made his acquaintance two years after my arrival in Denmark. He was a tall, stout man, heavy, but with gleams of wit. He was devoted to the chase, and told most amusing stories. One very cold day, when my husband was out shooting with him, he said : ' This is nothing to the day when Fredericksburg was burnt down. It was so cold then, that the water from the fire-engines froze into arches as it was spurted into the air, and therefore the castle could not be saved.'

The Queen Dowager Amalie was the widow of Christian the Eighth. She was a handsome and most amiable old lady, very simple in all her ways, and extremely interesting when she spoke of her younger days.

Princess Anne of Hesse, whom I had known so well at Berlin, was now living at Copenhagen, and this to me was a great help and comfort. Her husband, Prince Frederic, was the brother-in-law of Prince Christian (afterwards King Christian the Ninth). They had a fine palace in the same street in which the Legation was situated, and I often went to see this Princess, who was not only a charming woman but a great musician. There I frequently met Rubinstein, who was then quite a young man with a big mop of curly brown hair. He and the Princess used to play together, whilst I sat on the floor and played with the children and listened to this enchanting concert.

I need not say that much my most interesting experience was my visit to Princess Louise (afterwards Queen of Denmark). Her Royal Highness had asked me to come quite informally, as she knew my husband so well and had often allowed him to visit her in the same way both in town and in the country. The Princess was still a very pretty woman, with fine blue eyes and a good figure. Prince Christian came into the room whilst I was with the Princess, and we talked of his brothers, whom I remembered seeing in their smart Hussar uniforms as dashing young officers at my father's house in the country, when they were quartered near there, and also of his sisters, whom I had seen quite lately. There was a delightful charm of simplicity and kindness about Prince Christian which won all hearts, and the patriarchal and unostentatious setting of the family life of this Royal couple was most attractive. After I had been with Princess Louise for a little time, I said that my husband had so often spoken to me about Princess Alix that I hoped I might be allowed to see her. I was delighted when she came into the room, for I saw in her all the promise of her future loveliness and goodness. She was like a half-open rosebud, and so simple and child-like in everything. Later on I made the acquaintance of the other children. The eldest son (now King of Denmark) was then a good-looking stripling of seventeen, and Prince Willy (now King of Greece) a boy of twelve or thirteen, full of spirits and mischief. Princess Dagmar (Empress Mother of Russia) was quite a child still, with splendid dark eyes. Princess Thyra (Duchess of Cumberland) and Prince Waldemar were almost babies. It was charming to see the still youthful parents and their half-grown-up and growing children all so happy and united together in such natural, healthy, simple surroundings.

I need hardly say that after this visit my

correspondence with Princess Alix and the Princess (who by this time had, by the death of King Frederic William the Fourth of Prussia, become Crown Princess) became very lively. It is so full of intimate detail that I can only give short passages from the letters I received. I had many opportunities of seeing Prince and Princess Christian. The Prince sometimes came to see me, and I learnt to appreciate more and more his sterling qualities.

The Crown Princess wrote to me in the spring of 1861 :—

You must not be angry with me for not having written and not thanked you myself for your dear, most interesting, and most excellent letter. How often I have positively longed to be able to write to you. But I was exhausted in body and in soul in England, and since I am back from there. Now I am better, but still so sad ! [The Duchess of Kent had died in March.]

I have so many worries of every kind which take up all my time ; therefore, dear heart, you must pardon a very confused letter. . . . I am especially grateful to you for your last letter, which is so full of the business I have so much at heart. I own that my interest increases the more I hear of the person in question, and also in England much good has been heard of her. What a pity were she to make another marriage. [I had told the Princess that I heard some rumours of this kind.]

In the first place it would be desirable to find out whether she is not coming some time to Germany. I should be so enchanted to make her acquaintance.

You have a certain talent in making naïve remarks.

I should have no objection to your compromising *me* slightly, not as an official person, but as *my* friend, and if you were to be a little indiscreet about my interest in the young lady.

The result of these letters and some more visits I paid to Princess Christian was that an arrangement was come to by which the Crown Prince and Princess were to announce themselves for a few days at Strelitz, whilst Princess Christian, accompanied by her two daughters, was paying a visit to her relations there. The Grand Duchess of Mecklenburgh was the Princess Royal's cousin, and it was quite natural that she should wish to go and see her.

The utmost secrecy was observed; only Prince and Princess Christian, the Crown Prince and Princess, and my husband and myself knew.

It was necessary to be very careful, for we all were aware that this marriage project just as the Schleswig-Holstein question was seething might raise great political objections in Germany.

I confess that I awaited the Crown Princess's first letter after her visit with great impatience, but quite without any fear. It came the moment she returned from Strelitz :—

Quite enchanted I returned from Strelitz, and you are the first to whom I hasten to impart my impressions. Princess Alix is the most fascinating creature in the world ! You did not say nearly enough. For a long time I have not seen anybody who pleased me so much as this lovely and charming girl. Not to speak of a Princess.

Princess Alix and I got to know each other very soon, and in those few days I have got to love her very dearly ; she is simply quite charming. I have never seen Fritz so taken by anybody as he was with her.

.   .   .   .

I will only add now that I found Princess Christian very amiable and agreeable, and the little Dagmar a duck.

A few days later the Crown Princess wrote again :—

I shall now go to England and beg of you to tell Princess Christian this, and to add that I shall not fail to tell my parents of the favourable impression which the young Princess Alix has made on Fritz and me   I am sorry to say I am not certain whether Fritz can come with me ; to leave him behind would make me very unhappy, for I can enjoy nothing when he is not there, and shall feel lost even in my dear home if he is not there. Please write soon again.

Soon after the Crown Princess's arrival in England I heard that both the Queen and the Prince Consort were very much in favour of the marriage, and quite delighted with the account the Crown Princess had given of Princess Alix. It was then settled that some time in the autumn the Prince of Wales was to meet Princess Alix, as if by chance, somewhere in Germany.

Eventually the beautiful old Cathedral of Spiers

was chosen as a trysting-place, and, though the interview was quite short, the impression was a lasting one.

Everything in this Royal romance seemed to be progressing most favourably. The Prince Consort especially seemed most anxious for its accomplishment, when suddenly, like a thunderclap out of a blue sky, came the news of his death.

His illness had been hardly noticed in the papers, and the tragic ending of it was quite unexpected. Everybody felt what a fearful blow it would be to the Queen, for her happy married life had been a bright example to all her subjects. My thoughts were continually with the dear Crown Princess, who was singularly devoted to her father, with feelings in which love, respect and admiration had an equal part.

Princess Anne, the friend and cousin of the Crown Princess, felt this acutely, and wrote to me a day or two after she heard the sad news :—

I must tell you how wretched I am about my beloved cousin. To lose a father whom she loved so immeasurably ; so young, so unexpected, so sudden and terrible . read and see how utterly wretched she is. . . . If you have any details about the illness, the death, and the state of the poor, deeply tried Queen, I should be so grateful to you if you would keep me informed, as the Prince and I and all of us, as you know, take the sincerest interest in this painful event.

My husband was terribly shocked and grieved at the death of the Prince Consort, for whose high abilities he entertained the greatest admiration. I think it will be interesting if I give some extracts of letters from Countess Bluecher to him, as they corresponded much at that time.

Countess Bluecher (*née* Dallas) had been for many years a trusted and devoted friend of the Queen and Crown Princess, with whom she often spent many months at a time. She wrote from Berlin, the 15th of January :—

I wish I could give you a better account of our dear Crown Princess here. She is very miserable and has bursts of grief which are painful to witness. I don't think she will recover any settled composure till she has seen her mother again and talked over the sad past. Her health at present is very good, but I am always in fear that the continual emotions may be detrimental to her. She certainly has the kindest and most devoted of nurses (I may almost say) in the excellent Crown Prince, who seems to think of nothing else but how to try to alleviate her sorrow

And then a month later Countess Bluecher wrote from Windsor ·—

February 25, 1862.

You will like to hear what are my impressions of the state of our beloved Queen. I found her looking much *older* and with a careworn impression, but she appears in health and her state as natural as possible, I think, if one considers that it is only a little more than two months since she lost all she loved best on earth. The Queen talks much of the Prince's illness and death with calm and resignation, and then falls into other subjects, of which she speaks with composure and interest.

I can conceive nothing more admirable than her demeanour. She lives entirely with her children, seeing the members of her household at times, as well as the Ministers, and she has often one or the other of her ladies at dinner. Can more be expected! One is filled with grief and sympathy when one looks at the Queen in her widow's dress and thinks of the weight of affliction she has to bear. . . .

As the summer approached I had urgent calls from the Crown Princess, who wished me to spend some time with her at Potsdam. I was most anxious to obey, and I started for Berlin the beginning of June.

Some extracts from my letters to my husband will give a more vivid picture of the sad state I found the Crown Princess in than I could give in writing from recollection after so great a lapse of time :—

POTSDAM, 8/6/1862.

.   Here I found the dear Princess all kindness and love ; poor, dear Princess. She spoke of those happy days we spent together, but she said she would not speak of her loss that evening. The first thing almost she said was that I was to tell you that you must come to Berlin on your way to England and stay a day, as she was most anxious to speak to you about several things. . . . It's about Princess A.'s marriage ; she wants you to remove the political scruples and difficulties, for the Crown Prince and Princess think it might lead to trouble in Germany.

POTSDAM, 10/6/1862.

. Boykins [this was my little son whom the Crown Princess had insisted upon my bringing with me] meets with admiration wherever he goes. Yesterday the King [who became the Emperor William] asked to see him, and the moment baby came in he said, ' He has got his papa's beautiful eyes,' and then he got up from his chair and made me a low bow, and said, ' Je vous en fait mon compliment ! '

Poor dear Princess ! she feels so lonely sometimes, and now she is getting back into all her old ways with me she feels it more and speaks of things she generally never mentions. She showed me yesterday a beautiful coloured photograph done after the Prince Consort's death, and she had some of his hair, which she kisses and cries so much, poor dear. She says she never can be happy again, and that with him she has lost everything. Certainly with him she has lost her chief counsellor and stay.

June 16, 1862.

. . . The Princess gave me to-day a heartrending letter from the poor Queen to read. I could not help crying whilst I read it. . . . She says her pulse is 90 instead of being 75, and she says she feels so weak. She writes so touchingly and naturally.

June 24, 1862.

. The Crown Princess tells me that the Queen goes to Windsor on the 21st and to Scotland on the 22nd, and we must manage to be there before that time. There is such good news about the Prince of Wales, and the Queen calls him her dear darling boy, whom she always wished to see thus excellent and grown up beside his adored young father. . . .

I had regretfully to leave the dear Crown Princess, but not before matters had so far proceeded that it was arranged that some time in September, whilst Prince and Princess Christian and their family were taking sea-baths at Ostend, the Queen should pay a short visit to her uncle, King Leopold, at Brussels, where a meeting was to take place.

Whilst I was staying with my relations in Saxony the Crown Princess wrote to me :—

. . . You will have heard what a truly terrible misfortune has fallen upon my poor mamma in the death of General Bruce [the Prince of Wales's Governor]. It is a hard blow, an irreparable loss . . . which pains me unspeakably. Every misfortune appears now to fall on our family, which formerly had no idea what unhappiness was. The Queen has written to me several times with such contentment about my brother ; the feeling between them is such a good one that I cannot help copying out for you a passage from mamma's letter, because I am certain that you will rejoice with me over it ; then there is a message from mamma to you, which I also give verbatim. ' Bertie goes on being as good, amiable, and sensible as any one of us could wish. It is such a comfort to feel that dear General Bruce's anxious efforts and wishes have not been in vain. Bertie is most anxious about his marriage, and hopes it may be in March or April, and has bought numbers of pretty things for the young lady '

It appears to me no one could wish for anything better. The expression of these words is so just, and yet so gentle and loving. God protect my beloved brother and the dear lovely young creature, and unite them to their happiness and the welfare of England. . . .

As soon as my husband was at liberty to leave Copenhagen, we went to England and were at once invited to Osborne.

We both of us had several long and interesting interviews with her Majesty, but always apart. The Queen used to sit near the writing-table in the room which was the Prince Consort's study. She looked very much crushed and sad, but always brightened up when the Prince of Wales's marriage was the topic of conversation. She told me that she felt it a sacred duty to do all she could for this marriage, as the Prince Consort had wished it very much, for he had been so taken with all he had heard about Princess Alix. The Queen said it was her desire that we should accompany her to Brussels ; as we knew the Danish Royal Family so well, it would make things easier. I naturally kept Princess Christian informed of all I saw and heard, and during the following weeks our correspondence was a most lively one.

There was so much to arrange and to think of, and though both Prince and Princess Christian were so happy at the prospect of this marriage for their beloved daughter, they were also anxious not to advance themselves too much. Also a good many political and other impediments had to be overcome, but at last both the Royal Families were assembled at Brussels under the wise and kind auspices of King Leopold.

The first meeting between the Queen and Princess Alix took place one morning in the King's writing-room, where all his children and the Danish Royalties were assembled.

The Queen sat in a small boudoir adjoining this room. I was alone with her. Her emotion was very great, and, suddenly bursting into tears, she said, ' Oh, you can understand what I feel. You have a husband you love, and you know what I have lost.'

I was so deeply moved myself at seeing the Queen's grief and emotion that I could say but little to comfort her. The happiness she hoped for, for her beloved son, recalled to her memory her own perfect union, so suddenly broken up. . . . It was a relief to me when a page came in to say that all the Royalties were assembled. The Queen motioned me to precede her, which I did, and after presenting Princess Christian to her I retired to the little boudoir again, as I thought my presence was quite unnecessary. I sat down, tired by the journey, the continual driving to and fro between Brussels and Laaken, where the Queen lived, and I suppose, above all, by the anxiety I could not help feeling about a thing I had so much at heart, and which for the last year had filled my thoughts so much.

It will therefore be readily believed that when after half an hour the Queen returned to the boudoir quite enchanted and immensely pleased and delighted with Princess Alix, I felt sincerely happy.

The next day there was a great *déjeuner* at Court. After it the guests walked about in the gardens. It was then the Prince of Wales proposed to Princess Alix, and immediately after this the engagement was made public. It was touching to see the Queen's delight at the prospect of her son's happy marriage, and it was with a lighter heart that she continued her journey to Reichardtsbrunn to pay a visit to her brother-in-law, the Duke of Coburg.

The Queen naturally wished to make a closer acquaintance with Princess Alix before her marriage, and it was therefore arranged that the young Princess should pay her a visit at Windsor in November.

I was the first to inform Princess Christian of the excellent impression she had made, and Princess Christian answered :—

Heartfelt thanks for the good news, the first which I received, and which gave me great pleasure naturally, especially that everything went off so quietly, for I do not wish her to be seen in England before the marriage. I thank you also for the paper (with the Prince and Princess's portraits in it), and to read this yesterday (the Prince of Wales's birthday) on the important day, appeared to me a good augury. God bless the dear young couple. My dear daughter telegraphed to me yesterday evening, as on the day on which she could not think of him apart from me. . . .

The Prince of Wales was not at Windsor during the Princess's stay, but when Prince Christian came to escort his daughter back from England the Prince joined them at Calais and travelled back two days with them.

The Queen, with her wonderful forethought and knowledge, made all the arrangements for the marriage. I possess a large batch of letters from General Grey, the Queen's Private Secretary, which are simply transcripts of her wishes and orders, and in which she goes into all details with the utmost clearness and method.

The wedding day was eventually settled for the 10th of March, but there were some fears that the elements might interpose at that early season, for communications with the mainland were sometimes interrupted for many days by great icefloes. Fortunately this was a mild winter, and such a *contretemps* did not occur.

My state of health at that time precluded my accompanying the Princess Alix to England, which I regretted very much ; but I went to bid her good-bye at the Palace, and found her very bright and cheery. She wore a dress of brown silk with white stripes, and one of those natty little bonnets which seemed to sit better on her head than on anybody else's. Even in those early days I was struck by the extreme neatness and taste of her attire.

My husband was entrusted with all arrangements

for the Princess's journey, and I will give a few extracts from his letters.

After saying how well the Danish Royal Family was received everywhere in Denmark, he writes from Hamburg :—

The Princess behaves with great dignity and affability to all deputations, etc. We dined at the Duke of Gluecksburg, at Kiel ; the Schloss was crowded with young ladies all up the staircase, etc. . . .

And then from Hanover :—

There was a guard of honour, and everything that was proper. The King visited the Royal Family soon after their arrival, and they dined with him afterwards. . . .

On board the *Victoria and Albert* he continues :—

This is something like travelling on board this yacht, with every comfort and luxury one can possibly think of.   On arriving at Flushing, the *Resistance* and *Revenge* manned yards and saluted us. We stopped the engines so as to drift by them slowly. The men were facing us as we approached, and on our passing they turned round as if by magic. . . . The Princess stood on the paddle-box, and bowed very gracefully. . . . All the officers on board think Princess Alix charming.   A woman in the crowd at Cologne said, ' Oh, this is a dear little thing ! ' . . . We have just got under weigh and are steaming up to Gravesend. . . . The Prince of Wales is to come on board at 11.30. . . . The Mayor and Corporation of Margate came on board with an address, with which I found Princess Alix pounding Prince Willy's [King of Greece] head.   They are all very jolly and nice together.

WINDSOR CASTLE, *Sunday, March 8.*—As for yesterday, I shall not attempt a description of it . . . such a crowd is almost beyond imagination . . . I have just been to see the presents . . . the tiara given by the Prince of Wales is splendid.

Here I was called to the Queen. She said she was so sorry you had not been able to come. . . . I was with Her Majesty for about half an hour, and it is impossible for me to tell you all we spoke about. She says Princess Alix is quite like one of her own daughters. She is very fond of her indeed. . . .

March 10.—It is all over. . Such a magnificent sight I could never have dreamt of as that in St. George's Chapel. They both went through the ceremony admirably. She looked beautiful, and spoke out capitally. Everybody is in rapture both at her looks and behaviour and bearing. . . .

I have only given short extracts from these letters, which were full of most interesting details.

The many deeply interesting letters from the Crown Princess and a still larger number from Princess Christian, Countess Bluecher's letters, and very long and important ones from General Grey relating to the political situation as affected by this alliance, will in future times form a very important addition to the history of that day, and throw many and quite unexpected lights upon some of the events and persons who played a part in these negotiations, some of whom I have not even mentioned.

This Royal marriage absorbed so much of my

attention and interest during· the first two years of my stay in Denmark that I have not been able to give any idea of the country as it then was, or of the social life at Copenhagen.   In the next chapter I will try to recall my impressions of some other interesting events which I witnessed there, and of the wonderful northern nature of which this was my first experience.

CHAPTER V

THE previous chapter related how my husband in his capacity of British Envoy to Denmark had accompanied the ' Sea-kings' daughter ' to her future home.

He had hardly returned to Copenhagen when another question concerning European politics, and particularly the Danish Royal Family, began to occupy the public mind. This was the choosing of a king for the Greek throne. King Otho of Greece having been deposed by his subjects in 1862, a provisional Government was formed and a Constitutional Assembly elected, in which the names of various members of reigning houses were discussed as eligible occupants of the Greek throne.

The Prince selected was Prince Alfred of England (later Duke of Edinburgh and Duke of Coburg-Gotha), and a formal offer of the Crown was made to him. Apart from other considerations, such an offer could not be accepted owing to an understanding between the Great Powers that no member of any of their reigning houses should accept the vacant throne.

The choice eventually fell upon Prince William, second son of Prince Christian of Denmark, who was then in England for the marriage of his daughter. Earl Russell, Minister for Foreign Affairs, brought the subject under the notice of Prince Christian through General Oxholme, the Prince's trusted friend and adviser. Sir Augustus Paget was at the same time instructed to lay the proposal before the Danish Government.

I may as well say that Prince and Princess Christian were from the beginning very averse to the idea. Their family life was a very happy one, and the thought that their son, not yet grown up, was to take up so arduous a position so far away was a most painful one to them.

Monsieur Hall, Minister for Foreign Affairs in Denmark, showed considerable surprise, accompanied, however, by a certain admixture of pride and satisfaction, on the proposal being made to him, and promised to bring it immediately before the King, Frederic the Seventh, who was then at Fredensborg, fifteen miles from Copenhagen.

It was agreed that no decision should be taken until Prince Christian's return from England; there was, however, some soreness on the part of the King at no communication having as yet been made to him.

Sir Henry Elliot was sent out on a special mission to Athens, with orders to enjoin patience upon the Greeks; but even whilst matters were thus in suspense at Copenhagen the news suddenly arrived that the Greek Assembly had proclaimed Prince William as their future King, under the style and title of King George the First, and that a deputation was about to start to make the formal offer of the Crown to the Prince.

It is impossible to exaggerate the consternation and dismay which this announcement produced upon the King and the Danish Government, for everything connected with this matter had hitherto been treated in the most secret and confidential manner. Monsieur Hall at once called upon my husband to express the surprise and annoyance of the King as well as his own, and seemed to imply that Sir Augustus had been guilty of indiscretion, which impression he, however, was able to remove at once by reading to the Danish Minister his telegrams and despatches to Lord Russell.

Sir Augustus now received the most urgent instructions to secure the acceptance of the Greek Crown by Prince William.

He had already taken steps to assure himself of the assent of the King, which was formally given, subject to Prince Christian and his family acquiescing. Up to this time Prince Christian had not communicated with the King on this subject, and the latter was considerably irritated.

All that was known of Prince Christian's sentiments was that he was opposed to his son's acceptance, and he was backed up in this by public feeling in

Copenhagen, and by the members of his own family—
namely, the Landgrave and Landgravine of Hesse,
parents of his wife, and Prince Frederic of Hesse, his
brother-in-law, who all deprecated it, as well as some
of the Prince's most intimate friends and advisers.

Prince Christian was indeed in a most difficult
position, and when he returned on the 4th of April
(1863) he at once came to see my husband, who was
in bed with a bad attack of intermittent fever, in
order to talk matters over. The interview lasted
over two hours, and there was another one later in
the day ; after which Prince Christian, coming into
my room, complained to me that he had been most
unfairly treated in matters having been pushed so far
without its having previously been ascertained whether
he was a consenting party or not.

The Prince, in order to prevent this separation
from a beloved son, put forward wholly unacceptable
conditions. My husband had, however, found out
that Prince ' Willy ' (as he was always familiarly called)
was, with the enterprise natural to an intelligent lad,
anxious to assume the proposed dignity, and the
young Prince, meeting him one day skating on the
ice, confirmed this to him, upon which Sir Augustus
said: ' If you will stick to it, Sir, I promise to pull you
through,' and the Prince assented.

This strengthened my husband's hands in conducting the negotiations, which, however, were strenu-
ously opposed all through. It was an arduous task,

requiring much patience, perseverance, and delicate handling, but it was accomplished.

The Greek deputation arrived at Copenhagen on the 25th of April, and were most graciously received by the King on the 27th. We gave them a dinner, and, unaccustomed as I then was to southern types, I thought I had never seen before such an assemblage of romantic, adventurous, but rather terrifying countenances. Old Canaris, the head of the deputation, sat next to me, and he did not know one word of French or English, so we conversed by signs or in a ghastly jumble of Italian, Latin, and ancient Greek. Canaris had been one of the leaders of the War of Independence, and had sacked, pillaged, and burned to his heart's content. To me he was benign.

Some knotty points still remained to be settled. The deputation complained to Sir Augustus that they had been unduly hurried on their journey before things had been settled, and they even threatened to leave Copenhagen without making the offer unless everything was arranged within a few days. The situation was most embarrassing, for England was in a way standing sponsor to this affair; and though both France and Russia guaranteed 4000*l.* a year to the Prince in case he was deposed, they did not otherwise take any active part.

At last all the difficulties were removed, and the formal ceremony of the acceptance of the Crown of Greece for Prince William by the King of Denmark

took place at the Palace of Christiansborg on Saturday
the 6th of May, in the presence of all the Princes of
the Royal Family, the Danish Ministers and State
Officers, and the Ministers of the three protecting
Powers.

Lord Russell, who was extremely popular with all
those with whom he had to do on account of his good-
nature and kind heart, had, however, sometimes a
very peculiar way of showing his regard. My husband
received from him the entire approval of Her Majesty's
Government for the manner in which he had conducted
these negotiations, but as a reward he was to accept
the Mission at Athens in order to ensure things going
smoothly there in the beginning! Athens was in
those days only a third-class Mission; Lord Russell,
it is true, offered to raise it to a first-class one; and
my husband was to receive the G.C.B., so that there
was to be no misunderstanding in the eyes of the
world. Still, Athens was very much less in importance
than Copenhagen. My husband accepted reluctantly.
To our great relief, however, the Queen thought Sir
Augustus's presence at Copenhagen just then of so
much importance that the arrangement did not take
place.

King George left Copenhagen on the 17th of September for Athens. He was accompanied by Count
Sponneck, a very clever man, as confidential adviser,
but he did not turn out a success, and he returned to
Copenhagen within less than two years.

Some of General Grey's letters (at that time Private Secretary to the Queen) throw interesting sidelights on this question.

General the Hon. Charles Grey to Sir A. Paget.

[Private.] BALMORAL, *May 19th*, 1863.

Your account of your Greek difficulties interests me, and also amused me very much.

Amused me, for I had found in many of the telegrams and despatches many of the selfsame suggestions I had made from Brussels, with a view of smoothing matters for the acceptance of the Greek throne for the Duke of Coburg [this was not Prince Alfred of England, but his uncle, the brother of the Prince Consort], the only difference being that while my suggestions were pooh-poohed, yours met at least with respectful consideration. But Lord Russell had not then learned that it was not quite so easy a matter to find a Sovereign for Greece, and that the Duke was not so far wrong when he said that there were certain questions which must be satisfactorily answered before any Prince, not a mere adventurer, would consent to accept so precarious a condition as that of King of Greece. Of this I am certain, that had half the disposition been shown by our Government in the Duke's case to remove the difficulties, that has been shown in Prince William's, the Duke at this moment might have been King of Greece. The Duke retaining his own German possessions, he asked no retiring allowance in case of dismissal, but he asked for a sufficient Civil List; and this I suggested, as you did, should be secured on the revenues of the Ionian Islands. He asked for the means of reorganising the army, without which it was vain to try to restore order or to keep the 'Grand idea' in check, and the backing he sought might, I suggested, be given by the non-withdrawal, for a certain period, of our Ionian garrisons and the presence of our fleet ; but our Government met all these not very unreasonable requests with the shortest and coldest answers. He must accept the throne of Greece, purely and simply, trusting to his own resources to work out his salvation, and was coolly referred to the money market, ' though he would doubtless have to pay high interest,' for any pecuniary aid he might require.   But at this time Lord Russell thought there were fifty stray Princes eager to don the Greek diadem

If we put a King on the throne of Greece, to restore order to that country, to maintain the peace of the East in spite of the insane Greek desire to disturb it, we ought at least to give him some support in upholding our policy, and secure him, as far as we can, from the fate of Otho.

That fate would be a certainty for any Prince thrown as naked as Ulysses on the coast of Phocea, with none but his personal resources. . . . ' That most tiresome question,' as King Leopold most justly calls it, of Sleswig-Holstein, seems to come again into prominence, and the debate the other night in the Lords is not, I fear, calculated to make its settlement more easy.   There will be a great deal of talk before the threatened exclusion, unless, indeed, matters go on so rapidly at Berlin that Bismarck may think Prussian action in Holstein a desirable diversion from their home disputes.   I have never believed that such a contest as the King has engaged in with the Chambers would go on long without getting beyond mere words.   The last telegrams from Buchanan point to the imminence of a dangerous crisis, and whatever the immediate consequences *may* be, I have no doubt as to what the ultimate results *must* be.   I only hope our Crown Prince and Princess may not be involved in the misfortunes which, sooner or later, the King is sure to bring on his family.

May 21st, 1863.

. . . The Crown Princess telegraphs to the Queen that she knows of no intention that makes any change in their own line necessary at present. Buchanan speaks of a closing of the Chambers, Ordinances altering the Articles of the Constitution, restricting liberty of the Press, &c., &c.   CHARLES GREY.

General Grey was an exceedingly clever and moderate man, trusted by the Queen entirely and without restriction. He belonged to a family of statesmen and had always been in the midst of politics, yet it will be seen how little even he understood Bismarck's ulterior views or the character of the King of Prussia, that King whose memory as Emperor William the First is even now cherished and revered by every patriotic German heart.

This now almost forgotten question of Schleswig-Holstein had, at that time, been brewing and simmering for several decades.   It was a most intricate one, and I have heard it said that Mr. Morier (later Sir Robert Morier and Ambassador at St. Petersburg) was the only Englishman who ever understood it.   In some ways it resembled the Boer question, and quite especially in the manner in which it roused the violent partisanship of nations who really had nothing to do with it.

At the time of the Prince of Wales's marriage

Lord Russell had promised my husband to grant him a long leave of absence for the next winter, as he suffered much from ague at Copenhagen. These new political complications, however, put that out of the question for the moment, and I therefore went with my two children to pay a visit to my relations in Germany. I give some extracts from my husband's letters and my own, to show how high the feeling ran both in Germany and in Denmark, and what a maddening, never-ending, protean question it was.

Sir A. Paget to Lady Paget.

October 12th, 1863.

I am trying hard to get a concession out of these people, but I don't know whether I shall succeed. This business is really enough to tire out anyone, and requires a larger stock of patience than, I am afraid, I shall ever possess. . . .

October 13. . . . I was at Hall's [Danish Prime Minister] at 9½ this morning, all the way out at his country-seat. Oh, dear! I wonder whether any good will come of it at last. It has been necessary to employ the battering-ram [this was an expression invented, I think, by Mr. Lytton, then First Secretary at Copenhagen, and used in fun by all the Secretaries when Sir Augustus got very angry] very copiously, and somebody's hair stood very much on end. [M. Hall had a way of ruffling his hair when he was agitated.]

October 15. . . . I have got something from the Danes, and if the Germans really wish for an excuse not to proceed with hostile measures, it will be enough to enable them to be peaceful. . . .

October 20. . . . My spirits have been somewhat damped by a communication from Hall. It's always the same thing ; they lead you to hope that they are going to follow your advice, and when it comes to the point they don't do it, or do it in a way that it's of no use. I am sick, sick, sick of the whole concern, and wish from my heart that I had nothing whatever to do with it

October 21. . . . I can only write a few lines, I have such an immensity to do. . . . I really am worried to death. . . . but there is no end to this never-sufficiently-to-be-hated question, and every day there is some new difficulty or confusion   but there is no option but to keep at wheel, and so the less said about it the better. . .

October 23. . . . I think if I am worried much longer as I now am with telegrams, &c., &c., I shall end by becoming a drivelling idiot. It beats the Greek question, which is saying not a little. . . .

October 28. . . . I am very sorry to hear your uncle [Count Hohenthal, Saxon Minister at Berlin, and *persona grata* at both Courts] has gone off with such warlike instructions, because I have been in hopes that if the Germans were reasonable what the Danes have now done would stop the execution.

November 2. . . . There is something about this business which seems peculiar to it—viz. that even when one thinks one has got everything all right it turns out that something has been omitted or put in a different way from what one had expected or been led to expect. It is very tiresome and disheartening.

November 3. . . . I suppose the Committee of the Diet will present their Report on Thursday, and that will give one some insight into the future.

November 8. . . . The Danes have really behaved very well in these last times, and though there has been occasionally some little trouble attending it, they have done all they could, and may now say all they have been asked. . . . I certainly never thought I should see the end of this question, and I will not be too sanguine ; but if Germany is only reasonable we are certainly further on the road to an ultimate solution than we have ever yet been. Lord Russell has come out wonderfully in this business, and it does him the highest credit and honour for having put it in such practical shape and disencumbered it of all its obscurity and complication. . . .

November 9. . . . The Emperor [of the French] has sent his invitation out for the Congress. The King here has got one, and is told, like all the rest, of course, that besides his Plenipotentiaries if he likes to come himself he'll be welcome. These people will, of course, accept, and it will be difficult for others to refuse, I should fancy so. I hope we may look upon execution as definitely set aside. . . .

November 13. . . . The truth of the proverb, 'Give a dog a bad name,' was never more fully proved than in the case of the Emperor's proposal for a Congress. . . . I think his letter of invitation, which you will have seen in the papers probably, an admirable one. It is impossible Europe can go on much longer as it is now—the Congress appears a chance, although a faint one, of a peaceful solution of many questions . . . it appears, however, that our Government is not likely to agree to it. . . .

November 15. . . . I have omitted to tell you that poor old Kongen [Danish for King] has been for some days very unwell with erysipelas in the face. The illness appears now to have taken the most alarming symptoms. A bulletin was issued this morning, from which it appears he has a great deal of fever, gets no sleep, and is delirious. We shall have a nice complication if he dies.

November 16.—Poor old Kongen died yesterday at 2.35 in the afternoon. I have been this morning to hear King Christian IXth proclaimed from the balcony of Christiansborg Slot. He appeared on the balcony immediately afterwards, and was loudly cheered. The poor old Kongen will be very much regretted, and deservedly so ; for notwithstanding many things, he had, as I have often said, many good qualities as a King. Prince Christian's accession takes place at a most critical juncture—it's quite impossible the execution can take place under the present circumstances, unless the German Powers have lost all their sense of decency. . . .

November 18   Your beginning about Holstein amuses me a good deal. You are right in the relative positions you assign to the Diet and to Denmark, in so far as the purely Federal question which extends to Holstein certainly is concerned . . . but there is also an International question on which the Diet and Denmark are on the footing of two independent Powers, and you would hardly have Denmark yield to everything in this, would you ?   The King has signed the new Constitution to-day. It is against his views, but the ferment throughout the country is such, he would not have kept his Crown if he hadn't. . . .

November 21. . . . Carl Moltke is to be Minister
for Holstein, which ought to please very much both
the Duchies and Germany . . . not, however, that
I expect anything that ever can or will be done here
will ever be useful as far as conciliation goes, for
Germany don't chuse to be satisfied with anything.
. . . I am sorry, by the by, to see that you are dreadfully tainted with German notions, and believe all
you hear on the question . . . for myself, I try to
take a calm and dispassionate view of things. . . .

November 24. . . . As you tell me seriously
that the impression in Germany is that the Augusten-
burgs will get the Duchies, I must tell you seriously
that your friends are as mystified on this subject as
on others. . . . I am really sick of all this cant and
sophistry. . . . I met the King yesterday, and walked
with him to the Palace. He told me he had received
the most kind message from the Queen on his accession. I am so glad of this, and it is, of course,
much better than having sent it through me. . . .

November 25.—Baron Carl Plessen, the great
Holstein man, has been sent for to undertake the
Ministry for Holstein . . his influence there is
immense ; and if he can bring his countrymen to
inform the Diet that they are satisfied with the security
for their interests, which his name will give them, and
that they don't wish for an execution, I imagine the
Diet, notwithstanding the belligerent propensities of
some of the minor German potentates, will find it
difficult to carry out their hostile projects. *Faisons
des vœux donc pour Plessen.* His presence here, at all
events, is a sign that amongst the respectable part of
the Holsteiners there is no sympathy for the Augus-
tenburgs. Not only is HE here, but also Count
Blome and Count Reventlow Crimonil.

November 27. . . . The resource I had some hopes in on Wednesday has failed. Plessen has refused positively to have anything to do with the Holstein Ministry under present circumstances. I had him with me for upwards of two hours on Wednesday evening, but all to no purpose. There is therefore only the chance of our mediation being accepted at Frankfort   Besides this, though it must not be mentioned at present, Russia has proposed to send special Missions here from all the Powers who signed the London Treaty to compliment the King, and that they should at the same time be charged to make certain representations. This is a very good idea.   Really, I never saw anything like the state Germany is in.   What on earth is there in this infernal question that can excite them to this extent !

Here follow a few extracts from my own letters to show what the feeling was in Germany at that time.

Lady Paget to Sir A. Paget.

KNAUTHAYN, *October 6th*, 1863.

. . My uncle [Count Hohenthal, Saxon Minister] says that nobody in Germany wants the execution, and a very little concession on the part of Denmark would prevent it ; but at the same time he says that nothing will set this eternal question at rest but a European war, which, however, the Germans would do anything to avoid at the present moment. ·

November 8. . . . How beautifully worded the speech of the Emperor [of the French] is—but does it not look very threatening ? · · ·

November 10. . . . At Berlin the speech has caused great consternation, for it seems to be such an impossible thing to bring a universal Congress together, and the end of it would be that everybody would have to submit to what the Emperor says. . . . I don't think any German Prince will go, for they look upon the proposal as more or less a trick, so that the Emperor may put himself above the others and bring a war on somewhere, for at peace he cannot live.' . . .

November 16. . . . My uncle arrived yesterday, quite unexpectedly, from Berlin . . he says Sir Andrew Buchanan [H.M.'s Minister at Berlin] never speaks of anything but the Holstein question, and is very Danish. . . . Since I am here, I rather see the Schleswig-Holstein question in another light. Till now I always understood that the German Bund and Denmark negotiated like two Powers on an equal footing ; but I find that here they consider that the Bund is the highest tribunal, to whose judgment Denmark is bound to submit as far as the Duchies are concerned, and if it does not, an execution takes place.

November 20. . I think if you trust to the generosity of the German powers not to go on with the execution you will be very much deceived, and from their point of view it would be wrong to let the right moment pass and allow the Germans of the Duchies to be oppressed as in the past. . . . I am dreadfully sorry for King Christian in this emergency. . . .

November 21. . . . The execution seems unavoidable since the King has signed the Constitution. Everybody here seems only too happy that the storm breaks there, and that the Congress question is forgotten. . . .

November 25   The irritation in Germany is very great. It is not at all certain whether France will stick to the Treaty of '52, and, indeed, M. de Talleyrand, at Berlin, behaves as if they were going to do quite the contrary. You'll see England will be left to fight it out alone. . The Crown Prince of Prussia has telegraphed four times to the Duke of Coburg to beg him to be moderate, and has not even received an answer. . . . I will return to you about the 8th or 9th of December; I'm only waiting for the Princess Royal to return to Berlin to go there for a few days. . . . The execution is unavoidable; the only person who has prevented it until now is Bismarck . . . it may even cost him his place if he holds out much longer. Even Sir Andrew, who is more Danish than the Danes, says that Bismarck is *tout à fait correct.* . . .

November 27.—Thank you very much for your letter and the article in the *Times*, which, however, does not in the least change my ideas. The article only just shows that the man who wrote it has not the slightest idea of German affairs; he does not even know the genealogy of the Royal Family aright, and calls the Landgravine the daughter of Frederic VI. I know more about the question than he does

It may perhaps appear from these extracts that I took too much a line of my own and ought not to have had any opinion at all, but it must be remembered that the Schleswig-Holstein question was one I had heard discussed all my life and belonged intrinsically to German politics. As far back as 1849, I remember my father travelling through the Duchies and telling us of many instances of oppression and injustice to which the Germans there were subjected. I can truly say that during the whole of that sad and difficult time I was only anxious dispassionately to get at the truth, which perhaps was an absurd pretension on my part, as so many clever people engaged in this controversy had never been able to do so. Yet my intention was good.

When I returned to Copenhagen it was to find Sir Augustus, Mr. Lytton, all the other members of the Legation, and the English war correspondents, whom we constantly saw, violently Danish. Their feeling was a chivalrous one, for they saw in Denmark a small country bullied by two great Powers. I myself did not think that the German procedure was always quite correct, but I knew also that at the real core of the question the Germans were right. However, I learned to be silent.

Twenty years later, one evening in Vienna, when my husband and I were talking over this question academically and dispassionately, he owned to me that, had he then been possessed of the information he now was, he would have taken another view of things.

This winter of 1864 was a sad and weary one. Everybody was in deepest mourning for the late King, and the war soon broke out.

I felt the keenest sympathy for the Danes, and quite especially for King Christian, whose kindness of heart, straightforwardness, and high sense of honour had endeared him to both my husband and to me.

I shall never forget the impression the first carts full of wounded soldiers made on me as they passed under our windows.   My heart went out to those poor men lying there and suffering for a cause which none of them understood on either side.   We heard that the Tyrolese and Italian regiments fighting with the Austrians expressed their astonishment at people going to war for so ugly a country as Schleswig.   A most pathetic incident was that of a poor young Lap woman just married, whose husband had to serve with the Danish troops.   He had gone to the war and she had accompanied him to Copenhagen.   During the three months of his absence she cried so much that when he came back she was blind.

The winter was a very severe one, and we were often many days without letters, once even for three weeks.   For eleven days during this time there was not even telegraphic communication, as the Germans had cut the wires.   Now and then a telegram reached us by way of Sweden, but it was very rare that even that way was practicable.

Prince Frederic of Hesse was in the habit of often coming to see me during this war.   A German Prince married to a Prussian Princess and brother-in-law of the King, he had many ties on both sides, and was generally well informed.   I remember that a week before the war actually broke out he paid me a visit and, walking up and down my room, he explained to me during two hours what madness it was in the Danes to try to hold the 'Dannewirke,' a huge fortification the manning of which would have required an army many times greater than the Danish one.

In England it was confidently expected that they would hold it for many months, and at the very least for six weeks.

Prince Frederic, whatever his other faults may have been, was a soldier and clever, and his reasoning was so cogent that I implored my husband to adopt his view and write in that sense to England ; but he believed the Danes, who were just then very bellicose, having received much encouragement from Lord Palmerston and Lord Russell, though I am bound to say that Sir Augustus told them on every occasion they must not expect anything but moral support.

The Dannewirke was not held at all ; it was abandoned before the Germans attacked.

Sir Augustus's sympathy with Denmark made him most anxious to induce King Christian to make such sacrifices at the right moment, as to ensure a more advantageous position in the future. One day when, after a long interview with my husband, King Christian came into my room, looking very tired and weary, he said : ' I have often been bullied and badgered in my life, but nobody has ever pushed me into a corner as badly as your husband has to-day.' I answered : ' It is because he has the welfare of

Denmark and your Majesty's happiness so much at heart'; and this was the plain truth, and the King said he knew that he was a true friend to them.

Lord Wodehouse, who later became Lord Kimberley, was sent on a special mission during the winter to get further concessions from Denmark. He was accompanied by his brother Henry, who was in the diplomatic service, Mr. Philip Currie, and Mr. Sanderson, both in the Foreign Office. They were all very pleasant, and the weather being very cold we used to go out on skating expeditions along the canals, which were spanned by many low bridges. Lord Wodehouse, who was a heavy man and a splendid skater, used to go first, and we all followed in crouching position, holding on to each other and shooting through at a great rate. Mr. Lytton was the only member of the Legation who did not skate, as he hated the cold and was not fond of exercise. On the more civilised parts of the ice we frequently met the Royal children, Princess Dagmar (Empress Dowager of Russia) and Princess Thyra (Duchess of Cumberland), accompanied by their brothers.

I remember this skating as the one bright speck upon the greyness of that winter.

For Lord Wodehouse it was also the only advantage he derived from his mission, for after three weeks he had to return to England without having obtained anything. The day after his departure, however, the knotty point was settled.

The only more or less quiet time which I can remember during the five years I spent in Denmark was after the conclusion of the war. A fine summer was brightened still more at its close by the first visit of the Prince and Princess of Wales, after their marriage, to Denmark.

Sir Augustus and I went to meet the Royal visitors at Elsinore, and as the *Victoria and Albert* steamed in, the fort, as well as the Danish men-of-war lying in the harbour, saluted. It was a fine day with splendid cumuli piled up against the horizon, and the solemn old castle and undulating hills covered with beautiful beech woods made a picturesque background.

The Prince and Princess were received on shore by all the Royal Danish family and at once carried off to Fredensborg, a castle towards the centre of the island.

I had been to Fredensborg once or twice during the reign of the late King when it was uninhabited and neglected. The place had an uncanny attraction for me—the park was vast and melancholy, and it was there that the unhappy Caroline Mathilda, the sister of George the Third, had principally lived, but not in the present modern palace. Of the one she had inhabited not a vestige is left, as the marshy ground upon which it was built has sucked it all in little by little.

We followed the Prince and Princess there for a

day or two, but the scene now was a very different one. Bright faces and happy voices filled the great and gorgeous rooms. The Prince of Wales, with the tact and kindness which always distinguished him, won all hearts, and the Princess was far more beautiful even than when she left Denmark, and the admiration of her country people for her and for Lady Spencer, one of the prettiest women in England, was unbounded. They were covered with splendid jewels and dressed in the latest fashions, which in those days were not disseminated everywhere as they now are. The King and Queen were radiant, especially as the Princess had brought her little son, their first grandchild, with her. It was a happy time for them and made up in some degrees for the sadness of past days.

The rest of our time in Denmark was politically uneventful. In the spring of 1866 Lord Clarendon appointed my husband to Lisbon. Before our departure we went to Bernsdorff to take leave of the King and Queen. Princess Dagmar had just become engaged to the Czarewitch, who died the following winter of meningitis at Nice. He was on a visit at Bernsdorff and looked very delicate indeed, the greatest contrast to his young *fiancée* in her bright pink frock, with the fire of life sparkling in her deep blue eyes and her rosy face framed in glossy dark hair.

We parted from the King with feelings of real regret and respectful friendship. He had always at the most difficult moments proved himself a thorough

Christian gentleman—courageous, truthful, gentle, and forgiving. The Queen I had always admired for her single-hearted devotion to her children and the charm with which she environed her family life.

The thing of which I retain the most vivid remembrance in Denmark is the first burst of spring. One day you have been out for an hour's exercise, muffled in your furs, the air as cold as ever, blowing, snowing, and not a hint of Nature awakening out of her long sleep. The next morning you open your astonished eyes upon a blue sky; the sun is shining, the birds twitter, the air is still. The fruit-trees stand in great masses of solid white against a steel-blue sea, and farther on all along the shore the great beeches shine in a billowy line of verdant gold, so resplendent that the mind can hardly believe the evidence of the eye. This magic, however, only lasts a few days; the leaves soon darken, and at the end of August already begin to be sere and yellow and herald the approach of winter.

CHAPTER VI

RECOLLECTIONS OF PORTUGAL IN THE SIXTIES

It was in the winter of 1859 that I first met the good and charming Princess Stephanie of Hohenzollern, the future Queen of Portugal, whose early and tragic death aroused at the time so much sympathy and interest. She was even then engaged to Don Pedro, an exceptionally gifted young Sovereign, whose head and heart gave promise of a most felicitous reign and happy days for the country he was to govern.

The Princess Stephanie was, when I saw her at Weimar, under the protection of the Princess of Prussia, later Empress Augusta of Germany. This kind and highly endowed Princess loved to have young girls about her, and as her own ladies were of mature age, she often borrowed me from her daughter-in-law (the Princess Frederic William of Prussia, Princess Royal of England), whose lady-in-waiting I was.

The Princess of Prussia had come to Weimar to be present at the birthday of her beloved mother, the Grand Duchess Maria Palowna of Saxe-Weimar, who was the eldest daughter of the Emperor Paul of Russia and the sister of the Emperor Nicholas. The Grand Duchess was a most venerable and dignified old lady, the very prototype of a great and benign Princess. Her children adored her, and the Princess of Prussia never missed coming to her mother's birthday wherever she might be at the time.

The Princess of Prussia had not, at that period, won for herself the sympathies of the nation, but those who knew her well appreciated her great qualities and were not astonished that, when more scope was given to them, as Queen and Empress, public opinion should have entirely veered round in her favour.

She had a slightly stilted way of speaking and a rather artificial manner, contracted from having been obliged as a child to make ' cercle ' before the trees of the parks belonging to the castles where the Grand-ducal family happened to be living, each tree representing a gentleman or lady of the Court, to whom she had to say an amiable thing.

It was the middle of a very hard winter and we started from Berlin in the dark, arriving at Weimar after midnight. During nearly the whole of the journey the Princess insisted upon reading out the papers to me, which she could only accomplish by sitting upon the arm of the seat, so as to get as near as possible to the dingy and dirty oil-lamp of the unwarmed ordinary railway compartment in which we were travelling. When I begged to be allowed to read out to her she said, 'No, no, dear child, you must not try your young eyes.'

The next morning when I went to the Princess's rooms I found the Princess Stephanie already there. She had come from her home at Duesseldorf, where she lived with her parents. Her father was the head of the Roman Catholic and non-reigning branch of the Hohenzollern and her mother was one of the three daughters of the charming Stephanie Beauharnais, the niece of Joséphine, and whom Napoleon married (very much against the young man's will) to the Duke of Baden.

The Princess Stephanie was to accompany the Princess of Prussia that morning to some function, from which I had been dispensed, as the day happened to be a sad and recent anniversary for me. She was dressed in a pink silk frock, in spite of the intense cold. The rest of her attire bespoke the Spartan simplicity in which she had been brought up. Her soft brown hair framed the round and childlike contours of her face. There was something angelic in her expression, which was most attractive and endearing. Two or three months later, as she stood decked out in regal splendour in the Hedwigs-kirche, the great Catholic fane of Berlin, she looked a beautiful young Queen. She was married by procuration to her brother, who accompanied her to Lisbon.

Don Pedro had sent rich and gorgeous presents to his bride, by the Duc de Loule, the Marquis de

Ficalho and many other Portuguese nobles, some of them accompanied by their wives, who were to be the Queen's ladies. The Marquis of Ficalho, who looked the very incarnation of one of Valasquez' portraits, high-bred, tall and extremely thin, with a pointed white beard, refused, when it came to his turn to kiss the Queen's hand, to kneel as the others had done. He said, 'Je ne m'agenouille que devant Dieu et ma Dame.' La Reinha Estafania, as she was now called, smiled and put out her hand.

This young Princess, who was as noble-minded as she was lovely, was carried off a few months after her marriage by a mysterious illness, perhaps diphtheria, which in Portugal was unknown. Don Pedro never recovered her loss, and when a little more than a year afterwards he fell ill of typhoid, to which one or two of his brothers succumbed at the same time, there were some who said that he had allowed himself to die, though others attributed his death to other causes.

When we arrived at Lisbon,[1] Don Luiz (Don Pedro's brother) had been on the throne about five years. He was a fair, fat, amiable, blue-eyed little Sovereign, fond of cooking German dishes in his own private kitchen, and with a quite remarkable talent for the violin.

[1] My husband was appointed as British Envoy Extraordinary (plenipotentiary) to Portugal in September 1866.

He had married, three years before, Maria Pia, the daughter of King Victor Emmanuel of Piedmont. She was fourteen when she arrived in Portugal. When I first saw her at the New Year's reception of 1867 she was seventeen. She startled me by her peculiar beauty. She was tall and stately, though very thin, but her shoulders were broad and she moved well. No smile ever flickered over her small pale face, which was overshadowed by a forest of reddish golden hair. Her turquoise-blue deep-set eyes gazed with a *farouche* expression, very like her father's, from under russet-coloured brows. She wore a pale blue satin gown, absolutely simple except for a piece of priceless lace swathed around her shoulders. Chains of pearls and rubies were wreathed about her head, her neck and arms. It was with difficulty that she could be induced to speak to strangers, perhaps from shyness, but she clung with passionate affection to everything Piedmontese and was very communicative to her father's Envoy and his wife, though she was an English lady. Report says that at present she clings with equal fidelity to everything Portuguese, and, indeed, she has returned to a transformed country; instead of Piedmont, she has found Italy, of which she even barely knows the language, much less the habits of the people! They, who knew her very well, always said that she was a very fine character.

She lived in the great and solemn Palace of the

Ajuda, where I sometimes went to see her ; for on every Thursday afternoon she received any of the ladies whom she knew. The Portuguese ought to be moved by the sad fate of this Princess, who came to them a mere child and felt so lonely and forlorn during the first years of her stay there that she wrote on the walls of her Palace the pathetic words ' Je m'ennuie ! ' ; and who yet has become so passionately attached to the country of her adoption that her exile from it, even after the ghastly events of some years ago, appears a crowning misfortune.

Though I do not remember ever hearing that there were any court festivities, and the King and Queen lived in the most retired way, they were even then very much pressed for money, and in a letter from Sir Augustus Paget, written to Lord Stanley, he says on February 26, 1867 : ' The intended journey of the King and Queen to Paris, London, etc., has now become pretty generally known and causes great dissatisfaction, at which one cannot wonder much in the notoriously impoverished condition of the Royal as well as the public treasury. To defray the expenses of the journey, the King has, it is said, contracted a loan in London, and it is well known that he is already much in debt. They are, I believe, to go to Italy after Paris and London.'

It will be seen by this that the financial embarrass-ments of the Royal family, which contributed so much to the present discontent in Portugal, dated already from King Manoel's grandfather, nearly fifty years ago.

A month later Sir Augustus refers to the same subject :—

I hear rumours that the King's journey abroad is to be given up and, considering his pecuniary position, it would be the wisest thing he could do. To obtain the necessary money he would have to mortgage the Braganza estates, and to enable him to do this he must apply for a law to the Cortes, as they are entailed upon his eldest son. If the application is made, it will be grounded on the plea that the money asked for is to improve those estates, whereas everyone knows the real purpose to which it will be devoted.

And then again on the 30th of March :—

There seems to be great mystery and uncertainty about the Royal movements. Some say the journey is postponed and my own impression is, that it forcibly must be so, but the Queen is exceedingly annoyed, and last night it was said no decision had really been taken. One thing is certain however, that they can't go without any money, and as the Royal treasury is as empty as the public one, this money will have to be borrowed, and moreover the sanction of the Cortes to the King's leaving the country must be obtained, and King Fernando's opposition overcome. I don't see how all this can be done in a week.

I will not enlarge upon a description of Lisbon, as all that ever can be said about it has been said by Lord Byron and Beckford, but I must dwell for a moment upon the ecstatic sensations the first experiences of the real South awakened in me after having passed so many years in the extreme North.

I had at Southampton retired to my cabin amidst bitter November sleet and rain. When two days later I emerged on the sun-bathed deck to listen to the strains of music and inhale the scent of orange groves which came wafted on a gentle breeze from unseen shores, I felt intoxicated with happiness. Another day brought us to the mouth of the Tagus, and there we were informed that we should not be allowed to land at Lisbon, but must undergo five days' quarantine on the opposite shore, because, though we had a clean bill of health, the cholera had been in England in the summer.

We had to go into the Lazzaretto, a kind of fort on a cliff overlooking the Tagus, a place where one was much more likely to catch an illness than get rid of one. The discomfort of this establishment cannot be described. The beds were simply boards with coarse sheets over them. The furniture was of the most common and uncompromising kind, the food absolutely uneatable ; in fact, it was an establishment for fleecing the wretched foreigner whose ill luck lands him into this den, for the prices were far above those of the most sumptuous hotels in Paris or London. Whilst shut up in this prison we were not allowed to see our friends except across an abyss about twenty feet wide and with gratings on both sides, through which we had to shriek out.

In a private letter to Lord Stanley, Sir A. Paget, after touching upon the extremely antiquated and inconvenient custom-house regulations, goes on to say :—

I don't know whether it is because I have been a recent sufferer, but I certainly feel very strongly that if ever the present negotiation takes a practical turn we ought to insist upon the modification of their sanitary laws. Here we have in a free and constitutional country a body which, avowedly totally independent of the Government, is exercising the most unlimited powers in the most arbitrary manner. You can have no conception the injury it does to trade, not to speak of the inconvenience to travellers. It is atrocious that people coming from a clean port and in a ship with a clean bill of health should be subjected to be detained for any number of days in prison, at the caprice of this medical board, and as the term of observation is generally longer for merchandise than it is for passengers, the annoyance and loss to the mercantile community is much greater.

This horrible quarantine was the cause of my missing one of the most remarkable sights of the nineteenth century—the shower of falling stars which took place at midnight on the 14th of November 1866. The hours dragged on so slowly that I sought consolation in sleep.

We were not allowed outside the prison walls, and the only place we had to pace about in was a small sandy court.

We departed with sighs of relief, but not without my husband leaving many forcible wishes behind him, for an unwashed nation, that dared to lock up clean and healthy English people in their disgusting Lazzarettos. We lived at first in a large hotel which stood on the square where we landed. On waking the first morning, I was fascinated by the charm of outdoor southern life. The noise, the bustle, the colour under the blue vault of heaven, with a sun such as I had hardly ever seen in July, and all this in the second half of November! There were half-naked fishers with their nets and Callegos women gracefully balancing great water barrels on their heads ; children selling lemons and oranges and fruit of which I did not even know the name, women with the straight black cloaks and white kerchief on their heads, a dress which in Portuguese is called ' Capot e lenzo,' and the fan, without which no lady or beggar-girl is ever seen, and men screaming out their wares with strange wild cries, which I never learnt to understand. It all appeared enchantment to me. We at once set to work to find a house, for though Lord Stanley had told my husband we were only to stay six months at Lisbon, a change of Government during that time might have also changed this disposition.

We soon found a very delightful house high up

in the Rua San Francisco, where it widens into a little square. Though only a stone's throw from the most animated part of Lisbon, I never, during the six months I was there, saw a carriage pass, except those that drove up to our door. It was utterly deserted. The house itself put me in mind of a gilt cage, it was so smart and frivolous. It was full of light and sunshine, but its great charm was a little garden which seemed to hang in mid air almost above the Tagus. Fathoms below, roofs were piled upon roofs, and the eye ranged over the half of Lisbon and the wide blue river to the marble walls of the Almeida and the purple lines of the Arrabidi mountains.

In the garden stood pepper-trees, magnolias, and aromatic shrubs ; the walls of the house, which on two sides formed the boundary, were covered with camellias as large as saucers, ranging from pale yellow to flaming red ; and the mauve blossoms of a wistaria fell in thick fringes over the slender banisters which encircled the garden east and west.

A rather unpleasant surprise was vouchsafed to us when we proposed giving our first dinner. We found that all our plate-chests had been rifled in the custom-house. Nor were we able to recover any of the stolen articles, though we engaged detectives, who traced them, but after some time gave us to understand that they were under orders to desist.

There was no real political work in Portugal, but

a number of rather annoying current questions ; and the dilatory and not very straightforward dealings which my husband had to encounter tried his patience to the utmost. I will give some extracts from his private letter to Lord Stanley in which he speaks of the affair of Consul Vines, and which will give a picture of what the state of things in Portugal was then. After having said that the Prime Minister, M. Cazal Ribeiro, whenever a thing does not go as he wishes, ' speaks more like a disappointed child, who has been baulked of a pretty toy, than a sensible man having the interests of his country at heart,' he continues: ' I am afraid this affair of Consul Vines will give a great deal of trouble. . . . Even taking the Portuguese version of the case, I do not, I confess, see that they have much to allege against him, and certainly their secret and underhand proceedings are not to be justified.' It appears that Mr. Vines had stated that the ill-feeling against him had been got up by one of the members of the Cortes and that M. Cazal Ribeiro had been strongly influenced by this and had taken part against him.

Sir Augustus continues : ' However all this may be, I perfectly understand that we must try for a peaceful settlement of the affair, and I shall again call upon M. Cazal in a day or two, when perhaps he may be in a more reasonable temper than he was just after his disappointment about the treaty.'

Then a few days later :—

I send you the result of my appeal to M. Cazal Ribeiro in the case of Mr. Consul Vines, and it has been, I am sorry to say, very unsatisfactory. Everything which has been done is, according to him, in conformity with the usual mode of procedure and law in Portugal, and the report of the legal adviser to the Legation supports his assertion.

I can only say under these circumstances that it is a great pity we gave up Conservatorial Court, for a more unjust system of procedure it seems to me difficult to imagine. Conceive an accusation brought against a man in England, the magistrate conducting a secret trial—behind his back and unbeknown to the accused, and consigning him to the Old Bailey on the evidence produced in this secret ordeal, which he has no opportunity of replying to. To me it seems like condemning a man without any trial at all, for, of course, when the real trial comes on, the bias of the jury must be against the accused by reason of the verdict already pronounced against him, which verdict has been obtained behind his back. M. Cazal Ribeiro says such is the universal law on the Continent. I know not how this is, but if it's the case it is another reason why I thank God I'm an Englishman and not a foreigner !

M. Cazal Ribeiro disclaims, as you will see, any personal feeling in the affair, and it is possible that he speaks the truth, but the visit I received from the Deputy of St. Michaels will not fail to strike you in connexion with what Mr. Vines says, as to his being employed in the business.

How this business ended I do not remember, nor do I find any more allusions to it, but in the next letter Sir A. says :—

I wish I could think that I take too gloomy a

view of the state of things, but all my information is derived from the most authentic sources, and there can be, it seems to me, but one inference. No wonder, as you say, that we find so much difficulty in getting our claims settled. If they would only be good enough to answer, it would be something, but they don't even condescend to do this. I have three cases now to which I can't obtain a reply, notwithstanding my repeated applications. Cazal thinks, I suppose, that if he can only get to the day of his departure with the King, he will be all right, at all events for some weeks. I do not wish to appear cynical in my despatches, but the fact is, the whole machine is rotten from top to bottom, and it is such a pity, for there never was a country possessing more natural elements for prosperity. There is said to be a great deal of agitation in the country, especially in the north, but I shall not be surprised to see it settle down.

There is no doubt that a country which once had the mines of Golconda at its disposition, and suddenly lost this source of untold wealth, was in a most difficult position, and the nation's character, or rather want of character, failed to adapt itself to the new situation.

Nobody can tell into what the recent events in Portugal will develop, but there is no doubt that this splendid country, administered by an incorrupt, intelligent and frugal Government, might, like Egypt, be transformed out of poverty and misery into one of the most thriving, most prosperous and happy countries of the world.

M. Cazal Ribeiro may have been very tiresome

in business, but he afforded us constant amusement ; the clever and witty American Envoy, Mr. Harvey, was quite especially entertained by the Prime Minister's vagaries.

M. Cazal was still young, small, dark, slight and alert ; he was involved in everlasting flirtations. At that time he was devoted to a piquante brunette, who, however, showed a certain 'penchant' for a very young, good-looking and lively attaché of our Legation. He was a mere boy, and spent the time, during which he did not copy despatches, in the nursery playing with my children. He was, however, a thorn in M. Cazal's side. Mr. Harvey, who was just as much tried by the latter's business methods as my husband was, mischievously encouraged this sport, and I, who had not forgiven M. Cazal for baulking us in the recovery of our plate, own to having thoroughly enjoyed the fun ; besides which, whenever he came to dine with us, I used to vex his spirit by saying it was so fortunate we had that fine Government plate, or we should not have the pleasure of seeing him at our table, as all our plate had disappeared in the most mysterious way. Mr. Harvey used to be in fits of laughter when at balls and parties, assidu-ously frequented by M. Cazal, he peered round the doors trying to avoid me. The whole thing was infinitely droll, more like the happenings in an *opéra bouffe* than in real and serious life.

Lisbon was, during the winter, a very gay town.

Society appeared to me to be a mixture of Louis XV manners and usages and Alice in Wonderland. It was a never-ending source of surprise and amusement to those who had sufficient sense of humour and romance to see the picturesqueness and not mind the inconvenience. Countess Penafiel gave brilliant balls. She was the daughter and heiress of Count Penafiel, and had fallen in love with a penniless Brazilian, whom she was forbidden to marry. She did so, however, after her father's death, and the hospitality and extravagance of her house was unbounded. Then there was the Duke of Palmella, who also held his title from his wife, a very frequent occurrence in Portugal. The Duchess was a nice quiet woman, half English through her mother. Their dinner parties were what one might imagine banquets to have been in the days when Portugal held sway over Peru. The viands were, it is true, rather weird and eerie, but the topaz-coloured port flowed in goblets, dusty perhaps, but of untold value. Golden pheasants sat, feathers and all, on platters of embossed vermeille, and there were other contrivances such as are only recorded at marriage festivities in the Middle Ages.

The King and Queen never appeared in society, but the King's father, Don Fernando, a very clever, agreeable man, went to great Portuguese houses. He was very tall and good-looking, and spoke German with the strongest Coburg accent. He was married morganatically to a German actress, whom he had created Countess Edla, but he did not then, as later on, introduce her into society. Lisbon was not yet ripe for this innovation. He lived at Cintra, in his castle of La Penha, on one of the highest peaks. The steep slopes of this mountain are covered with gigantic camellia-trees, which are studded with thousands of coral blossoms all through the winter. Under them grows the aromatic white Mediterranean heath, often six feet high.

There were many very beautiful women at Lisbon in those days. The most remarkable one was the Marchesa Ficalho, who looked from head to foot like the 'Donna Inez' of Romance. There were also some very good-looking Spanish exiles, driven away from Madrid by the constantly changing régime. The diplomatic corps was particularly well composed, and lived together in amity like a large family. The Russian Legation, especially, was a great resource. Both the Minister and his wife were Poles, who spoke English to perfection. They were a middle-aged couple, and spent their life under a pear-tree in their garden, where they gave everybody who came to see them an excellent cup of caravan tea. Their hospitality was unbounded, like the kindness of their hearts. They, as well as their secretaries, were great whist-players, in fact everybody at Lisbon was, and when one went to a party all the rooms were filled with innumerable whist tables, and there was hardly anybody to speak to.

Prince Alfred (Duke of Edinburgh) came with his ship and remained about a month. He and his suite went out a great deal and were most popular in society. Many of our men-o'-war used to come and lie in the Tagus, and we sometimes went on board for Divine service, which I always thought most impressive in those wonderful surroundings.

The English church at Lisbon, situated at the highest point of the town, stands in the most beautiful cemetery in the world. Huge cypresses rise into the translucent sky, and scarlet geraniums, with stems as thick as trees, wind in and out of the deep green branches and cover every marble tomb and iron railing. Beyond the whitewashed wall, lavishly draped with crimson bougainvilleas, the azure river melts into the azure hills. The glow and richness of all this red and blue and deep green, with little patches of pure white wall, is such as no words can render. The peace and brightness of this God's Acre is very touching. Many English are buried there, for Lisbon always was full of them.

Once only I was induced to go to a bull-fight, for I was told that there was no cruelty attending them, as the horses that were used were good ones and never were hurt. Unfortunately for me, the first bull that came into the ring was a very savage one, and immediately badly gored a man, who was carried away, upon which he turned upon another one, whom he killed. I fled, wondering what people could find in such pastimes. It is certain that such spectacles must rouse cruelty, the worst of all passions, in the breasts of the onlookers, and very much retard the moral advance of a nation.

All the accounts of the great earthquake of 1758 had a weird fascination for me, and the fact that the word 'earthquake' could never be mentioned at Lisbon, as it was considered as tempting Providence, made the fascination even greater. I visited with curiosity the ruins of the Carmine church, which was still lying as it fell, and any other vestiges I could find of this fearful commotion of nature. A tidal wave sixty feet high swept up the Tagus and over Blackhorse Square (thus christened by the British tar on account of the equestrian statue in the middle) and swallowed up 20,000 people. The impression and the horror have never been effaced from the minds of the people, and a stranger who dares to allude to an earthquake is at once peremptorily silenced. The old gardens of Lisbon had a most mysterious attraction for me. They had been laid out in the splendid days, when the gold mines of Peru were at the disposal of the great nobles, but now no mortal foot ever trod their moss-grown paths, except the girls who gathered the lemons and oranges. They were full of thick high hedges, moss-grown statues, and quaint devices, and my children and I used to run along and play amongst their enchanted green mazes, without any fear of ever being disturbed.

Sometimes we drove to the beautiful Moorish cloisters of Belem, with the fountains and the rose trees in their courts, or to the shore beyond, where the Tagus flows into the Atlantic, the very place where the Royal fugitives embarked the other day.

Some miles inland lay the vast gardens of the Countess Farobo, a very great lady, whose husband had long been Governor of Madeira, where they dispensed princely hospitality to all the English wintering there. These gardens were full of strange, wild, untended flowers, even in the middle of winter. The Portuguese ladies never had a flower in their rooms, for they feared their strong scent, but finding that I loved them they filled my house with nosegays.

Only those who have taken the trouble to visit some of the palaces and gardens around Lisbon can understand the subtle old-world charm which emanates from them.

One day I persuaded our Italian colleagues to accompany us to the Palace of the Almeida, on the opposite side of the Tagus. They kept us waiting a long time and, when they joined us, one of their secretaries, who was a Florentine and had the wicked tongue of his birthplace, confided to me, that what had made his chief late was that he could not manage to concoct a despatch in Italian. Count Cavour had just then put an end to the optional writing in French, which had been allowed to Italian diplomats, and the North Italians were in despair, as many of them were incapable of writing their own language, and among their number was our poor little friend, who was a Genoese. This day another terror was added to his woes, for the playful Dolphins would pass and repass under the bows of our little craft bumping up against her, and my husband amused himself by telling stories how they sometimes even upset a boat. He was terrified.

As we neared the shore, I was absorbed by the Almeida, which stands like one of Claude's ideal structures close to the margin of the water, the little wavelets lapping over the lower steps.

There were great flights of stairs, and tall columns and porticoes, all of sober grey, and the whole was entirely forlorn and abandoned. At the back a wilderness of myrtle hedges as high as houses, carpeted with spring flowers, led one up into the hills.

Another Royal Palace, **Quelus,** is the Portuguese Versailles. Here the rooms **are** partly furnished in a quaint unreal kind of way, a sort of French exotic Louis XV. The gardens are famous for their waterworks, and out of every stone, and bush, and statue, a shower of spray is thrown up. I strayed out of the formal gardens, away from my friends, attracted by **the** most delicious overpowering scent of orangeblossoms, and I came to a grove, a wood, a forest, of orange-trees, such as I had never beheld before. The thick-stemmed trees, with their shining foliage, white

L

flowers, and heavy golden fruit, seemed to stretch for miles. The branches were bowed down to the ground with the weight of the fruit, and the ground was strewn with white blossoms ; I thought myself in fairyland. What makes Quelus so curious is that it lies, a green and luxurious oasis, amidst a desolate desert of sand and rock.

There were hardly any railways in Portugal in those days, and the *posadas* (inns) were of the most elementary description, and all of them infested by a ferocious kind of little scarlet sand-flea. In despite of these terrors we made several rather long excursions into the inland provinces. We went to see the famous shrine of Batalha ; and to get there we traversed an entirely uncultivated and desolate country, sometimes coming to a squalid village crowned by the ruins of a medieval castle and peopled by swarms of filthy half-naked beggars, who insisted upon thrusting their maimed and distorted limbs into our faces, as the horses were being changed. Disgusting and repulsive as these poor wretches were, I remember one exception, a little boy who touched me very much. We met him at the bottom of a long hill which we had to ascend. There was apparently no house near to which he might belong. He was barefoot and hardly clad at all, he had fair hair and blue eyes, like many descendants of the Visigoths, and his age might have been five or six. As his little limbs were all in perfect order I suppose he thought it useless to beg and vociferate, so all he did was to fold his little hands together, as if he were praying, and to follow the carriage silently in this attitude I need not say that he did not do so in vain.

On the afternoon of that day, as we were driving on and on through the dreary brown undulating fields, I suddenly saw, close before me, or more truly, just below me, a vision which seemed too surprising to be real.

The land fell very abruptly, almost like a quarry, only instead of stones there were the never-ending cornfields, and out of the middle of this cup, not a quarter of a mile in diameter, rose the spires and towers, the roofs and columns, the arches and cloisters of world-famed Batalha, so beautifully bewildering to the eye, so utterly unlikely to the imagination, so entirely different from anything I had expected, that my breath stopped for a moment, and the only word I could formulate was an exclamation of surprise. Even now, after so many years, the impression is quite fresh in my mind, but no words can describe or render this unique work of the human brain and hands, built up to the glory of God.

Here the Gothic Moorish style is melted into perfect harmony, and whilst the inside of the Cathedral is mystic and solemn in its noble simplicity and carries the thoughts and prayers of the devout upwards, without distracting them by a single detail, there is not one foot, nay, I may almost say inch, of the exterior that is not worked and wrought over with the most elaborate design and beautiful tracery, as if to say to the world, ' Behold ! can the house of the Almighty be decked out more wonderfully than this one is ? ' As I gazed at these marvellous cloisters and courts, now overgrown with giant nettles and tangled thorns, I felt almost giddy with the wealth of new-found impressions which rushed in upon me, and I looked in wondering silence upon the richness and lightness of the ornaments ; no ancient lace is more delicate in design.

The most astounding part of this indescribable fane is perhaps the ' Capella Imparfeita,' which lies on the south side, and never was finished simply because it was not possible to finish it, such is its unbelievable elaborateness. Conceived by the brain of an enthusiast it can only have been put together inch by inch by hands as patient as they were dexterous. It is so unlike anything else in the world that it is useless to try to describe it.

Lisbon might, I think, have appeared an uneventful place in the long run to those who did not appreciate its perfect climate, its southern splendour, and the old-world picturesqueness which lurked out from amidst much that was repulsive and unlovely to our northern sense of cleanliness and order.

A few men in society were cultivated and well-mannered, and some of the ladies who had travelled and seen other countries were pleasant and distinguished, but the great mass of people struck me as a very mixed race, very *arriéré*, as the French would say, and entirely given over to the pursuit of material profit, no matter how it was attained.

We were extremely fortunate in the composition of the staff of our Legation. Mr. Lytton (later Lord Lytton, Viceroy of India) was first secretary. He had served in the same capacity at Copenhagen when we were there, and we now made the acquaintance of his charming wife.

A very old and close friendship united him and my husband. It had begun when they were quite young men at the Hague, and continued at Copenhagen. It lasted true, warm, and sincere until the younger friend passed over—a loss which created a sorrowful void in the last years of the elder one's life.

Mr. Lytton's delightful conversation, keen sense of humour, brilliant imagination, and above all, his warm heart and affectionate disposition, endeared him to all who knew him. His very peculiarities and oddities only made him more attractive. The Lyttons lived at Cintra, and many were the happy hours we spent together in those fairy woods.

When in the spring, barely six months after our arrival, my husband was appointed to the Legation at Florence, which had just become the capital of Italy, I was of course delighted, but I could not repress a sigh of regret for Lisbon's serene skies, its sunlit gardens, with their unreal, dreamlike fruit and flowers, and, above all, the stately azure river on its eternal journey to the ocean.

There is a Portuguese word, ' *saudades*,' which perhaps best rendered my feelings. It is untranslatable, but unites within itself something of the German *Wehmuth* with the English ' longing ' and a spice of other emotions for which I cannot find expression.

CHAPTER VII

WHEN FLORENCE WAS THE CAPITAL

IT had always been the wish of my heart to go to Italy ; and when my husband was named Minister to the post of Florence, at that time a most interesting one, we were both delighted.

As during that summer of 1867 the cholera was devastating Europe, I took my children, household and all worldly belongings, by ' long sea ' from Lisbon to Leghorn, whilst my husband went to England to kiss hands on his new appointment. When I arrived at Leghorn I found everybody paralysed with terror. The Italians are a very emotional race, and in those days the Government had not learnt to keep things that might affect the public mind out of the papers.

Everybody was talking of a party which Prince Doria had just given, at his lovely Villa of Albano, to the cream of Roman society, and whilst his guests were chatting on the terrace some of them observed the so much feared blue mists creeeping up towards them out of the Campagna. The next day a number of them, Princes and Princesses, Dukes and Cardinals,

151

were dead! At that time disinfectants and pre-
cautionary measures were unknown in Italy, and
nothing was done to mitigate the evil; the poorer
classes especially were mad with terror.

I retired with my children to the Baths of Lucca
till the great heat was over. The whole place still
bore the stamp of Byron's and Shelley's days. It
had long ceased being the fashionable resort it once
was in the thirties and forties, and the only diversions
were the weekly receptions of Princess Corsini, the
greatest lady in Tuscany, at her Palace in the Piazza,
of the part of the Bagni called 'the Villa.'

I was taken to see her by a mutual friend; and
though the wife of any. Minister accredited to King
Victor Emmanuel must have been abhorrent to her,
she was most amiable to me, and we became in future
the fastest friends. I was ushered through a long
suite of rooms into the one in which the Princess sat
enthroned in a gilt chair in the midst of her devotees.
The room was quite bare like those we had come
through, but the walls were hung with a sumptuous
damask. The guests were seated on smaller gilt
chairs than the one the Princess occupied, the chairs
were disposed in a circle, and everybody took their
place according to their rank.

The Princess addressed her visitors with great
dignity; she was a frail little woman, covered with
jewels like a Madonna. The Prince, with a yellow
silk wig and nankin trousers, stood about, throwing

in a word here and there. They had shortly before lost their only son, heir to their immense fortune, at the age of nineteen, just as he was going to be married to one of the daughters of Queen Christina of Spain. They were the type of what was then called in Florence the ' Codini aristocracy.' They clung to their Grand Duke, and Victor Emmanuel was only King of Sardinia to them.

When I first went to Florence there were a great many of the old families who would not go to Court —if a Court could be said to exist at that time. King Victor Emmanuel, when he was not chasing the steinbock or the chamois on his beloved mountains, used to drop down to his capital for a day or two, only to see his Ministers and then disappear again. Once or twice during the winter months he gave a ball at the Pitti Palace. He loathed these functions, and stood for the short time he remained at them on a kind of daïs at the end of the room, surrounded by his staff, scowling, or rather glaring, at the dancers.

Such was the crowd at these balls—for it must not be forgotten that Italy is a democratic country— that a space had to be roped off in front of the daïs. Within this space, on the right, chairs were placed for the diplomatic corps, and on the left the Knights of the Annunciata and their wives and other great Italian functionaries were seated. Every now and then the King sent messages to the ladies within the ropes to dance before him. Many of them were old and portly and had not danced for twenty years. Outside the ropes the crush was indescribable.

Being filled with a thirst for information and a spirit of enterprise, I insisted, at the first ball upon leaving the protection of the ropes to inspect the other rooms and galleries of the far-famed Pitti Palace. I was told it was an impossible undertaking, that no lady had done it before ; but I remained firm, and four gentlemen ˎvolunteered to accompany me. I took the arm of the Duc de Rivaz, at that time Spanish Minister at Florence ; he was a poet of no mean order, the very best type of a high-born Spaniard, dignified, silent, most courteous, tall, pale and red-haired like a portrait by Velasquez. A Neapolitan senator, full of fun and go, carried my train, and two other gentlemen went, one before me and the other to protect me on my right. I laughed at first at all these precautions, but saw very soon that they were by no means exaggerated, for the moment we got into the surging crowd beyond the ropes, I should certainly have had my dress torn off me, as well as my jewels and laces, and it was only by main force that we got into another room, where it was easier to move.

Italy being so democratic, the guests at these balls consisted of every class of people, mostly men. I saw some in coloured ties and trousers, some in jackets and hobnailed boots, women in the most impossible attire, with striped blankets over their shoulders in guise of a shawl. Some wore mittens, and a camellia in their hair seemed to be the only effort at any kind of ornament which they had made. It was impossible even to approach the room in which the refreshments were, for a free-fight went on there all the time. I was told that the knives and forks were chained to the buffet, and that many who left had the necks of bottles sticking out of their coat-pockets. King Victor Emmanuel was a very generous Sovereign and whatever he did, he did splendidly, and his famished subjects were grateful. There was no lady at the Court, which was a purely military one, and so things went on merrily and without any restrictions. I may here mention that the King's civil list was a far larger one than Queen Victoria's, though Italy is a much poorer country than England. I believe it is the case that the more democratic a country is, the more they spend on their Government.

When I returned to the ball-room it suddenly occurred to me that I ought to be presented to the King, so I asked the Marchese Gualterio, Minister of the King's House, to proffer my request to his Majesty. I thought he looked rather embarrassed, but as I believed I was only doing the usual and right thing, I took no notice. After a while the Marchese returned with this message: ' His Majesty will be delighted to make your acquaintance, but not here, as it would entail his making the acquaintance of the other ladies of the diplomatic corps, and he does not feel equal to that. Will you go and see him to-morrow morning at ten o'clock ; Sir Augustus is to accompany you.'

Punctually at twelve o'clock the King, followed by his suite, retired from his daïs, which he had never once left, the ropes were withdrawn, and to my utter astonishment every diplomat seized hold of his wife or daughter and, taking them under their arms, they rushed down, helter-skelter, a small backstairs to the court where their carriages were standing, before the crowd streaming down the great staircase could block the way.

The next morning at ten o'clock I was sitting on a divan in a room in the Pitti Palace waiting till the Council of Ministers should be over. It was a well-known thing that the King, whenever he received ladies, always appointed ten o'clock; but they were not often ladies who belonged to what is called society, nor were they ever accompanied by their husbands, if they had any ; it was therefore not to be wondered at that when the door of the council chamber opened and one Minister came out after another they stopped breathless with astonishment at seeing us seated there. We were immediately ushered into the King's presence. He was sitting at the head of a long green table and made us sit down at each side of him. He at once began to explain why he had asked me to come to him instead of making my acquaintance the night before. He said that all those ladies intimidated him, and as for the old and plain ones (with a grimace) really it was *plus fort que lui*, he could not do it. He rolled his eyes, which were blue and rather bloodshot, and rumpled his hair all the time he spoke. His hair had originally been red, but he now dyed it black, because it was turning grey. He also had a huge black moustache and Imperial, his face was red and he was stout, but looked strong and healthy. He was dressed in some loose garments all made of black broadcloth, and I noticed how little white there was about his thickset, short neck, from which hung a wide black silk tie.

Everybody knows the fascination the ' Re Galan-tuomo ' exercised over those who approached him in those days. His genial address, his generosity, kind-heartedness and mother-wit won all hearts. What did it matter that his private life was not without reproach, or that in conversation he often drew the long bow, or paid without asking the debts of anybody who approached him in the right way ? He had all the qualities and defects dear to the Latin heart.

I soon forgot his extraordinary and rather terrific aspect and laughed heartily at the astounding statements which he poured forth during three-quarters of an hour. One of them was a detailed account of how the Sicilian women, his new subjects, cooked and ate their enemies during the Garibaldian invasion.

Another funny episode was the following, which, however, requires a little explanation. Before every

Pitti ball a list of the foreigners who want to be invited is sent to every Legation, and the Minister has to stand sponsor for the respectability of his compatriots. I knew nothing at all about this, but my husband had struck out the name of a person whom he deemed unfit to be asked, though he knew she was not unknown to the King.

His Majesty suddenly faced round upon me and shouted in his stentorian voice, ' *Ah, vous avez biffé le nom de Madame Z—— de la liste ! C'était bien cruel ! J'ai envoyé ce matin mille francs à ce pauvre diable pour la consoler !* ' I was not yet inured to this southern *désinvolture*, so I rather gasped, but the King went on chattering and laughing as if he had said nothing extraordinary.

The King was at that time married (religiously) to a very handsome but quite uneducated woman, called Rosina, by whom he had several children whom he loved dearly. Rosina would have been Queen of Italy if the King had ever found a Minister foolish or subservient enough to countersign the Civil Marriage Act.

The King had the qualities of a great Sovereign and founder of a throne. His indomitable courage carried him through all his difficulties, but both he and Cavour forgot that they were not immortal and that they had built up an edifice which would require strong shoulders to carry it. Thus it has happened that the growth of Italy has not been such as its makers might have wished, though the splendid talents and capacity of the race encourage one to hope that the present phase is only a passing one, and that Italy is suffering, though in rather a more acute form, from the troubles which are spread more or less over the whole of Europe.

When we arrived in Florence it had only been the capital for a year or two, and there was about the exquisite city '*pulita quanto un gioello,*' as Benvenuto Cellini terms it, that subtle but saddening charm pertaining to all beautiful things which one knows doomed to be adapted to modern exigencies. Already the noble old walls were beginning to fall, to allow of more extended traffic, and, instead of them, wide boulevards, icy and windy in winter, hot and dusty in summer, began to encircle the town. Many of the old palaces and convents had been converted into barracks and Government Offices, and in several places the alien want of taste imported by its northern masters had begun to show itself in Tuscany.

To anybody used to the order and stability of a town like London, Berlin, or Vienna, it would be difficult to give an idea of the chaotic state which a change of capital produces. We went through it twice—once in Florence and later on in Rome.

Like most Englishmen, my husband had a great sympathy with United Italy, and the Italians at that time were still grateful to England for the moral

support she had given them and which had been such
a great factor in their unification. It was therefore
only natural that all the most prominent Italian
statesmen, politicians and patriots congregated at
our house. One of these men was Marco Minghetti,
who had been Prime Minister a few years before, but
was turned out on his signing the unpopular September convention which made Florence the capital.
He was the most eloquent of many eloquent speakers,
his enunciation was smooth, calm and clear, he never
gesticulated, and the words dropped like rounded
pearls from his lips. Every sentence was beautifully
rounded, he never repeated himself, and his images
were elevated and ideal. His speeches gave me the
idea of a rivulet flowing, full and limpid, through
meadows enamelled with flowers ; they created a
sense of the beautiful, the pure and good. Standing
immovable, with his right hand hidden in his waistcoat, he gazed upwards with clear brown eyes, ever
following an ideal and never despairing. The Italians
called him *Il fanciullo eterno*, because of his naïve
faith in goodness, a faith so rare with them. He
belonged to a well-to-do bourgeois family of Bologna,
and had been brought up in antique simplicity. He
told me himself that fires and carpets were unknown
in his father's house, though Bologna, situated on
the northern slopes of the Apennines, is perhaps the
coldest town in Italy. The family always dined with
their fur coats on, and the men with their hats on

their heads. The extreme frugality of Italians in those days explains how it was that so many exiles lived on next to nothing for a great many years in foreign countries.

The foremost patriot amongst Florentines was Baron Ricasoli, always called ' the iron Baron ' from his absolute inflexibility of principle. Rigidly straightforward, entirely honest, and owner of large landed estates, he had a great weight in the country, but was more feared than loved. When not called by political business to the capital, he lived at his Castle of Broglio, which stands on a rock over Lake Trasimene. He never appeared in society, and curious legends, to which I will allude at another time, were woven about his name. He was an aristocrat of aristocrats, but refused to don a uniform when he went to Court, though a staunch Monarchist, for he said no Ricasoli had ever worn any king's livery.

Quite different from him, but equally deserving of his country, was another Tuscan, Ubaldino Peruzzi, then Syndic of Florence, the wittiest and most brilliant man in conversation and of marvellous *finesse*; a Florentine to his finger-ends, but of the very best type. He was devoted to his native city, and spent his life and fortune in beautifying it, without ever securing the gratitude of his fellow-citizens.

Then there was the brave soldier and *preux chevalier* General La Marmora. He was a Piedmontese and had fought many battles for his country, and

M

also played a certain part in politics. Married to an Englishwoman who had long ceased to be young and never had been pretty, he was always at the feet of the most charming women in society.

There was one political man who, as far as I remember, never crossed our threshold, and that was Ratazzi, the Prime Minister of that day. King Victor Emmanuel was most partial to him, though nobody reposed any confidence in a man who, though full of ability, was quite devoid of principle. He was a lawyer by profession and belonged to what is called in Italy *il mezzo ceto*. He was able always to adapt himself to the exigencies of the moment and the requirements of party. He was the first of the long list of men of humble birth who was made a Knight of the Annunciata, and raised, together with his wife, to the rank of cousins of the King. In the case of Madame Ratazzi, this created a most embarrassing position, as even the large heart of Florentine society quailed at admitting her, and everybody was kept in terror lest, by dint of the high rank bestowed on her, she should try to force an entry into it.

Madame Ratazzi was the beautiful daughter of Letitia Buonaparte and Mr. Vyse, a long-time H.B.M.'s Minister at Athens. She first espoused an adventurer calling himself Count Solms, but soon separated from him and led an untrammelled life at Paris and Baden-Baden. When she married Ratazzi she was stone-deaf and no longer young, but she had large, innocent-looking blue eyes, and was an authoress. Some years later, when well past fifty, she gave birth, at Rome, to a daughter, to whom the town stood sponsor with great pomp, and who was called Roma. She was in the habit of receiving every evening in her spacious apartments the most advanced and turbulent spirits—political, literary, and artistic, nearly all men, and would ply them with copious, though elementary, suppers and Virginias—the strong and cheap Italian cigars which were the fashion then.

Florence in those days was full of eminent men whose names were in everybody's mouth, but all of them have disappeared long ago, and the present generation hardly knows anything of the one which made Italy. Most of these men had gone through the bitter school of adversity. They had been exiled, poor, and sometimes imprisoned. It is in adversity that the Italians shine most. They are patient, enduring, contènt with little, full of resource, and can turn their hands to everything.

I must, however, mention a man who, though not an Italian, played a large part in the unification of Italy, and that is Sir James Hudson, who had been English Minister at Turin and now lived in Florence. He was an intimate friend of my husband's, and we saw him constantly ; though he lived an absolutely retired life, he made an exception for us, and occasionally came to dine and meet old friends. He was a man of immense charm of manner, witty, genial and open-hearted, very good-looking still, with his snow-white hair and bright flashing blue eyes. His retirement from the post of Turin has always remained a mystery, but though he never said so, he must at times have regretted not to have been allowed to finish the work he had begun, and both King Victor Emmanuel and Count Cavour reposed the greatest confidence in him. He lived in a beautiful but most secluded villa, to which only his intimate friends were admitted. He had great artistic talent, and in spite of his solitude kept his mind alert and interested, as in his most active days. ' Jimmy Hudson ' was to all who knew him beloved and a bringer of sunshine.

Florentine society had at that time a decidedly political and official aspect, out of which, however, occasionally peeped the former Boccaccio colouring. The King, the Ministers, the Senators and Deputies, the army, the diplomatic corps, and the thousands of employés who are the curse of Italy, all had to be squeezed into that small town.

What had been Florentine society was wiped out, and only a few of the ladies, who belonged to families which had accepted the new order of things, ever appeared, except at some great balls given at the foreign legations, for they found it difficult to compete with the new and much more luxurious habits of the newcomers.

The most striking aspect of a Florentine drawing-room of that day was the immense preponderance of men—about nine to one lady. There was only one small set of about a dozen ladies and fifty men who formed real society. The ladies were all either clever or beautiful, and many of them young. The leader was Donna Laura Minghetti, a woman of great charm and originality. The men, if they were Italians, had all played some part in their country's history; there were statesmen and soldiers, senators and deputies, promising young artists, distinguished foreigners and diplomats, but politics were never mentioned in those days of repose, after the storm and stress of the last six or seven years.

Whenever a lady appeared at one of these small parties she was immediately conducted to a seat, and a gilt Chiavari chair, now a thing of the past, was placed before her to put her feet upon the crossbar, because the marble floors were icily cold and only imperfectly carpeted. A dozen men seized other Chiavari chairs and at once made a circle around her, and there she remained for the rest of the evening. Two women never sat together; if they wanted to talk they visited in the morning. It was a very restful and pleasant way of going into society, for one only had to sit and listen and be amused, very different from the undignified rush and push and agitation of the present day.

I disliked most the late hours. Mothers with daughters used to arrive at my balls at two and three o'clock A.M., and always wanted to dance till six in the morning, when it was the fashion to drive straight to the Cascine and breakfast there. Some ladies who had receptions every evening were never to be found before midnight, and they were nicknamed *les dames d'après minuit.* This was the only sign that remained of the Bohemian element of former days, when the *dame aux perles* and others of that ilk led society.

During the first spring that we passed in Florence the marriage of Prince Humbert to his cousin Princess Margaret took place. To please the Piedmontese, who were very sore at Turin being a capital no more, it was decided that the ceremony was to take place there, and all the Court officials and dignitaries, the Ministers and diplomats removed for it to Turin.

The journey at that time took the whole day, and we travelled with Count and Countess Usedom, old friends of ours from Berlin days. Count Usedom as Prussian Minister had played an important part in Italy during the war of 1866, and had a great position in his own country. He was not only a clever diplomat, but a man with a vast knowledge of art and literature. Very moderate and *liant* in all difficulties, he had often to smooth over those created by his witty but violent and imperious spouse. She was a Scotchwoman by birth, very original and amusing, and she spoke every language with the utmost fluency but quite incorrectly. On one occasion her carriage was held up during the Carnival in the Corso and not allowed to cut the string. White with anger, she stood up in it to her full height, and stretching out her arms, she shouted · '*Io sono la Prussia e si non mi lasciate passare vi metto tutti is prigione.*' ('I am Prussia and if you do not let me pass I put you all into prison.') The effect was magical, for it was soon after Sadowa.

Clothes had been a great preoccupation for these marriage festivities, and there were but few that at that time were wealthy enough in Florence to procure them from that great arbiter of taste, M. Worth, who ruled the ladies of the second Empire with a rod of iron. One day at Turin I entered Countess Usedom's room, for her apartments were contiguous to ours, and I found myself in the midst of a kind of battlefield of cherry-coloured ribbons and precious laces, which with a large pair of paper-scissors she was ripping off ruthlessly from one of Worth's choicest creations just arrived, simply because she did not like it. Only a woman of that day can appreciate the independence of spirit which could commit such a sacrilege. Personally I applauded her.

Princess Margaret was at that time barely seventeen. A slight, graceful girl, with a bright, vivacious manner. Her splendid fair hair waved thickly about her low forehead, her long, grey, almond-shaped eyes were fringed with thick brown lashes, and the full red lips, an inheritance from Austrian ancestors, were always smiling. Prince Humbert was a shy, slim young man, with rolling eyes like his father's and a heavy moustache. Though reticent with people he did not know well, he was capable of strong and lasting friendships and great devotion. It was well known that he too possessed the physical courage which has always been the patrimony of the House of Savoy.

It was in the month of April, and a lovely spring. Festivity followed festivity, and the old town of Turin, accustomed to the severe etiquette of the Sardinian Court, was so overwhelmed by young and democratic Italy that at some great civic function the ladies were nearly thrown down, had their jewels torn off, and the whole festival degenerated into a kind of bear-garden. Such things cannot be avoided in new and unregulated communities.

At Florence the main attraction consisted in a tournament in the meadows of the Cascine, a truly artistic sight, for the Italian moves in a fancy dress as if it were his own, and has the instinct of the part he is playing. Prince Humbert as one of his Piedmontese ancestors was a most picturesque figure.

The one who, however, attracted most attention during all the festivities was the Crown Prince of Prussia, later Emperor Frederic III. He was then in all splendour of his manhood and with the glory of Sadowa about him. He was so fascinated by Princess Margaret that he could talk of nothing else. He thought her so clever, so natural and winning. This was, I think, the first beginning of the intimacy of the Royal houses of Hohenzollern and Savoy which has been such a feature during the last twenty years. No other foreign Princess attended the marriage ceremonies, for several of the Royal Houses allied to that of Savoy had been alienated by the recent events in Italy, and they feared the displeasure of Pius IX, though it only applied to public events, for it was no secret that personally he had a leaning towards the Re Galantuomo.

It is a fact that at the time when King Victor Emmanuel still thought of remarrying, it was not the hand of a Roman Catholic Princess he sought, but that of Princess Mary of Cambridge, then in the full bloom of her youth and beauty. The negotiations advanced to a certain point, and were conducted by Count Cavour himself, through Lady Ely, Queen Victoria's lady-in-waiting and friend, to whom Count Cavour was personally devoted. They were, unfortunately for Italy, broken off, for it may be surmised with certainty that such a personality as Princess Mary's would have had a most beneficial influence on many problems in the country over which she would have reigned.

I must confess that, though we lived almost entirely in the society of politicians, I did not know much about or interest myself in political events. Nobody ever mentioned them in society, everybody seemed to rest upon their oars, and the art and beauty of Florence and its surroundings entirely absorbed me. I could think of nothing else, and found willing and learned cicerones to guide me amongst the Italian statesmen, though they sometimes asked smilingly whether I wanted to write a guide-book, for it was quite unfashionable, nay, I may say, unheard of, for ladies to meddle with art at that time. Things are quite changed now ; many Italian women not only take a platonic interest in art, but they have become executive, as is proved by the exquisite embroideries and woven textures produced under their direction by the wives and daughters of agricultural labourers.

Italy was then still to a great degree untouched; many of its masterpieces were left in the original places for which they had been wrought, and had not been taken to museums or dragged out of the country. I learnt a great deal about Italy from Lord Malmesbury, one of our most frequent visitors. He knew the country well and had lived in it and loved it when he was quite a young man. He had known the Countess Guiccioli (who at this time lived in her villa near Florence) very well, and from her gathered a number of anecdotes about Lord Byron, who had only died a few years before Lord 'Malmesbury first knew her. One she used to relate to show his love of animals was that every year a goose was bought to fatten for Michaelmas, but when the time came Lord Byron would not allow it to be killed. At last he travelled about with six or seven geese slung under his carriage. Countess Guiccioli later in life married the Anglophobe Marquis Boissy d'Anglas, but at that time she led a very retired life and never mixed in society.

Lord Malmesbury was much annoyed that, when Countess Guiccioli's memoirs appeared, she had left out all the amusing stories about Lord Byron which he had so often heard ; however, he himself had the same lapses of memory when he published his 'Reminiscences of an ex-Minister,' for none of the adventures and extraordinary experiences which he had related to his intimate friends appeared in them.

In those days Florence was not, as it now is, the playground of all nations just for a few weeks in spring, then to remain empty for the rest of the year. The real Florentines hardly ever left their palaces, except for a few weeks in October, and it was said of the Marchese Piccolellis (the stepfather of Countess Walewska, so well known in England) that he had never left Florence for twenty-two years except to drive his four-in-hand every day for an hour in the Cascine.

Florence always has been the preferred town of the English, and many are the interesting and illustrious names of those who dwelt there and still shed a romantic charm on the places where they lived. Mrs. Browning had died in the Casa Guidi only a few years before we came. Walter Savage Landor also lived no more on the southern slopes of Fiesole ; the Villa Bricchieri, where Owen Meredith had written his charming 'Good night in the Porch,' stood empty ; Clare Claremont had left the two rooms of the almost ruined old villa which she inhabited at Bellosguardo, and was a daily governess in Florence. What an ending for the mother of Allegra ! Charles Lever lived with his lively and witty daughters on the Costa San Giorgio, and Tom Trollope wrote his lovely little story of the Beata in the villa which is now a lodging-house in the middle of the town. That curious old artist Kirkup, whose name none remembers now, lived in two rooms over the Ponte Vecchio. He had been Sir Thomas Lawrence's most promising scholar, and had painted, or rather, drawn, all the beauties of the Court of George IV. They were exquisite, delicate drawings, and a few of them still hung in his bare and lofty rooms. He had the most wonderful occult library of that day, which unfortunately at his death was dispersed into unknown hands, probably for a song, for at that time nobody knew anything of occultism and spiritualism had not yet emerged from the phase of table-rapping.

I do not think a picture of Florence would be complete without my mentioning Lady Orford, who had lived there for a great number of years. She was an extremely witty and clever woman, charitable in deed and speech, but family disagreements had driven her from England when still quite young, with her two daughters, and sympathy had attracted her to Italy. She had in almost everything adopted Italian habits, and was one of the ladies who received after midnight ; generally only men, who did not even come in evening dress. At the end of the room was a long supper-table, with innumerable bottles of Chianti wine, hams and other cold meats ; the room was filled with the smoke of strong cigars, and the hostess herself smoked. We were in the habit of going there once a year, but by her express desire we announced ourselves the day before. Cigars were banished and everybody was in evening dress, much, I fear, to the discomfort of the company.

It was a careless life, full of charm, art and pleasure, that we led in Florence for the first two years, till we were suddenly awakened from it on the 17th of July 1870.

We had taken for the summer a beautiful old villa situated on the last spurs of Monte Albano, about twelve miles south of Florence. Built by the Grand Duke Francis, in obedience to a caprice of Bianca Capello's, it was said that from its balconies the Cardinal Ferdinand di Medici watched for the messenger coming from Poggio Accaiano in the valley below, where Bianca and her husband were lying sick unto death, after eating of the cherry-tart which either Bianca or the Cardinal had poisoned. As soon as Ferdinand became Grand Duke he resigned his ecclesiastical dignities, for he had never taken any vows, and married Christina of Lorraine, the grand-daughter of Catherine de Medicis, and they had lived in the spacious halls and galleries of this earthly paradise. Such it may indeed be called, for the eye roams from the fir-clad heights of Vallombrosa on to the Apennines of Modena, and farther still to the Apuan Alps. To the south the silver line of the Mediterranean, the Siennese hills and the mysterious plains and marshes of the Maremma were closed by cloud-crowned Monte Amiata, from the summit of which, it is said, on a clear day you can see the cupola of St. Peter's and that of Santa Maria del' Fiore, and the two seas which wash the Italian shores. A large golden full moon hung over the Val d'Arno as we sat with our guests on the spacious loggia, enjoying the sea-breeze which always rises at ten o'clock after a stifling day. Somebody was strumming Italian airs on a piano, and several of our friends strayed down the wide stone stairs on to the green lawn which surrounded the great castellated palace on all sides. Suddenly the music lapsed into a valse, and two or three couples whirled over the grass. The diamonds glinted in the moonlight on the ladies' hair and the large pearls shone on their necks, the warm scent of aromatic herbs, brushed by their flowing dresses, was wafted up to us, and over all lay the indescribable witchery of an Italian summer night.

A telegram was brought to my husband · ' War declared between France and Prussia ! ' It was like the blare of trumpets awakening one from sleep ! Though things had looked serious for some time, they seemed to have quieted down again. As soon as the

Hohenzollern candidature was withdrawn, search had been made for another king to fill the Spanish throne. My husband at once thought of the Duke of Aosta, and even went so far as to sound King Victor Emmanuel, who honoured him with his particular friendship and confidence, whether he would be favourable to the proposal. The answer was in the affirmative, and my husband wrote privately to the Secretary for Foreign Affairs (Earl Granville) to inform him of it. The reply was that it could not be considered. Yet, after all the misery and bloodshed of that terrible year, it was the Duke of Aosta who became King of Spain.

King Victor Emmanuel's sympathies, and certainly his gratitude, were in the beginning of the war on the French side, and so were those of society in general. All 'the smart set' who had often been to Paris, had been presented at the Imperial Court and invited to Compiègne, remembered the amusing days they had spent at what was then considered the centre of Europe. The common people all sided with Germany, very much as they did in England.

The French sympathisers, however, received a severe shock with the surrender of Sedan, as was also the case with the members of the French Legation at Florence, some of whom had played a not unimportant part at the Tuileries. From the moment the Emperor was taken prisoner their interest in the war became very platonic; they had, however, the *mot d'ordre* not to show themselves at any balls or parties. I had, at one of the first fierce battles around Metz, lost a most dear and near relative and never went out during the whole winter. Intimate friends used to come and see me, and the members of the French Legation were in the habit of doing so at least once or twice a week. One evening they were all assembled in my drawing-room, even the military attaché was among them, when my husband received a telegram. After a moment he read it out. It was the fall of Metz ! Nothing but this had been talked of for weeks, and though it decided the fortunes of the war, none of the Frenchmen seemed much pained, the Imperial feeling was too strong with them. It put me in mind of the *emigrés* in Condé's army during the Revolution, who had only Royalist sympathies and no French ones.

On the 20th of September the walls of Rome had fallen before the assault of the Italian soldiers, for France was unable to protect the Pope any longer. The determination to have Rome as the capital was the passionate wish of the whole nation, and not to be resisted.

The King was probably the one who least of all Italians wished for ' Roma Capitale.' He went there for a few days and hastily returned to his beloved mountains. He always knew that Rome would be fatal to him, and stayed there as little as he could.

In the spring of 1871 the whole machinery of the

capital was set in motion and moved to the Eternal City. *Fiorenza la gentile*, the home of art and flowers, was deserted, but not, I think, distressed, for deep down in the heart of every Italian lives the passion for his native city and the wish to keep it for himself ; and does not every Florentine know that, capital or no capital, Florence is the jewel of Italy ?

CHAPTER VIII

LA CITTÀ ETERNA

A REMINISCENCE OF THE SEVENTIES

IT was one evening at Copenhagen during the winter of 1861-2, when, talking to some diplomats of the posts they would prefer to go to, I exclaimed, ' The ideal post would be Rome as an Embassy. I mean to go there ! ' Everybody laughed, for all thought that such a thing would be impossible. Since the days of James II, no English Ambassador had been accredited to the Pope, and who could foresee in 1862 a combination of circumstances which would make Rome the Capital of United Italy !

This was the time of peace before the German-Danish war, which eventually led to the Austro-Prussian one, which in its turn caused the Franco-Prussian war by the transference of the centre of weight to Berlin. The Pope was well protected by Napoleon III, it seemed certain that his successor would continue the same policy, and the boldest imagination could not then forge a chain of events which would lead to Victor Emmanuel being proclaimed King of United Italy, in the space of less than nine years from the evening when I expressed my fantastic desire.

When on the early morning of Christmas Day, 1871, I saw the dome of St. Peter's float transparent and unreal in the icy crystalline air, as the train wound leisurely round the low green hills of the Campagna, I asked myself what would be our lives in this new Capital, where everything was still chaotic, and where there could be no precedents or traditions which would particularly affect us ?

We had come straight from England, with only one day in frozen Paris, where the ghastly destruction of the Commune stared one in the face wherever one went. The winter was a particularly severe one, and, as we drove from the station to our hotel, I noticed all the beautiful fountains (one of Rome's chief charms) were ice-bound and covered with long stalactites—a sight I only once saw repeated there, during our twelve years' residence.

The new state of things in Rome seemed to have attracted the whole world, and every hotel was full to overflowing. A great number of Royalties had congregated together. The Prince and Princess of Wales were to be seen every day in the churches and galleries with the King and Queen of Denmark and all their family, and the Queen of Hanover with her children. Indeed, it was there that the marriage of

Princess Thyra, the Princess of Wales's youngest sister, to the Duke of Cumberland (the King of Hanover's only son) was arranged.

I cannot now enumerate the many crowned heads that came to Rome that winter, and all the interesting men and women I caught glimpses of, for, being in very deep mourning, we did not go into society, and only met people casually on the Pincio, or at some church festival, or in a gallery.

The chaos of a new Capital cannot be described. Nobody seemed to know anything for certain, or where anybody lived. Everybody was house-hunting, and nobody could find a shelter. Prince Doria, whom I knew well from former visits to Rome, offered us the beautiful little Palace in the Villa Pamphyli, but there were no fireplaces, and none could be put in, on account of the decorations, and at last we rented from him his Villa of Albano, until we should find something suitable in Rome.

The Villa had lovely gardens, and was in an ideal situation ; and among my most cherished memories are the drives along the Via Appia Antica, on returning from Rome after a busy day, when I watched the sun sinking into the Tyrrhenean sea, and gilding with its last rays the long line of tombs which border the ancient way, the most mysterious, solemn, silent, and pathetic companions, to those who understand.

King Victor Emmanuel, who disliked Rome even more than he did Florence, and was in the habit of saying that it would prove fatal to him, only came from time to time when important business had to be transacted ; but the Prince and Princess of Piedmont lived in the Quirinal, and represented him socially. Masses of foreigners, especially English, wished to be presented at Court. The Princess very graciously received the English ladies in audience, and one of her own ladies, half English by birth, had undertaken to present her semi-countrywomen, when a good number of demands for presentations had accumulated. I need not say that as under the circumstances there was nobody to refer to, it was impossible to select, and the numbers grew every day.

Shortly after my arrival, I wrote to ask when I might pay my respects to Princess Margaret, at whose marriage I had assisted, and whom I had frequently seen in Florence. When I went at the appointed time, I was received by one of her ladies, who knew me quite well, but who, staring me in the face with frightened eyes, said: 'Oh, but it is much too early ! Duchess X, who presents the English ladies, is not here, and the others have not yet arrived ! '

'*Chère Princesse !*' I responded, 'I am not an English tourist, but Lady Paget, and I have come to my private audience.' Recognition then dawned in her face, and I only give this little incident to show the state of bewilderment everybody was in. I should like to mention one curious remark made to me by

Mr. Marsh, the learned and widely respected American Minister, after he had been in Rome a few years, which was to the effect that among all the Americans who had come there during that time, he had not been able to persuade more than two to go to Court. Considering that Rome is at present entirely under the American sway, and that numbers of great Roman families are composed almost entirely, as far as the ladies go, of Americans, this is remarkable, and shows how entirely social conditions have changed in the United States, as well as at Rome.

The Court of Turin had always been one where a severe and antiquated etiquette had obtained, and now this was all changed and upset by the advent of young and democratic Italy, with no traditions at all, and one had to be a genius of intuition and adaptiveness to steer one's way clear of all social reefs and shoals.

Everybody who remembers Rome in the Papal times would have been struck by the unique and picturesque solemnity of the social functions, the great bare, ill-lit, and unwarmed palatial rooms, the Cardinals in scarlet, the thrones in the princely houses, and the flock of retainers in gaudy, ill-fitting liveries. All this was suddenly swept away by a busy, clamouring, lively, dancing and dining crowd, by calorifères and gas; and all the hateful trash and frippery so dear to semi-artistic minds of the seventies adorned the walls. Poor Mr. Swinton, the once so sought-after painter of delicate portraits of the English beauties of the forties and fifties, but very feeble then, remarked to me, after paying a visit to the high priestess of this new departure, that he had felt like standing on his head at a bric-à-brac, gone mad. The description was accurate.

The Roman aristocracy had for so long looked upon themselves as a kind of power to whom the Ambassadors were accredited, and the foreigners who came to Rome had to make all the advances to be admitted to their houses, that the sudden change of scenery caused numbers of difficulties. The diplomats took their cue from the Court only, and modelled themselves upon the rules laid down by it, and they caused a good deal of friction. Then there was the diplomatic corps accredited to the Pope, which was not supposed to ' *frayer* ' with us, but amongst them were often old friends, and then the rules were broken. The younger members of Papal Embassies, especially of the French one, were to be seen daily at our house, and even went so far as to come to some of our balls given in the spring during race meetings, when the Italian Royalties were absent ; but I believe they were severely rebuked for these transgressions. Roman society was sharply divided between whites and blacks at first ; but even during the twelve years that we were in Rome most of the younger generation had gone over to the whites—not on account of any particular convictions, but simply because it was more amusing and there was more to do.

Looking back upon my life in Rome, it appears to me like a brilliant kaleidoscope, without any very salient points.

After the tremendous events and changes induced by the Franco-Prussian war, France had, for the first time after many years, ceased to be a menace to the peace of Europe, but the Emperor Napoleon was still living. On the 9th of January 1873 we were dining at the Austrian Legation, together with several members of the French Legation, when a telegram was brought to my husband, announcing the Emperor's death at Chislehurst. The French diplomats were absolutely indifferent, and I was particularly shocked by the frivolous remarks of one of the secretaries who had been an *intime* at the Tuileries, where he led all the cotillons, and had been loaded with benefits by his Imperial master.

As regards external affairs, the feeling of peace and relaxation in those days was very profound. Italy had, however, much to occupy her concerning internal affairs, and was especially harried by the brigand question in Sicily, which was a continual sore. I remember two young Englishmen imploring me to intercede with my husband to get them a permit ' to pick the brigands off about Mount Etna, it would be such fun ! '

Rome and the Campagna were also very unsafe. Minghetti, then Prime Minister, was knocked about and deprived of his watch and purse, one evening, in the Foro Trajano, as he was leaving the Palazzo Roccagiovine. Duke Grazioli, riding in his own park with his son and daughter, was attacked by brigands. I was never allowed to go out riding during our stay at the Villa Doria at Albano unless accompanied by a man with a revolver in the holster of his saddle.

Much to the discomfort of the Minister of Foreign Affairs, who hated captures of foreigners by brigands more than anything else, I evolved the idea of driving from Albano to Siena via Capraruola, the Ciminian forest, Viterbo, and the lake of Bolsena, the very worst district for '*malviventi.*' My brother and Lord X were my companions, and we had four fleet horses to our light carriage. Along the whole road were relays of *carabinieri*, and in the most ill-famed parts two of them accompanied us on horseback. We never saw a brigand, but our hotel bills were very much increased by these signs of our importance.

The diplomatic corps had been much modified since its departure from Florence. The Communard Comte de Choiseul, son of the famous Duc de Praslin who murdered his wife in Louis Philippe's day, had been replaced by M. Fournier, the friend of Renan. He was clever, doctrinaire, violent, and *cassant*; very cultured and intimate with all scientific and literary people. He was short, thin, pale-faced, and sharp-featured, and always put me in mind of the Girondin Manuel. He ought to have been clad in a long brown coat and cape, and a low, wide-brimmed hat. His wife, an excellent, simple woman, who adored him, used to pray that he should break an arm, because her happiness was too great. My husband, who had known the Fourniers at other posts, asked why it was not her own arm she prayed for. She did not think that would affect her happiness sufficiently, was her answer. Such elements did not blend well with sarcastic people of the world ; they were soon removed, and replaced by the Marquis and Marquise de Noailles. The Ambassador who, in spite of his aristocratic name, was supposed to have extreme revolutionary leanings, was gentleness itself, and allowed his wife, his son, his Embassy to do exactly as they liked, a *modus vivendi* not usually associated with the intolerant Republican. He was a man of great culture and literary talent, in conversation mildly sarcastic. He used to sit for hours inside my huge fireplace, smoking up the chimney, because he could not be one minute without a cigarette. The Marquise was a Pole, whose great beauty was now somewhat marred by too much *embonpoint* ; but the sway she had for many years, during the time of her widowhood before her second marriage, exercised over many hearts, still prevailed to some degree. She was by no means *collet monté*, but when the great portals of the Palazzo Farnese, which the French Government with true Republican generosity had secured and partly furnished for the Embassy, were thrown open every Monday to crowds less remarkable for quality than quantity, she used to select a friend, and, taking him to the long gallery, she pointed with lovely hands to some very *risqué* subject in Giulio Romano's beautiful ceiling, and, with black lashes dropped over blue eyes, she sighed wistfully ' Et dire que tout cela a été fait à l'instar d'un prêtre ! '

The dinners at the Farnese were unrivalled for gorgeousness, and all the official world was invited to them. They were sometimes enlivened by the son of the house, aged ten, careering round the table on his tricycle adorned only in his nightgown.

Mme. de Noailles, who was amiability itself to everybody, sometimes remonstrated with me for not being sufficiently catholic in my invitations. She used to point at me, saying: ' Regardez cette Ambassadrice qui ne connaît pas les Ministres.' This was in a sense true, for after the Minghetti administration had been replaced by one of a very different kind, the men who composed it never went into society or made any attempt to make my acquaintance, and the principal one amongst them was then coping with the difficulty of having three wives at the same time, one of them being an Englishwoman. I therefore saw no particular reason to take steps to know them. Germany and France were the rivals for popularity, but England could afford to stand by and look on, for all Italians of that generation knew her to be their true friend, who had powerfully supported them in their fight for unity.

Before leaving the French diplomats, I must mention Madame de Corcelles, the wife of the Am bassador to the Pope. She was a delightful old lady, who often visited me in spite of prohibitions. 'Car,' she declared, ' je suis la petite fille de Lafayette, et je fais ce qui me plait.' She never addressed the Cardinals as Eminence, but hailed them in cheery tones as her 'dear Cardinals.' When one day she visited Pius IX, he asked her whether she had seen all the sights of Rome. ' Oui, Saint Père,' she responded, ' mais ce que je désire le plus c'est de voir un conclave.' That Pope had the saving grace of sense of humour, and he it was who told the story.

Prussia never had had any Embassies anywhere, only Ministers plenipotentiary; but Imperial Germany was the first to recognise Italy as a Great Power, and to accredit an ambassador. For this important post M. de Keudell was chosen and accorded a triumphant reception in Rome, both at Court and in society ; for by this time all sympathies had shifted from France to Germany. Southern imagination invested M. de Keudell with Macchiavellian inventiveness and Talleyrand's astuteness. He was supposed to be Prince Bismarck's *alter ego*, whilst he was not even his replica on blotting-paper, and it was only the aura of the man of blood and iron which shone around him. In reality M. de Keudell was the simplest, most naïve, straight, and unsophisticated Prussian soldier, who had been translated into an ambassador's uniform.

I, who when I was a girl at Court, had once sat behind his square white cuirassier's back, as he with huge hands called forth in the purest, most soothing and classical way the melodies of Bach, Mozart, and Beethoven, soon discovered that the mystery of his appointment was to be looked for in the thrall which that divine music had exercised on the receptive mind of the great Chancellor. Besides that, M. de Keudell was discipline in person, and what more could be wanted ? He was enormous, over six feet, and more than broad in proportion. Out of a round bullet head with white or flaxen hair—I never found out which—shone a pair of small but very honest brown eyes. He was utterly without guile, and, being the doyen of the Ambassadors, would have had to cope with many difficulties of form and etiquette, had not his happy nature allowed him to float about in the situation in unconscious bliss, till his popularity landed him on some point of vantage. As Mme. de Keudell was always ill, her duties as doyenne of the ambassadresses devolved upon me, and I had frequently to confer with her husband, so as to take united action. I need not say that with such a man everything was easy as soon as he was quite persuaded that the proposed course was absolutely right and straight.

There was in those days a very large English colony in Rome, and also an enormous influx of tourists, many of whom brought introductions from people we barely knew. There were also those who had printed letters from the Foreign Office recommending them to the Ambassador's good offices and protection. These all imagined they had a right to be invited to what they termed our 'public balls' and receptions. To satisfy them was not easy, and when I insisted that, when the King and Queen honoured our balls with their presence, the ladies should come in full dress, and not, as they frequently did, in walking frocks with striped Como blankets over their shoulders and mittens on their hands, there was an outcry; but I felt it my duty to be firm. Nobody who was not in Rome in those days can have a conception of the numbers of English who invaded it. A good number came to see the sights, others for the Church functions; some came for hunting, and some for riding only, and never went to see St. Peter's or the Coliseum. Many spent all their time in picking up coloured marbles and drinking tea together, but all of them wanted to be amused in the evening, and, as there were hardly any theatres, the Court and the Embassies were the only resource, for the Roman houses were not open to them.

From November to June it was a continuous string of new faces, and the dinners, luncheons, concerts, and balls we had to give seemed unending. Lent brought no relief, for Rome was fuller than ever at that time. On every fine afternoon when there was no hunting all the best lawn-tennis players among

the young Romans assembled in our lovely gardens,
and crowds of ladies came to watch this, till then,
unknown game. The gardens, now alas! reduced
to a third of their extent, covered the grounds of
some ancient villa, and were bounded on the east by
the Aurelian wall and on the south by the Castro
Pretorio. Secular ilex avenues gave a grateful shade
in spring and summer, and led to a grove which in
June was paved with scarlet poppies, out of which,
at one's approach, arose clouds of white doves. The
place was so lonely during the first years of our tenancy
that when I walked there by myself in the gloaming
of a frosty winter evening I saw the foxes creep out
of the copses, seeking for some prey. All this has
gone, and so have the Ludovisi gardens and many
other haunts of the Oreads and Dryads. The Rome
of to-day knows those mysteries no more. When
first we lived in what was then the Villa Torlonia,
but which now has been the English Embassy for
forty years, it was surrounded by vineyards, out of
which loomed ruins and ancient monuments. For a
quarter of a mile there were no houses, and I was
constantly warned by my Roman friends of the
dangers I ran when returning late at night with my
jewels on from some ball or party. The servants were
terrified, and would not go messages after dark, for
high walls, with here and there dark recesses, lined
the road. The gentlemen of the Embassy, when returning in the evening on foot, took the precaution of

walking in the middle of the road, and carried heavy sticks. I confess that these first years in sunny, peaceful, untouched, and mysterious Rome, had a great charm for me. It was romantic, and one might, with a little imagination, have invested it with a spice of danger.

Then there were the long rides over the undulating flower-enamelled Campagna, the spins of twenty or thirty miles through fields of asphodel, tinted rose-red by the setting sun, for we defied the ancient Roman superstition of coming in at sunset. The Embassy, which was close to the Porta Pia, soon became a meeting-place for all our friends who liked riding, as the Campagna was an open book to us. My children brought their playfellows, and these little creatures, some of them on tiny ponies, tore across the smooth green grass, sometimes followed by a stream of huge white Maremma shepherd-dogs, at a pace which often made me tremble. Mothers confided their daughters to me, and many a marriage was thus made in the saddle under my chaperonage.

We knew the Campagna better than anybody in Rome, yet in spite of this we sometimes got into difficulties owing to the frequent changes of boundaries. One day I was riding alone with Dr. Nevin. He was the well-known and energetic incumbent of the American Church in Rome—very popular, and quite a character in those days, before a long illness sapped his powers. He had been a soldier, and through the War of Secession. He was a friend of Dr. Doellinger, and yet was well noted at the Vatican. He seemed to know most people, although he was very poor and went little into society. A lady once sent him a cheque for ten pounds anonymously, because his clothes were so shabby. I doubt whether he bought new ones with the money. He was very enterprising, and reasonable people thought him a little—extraordinary; he rode a little skinny mare, whom he apostrophised as ' Baby,' and who got over or under most things. That afternoon we had lost our way in the long valleys which extend from the monastery of the Tre Fontane towards Albano, when we suddenly came upon a great number of convicts digging up a large extent of soil, and, in answer to our questions, we were told that the monks were extending their eucalyptus plantations in that direction. These plantations have made this most insalubrious part of the Campagna quite healthy and very beautiful. In the distance we espied, near another gang of convicts, what appeared to be an Arab on horseback. Our curiosity being aroused, we put our horses into a canter, and soon came up with what we found to be a monk, a Trappist monk in a white cowl with a black stole over it. He was young and handsome, and as we approached he vainly tried to pull his narrow skirt down over his white cotton stockings. We asked permission to pass through the lands appertaining to the Abbey, and he courteously offered to show us the way. I made a remark to Dr. Nevin expressing my admiration of the monk's straight seat and manly looks, but my companion pointed to the purple tassels hanging from the hat, and said : ' Take care, he will understand.' At this moment our cicerone, galloping on before us, took a wide ditch in splendid style, and, flinging open a heavy gate to let us pass, bowed a low and silent adieu. As he drew his hand back from the gate, the sun glinted upon a great jewel in a ring, which revealed him to be the mitred Abbot of Tre Fontane.

This apparition left a vivid impression upon both of us, and Dr. Nevin took some trouble to find out who the young Abbot was before he became a religious. He was told that he belonged to a great Piedmontese family and was a dashing cavalry officer, and that a tragic love affair drove him, like de Rancé, the founder of the order, to become a Trappist. These monks have strict *clôture*, and are hardly ever allowed to speak. The Abbot only may go abroad.

M. Minghetti, for whom riding was the one re-laxation from his arduous work, was my constant and most staid companion, and used to exclaim, with his calm, seraphic smile: ' Ah, but this is not riding, it is steeplechasing ! ' ' Corrono corrono tutto il tempo come disperati ! ' (' They race all the time like mad-men ! ') Many were the interesting conversations I had with him during those rides. He had at one time, I think it was in 1849, been much in the intimacy of

Pius IX: in fact, he held a position of great trust and responsibility. One evening he was alone with the Pontiff talking of the threatening aspect of the political horizon, when the Pope arose, and, drawing aside the curtain, pointed to a brilliant star, and exclaimed: 'Look at that star! As long as it shines, none can hurt me.' Minghetti told me this to show how strong in those days still was the belief in stars. Napoleon III also had his star, and so had many others. Pius IX and Victor Emmanuel both had superstitions, of which, however, their successors were entirely devoid.

Though the Pope had twice excommunicated the King, they really loved each other, for they were made of the same kind of stuff, and both belonged emphatically to the days that are past and gone. Impulsive in action, *primesautier* and generous in temperament, they allowed themselves the luxury of sometimes letting their feelings deviate from what others might consider the stern path of duty. When King Victor Emmanuel died, his chaplain, against all rules, gave him absolution for everything, though he was under the major excommunication. The Pope sent for the priest, inquired most feelingly about the King's last moments, and when the chaplain confessed, Pius IX, with tears in his eyes, cried: 'Hai fatto bene! hai fatto bene!' ('You have done well! you have done well!') In another month the Pontiff followed the King.

The death of King Victor Emmanuel made a great sensation ; it was so unexpected, for he had a strong constitution and was not past middle age. A shiver of apprehension had swept over the Court when, at the New Year's reception of 1878, the Princess of Piedmont and all her ladies appeared in deep black with long *crêpe* veils, because some time before, the King of Saxony, grandfather of the Princess, had died. It was customary on these occasions to substitute white or grey for black. A few days later it was whispered that the King was ill, not dangerously, said the doctors, but it might become serious. Some said it was miliary, others talked of Roman fever, and the most anxious ones murmured something about perniciosa, that most dreaded of all fevers in Rome.

On the afternoon of January the 9th I was walking in the garden, and as I passed the iron gates a man galloped up and called out ' E morto il Re ! ' and then galloped on.

The effect of the King's death in Italy was a tremendous one. It was not only the personal glamour which surrounded him, but the feeling of security that his strong character gave to the still heterogeneous unity of the country, which was thereby abruptly shaken.

We went to see the King lie in State. He was so enormously swollen and disfigured by his illness that they had been obliged to raise the catafalque almost to the ceiling of the lofty hall, and had disposed his body so that it could hardly be seen; or the people, always suspicious, would certainly have said that he had been poisoned.

At the funeral the whole population stood for hours in the biting wind, silent and uncovered, in the streets through which the procession was to pass. One of the most touching features in it was the King's old war-horse, which he had ridden in many battles, immediately following the hearse, trapped all in black.

Rome had been fatal to this first King of Italy, as he always said it would be. His fervent wish to rest with his ancestors on the wind-swept Superga, facing the majestic chain of the snow-capped Alps, could not be gratified. His body was laid in the Roman Pantheon, into which the Roman sun and the Roman moon shine through the open roof, and where the waves of the Roman Tiber sweep the marble floors when the waters are high. When Pope Pius IX died, just a month after the King, this event, which had been anticipated for so long, with so many hopes and fears, and so much curiosity, created very little excitement. The King's death had dwarfed it, and it was the cross of Piedmont on the cross of St. Peter's to the bitter end. When Pope Leo XIII was elected, whom St. Malachi in his prophecies had qualified as ' Lumen in Coelo,' it was found that the noble family of the Counts Pecci, to which he belonged, bore a comet in a blue sky in their arms. The Pope's arms play a great part, for they are put up in many places, and over all the Embassies accredited to the Holy See. St. Malachi's motto for the present Pope was ' Ignis ardens,' and it was found that he belonged to a religious community who had for their badge a vessel with flames coming out of it.

As these prophecies, which I believe were made in the twelfth or thirteenth century, and first printed in 1595, are very little known, I will give those which are more or less in the memory of man, and which one can verify. It will be observed that there are only eight more Popes to come, and, considering latter-day events, these ominous predictions give one matter for serious thought.

Pius VII.   Aquila Rapax, alludes   to captivity with Napoleon.
Leo XII.   Canis et Coluber, alludes to arms.
Pius VIII.   Vir Religiosus, alludes to character.
Gregory XVI.   De Balneis Etruriae, alludes to place of birth.
Pius IX.   Crux de Cruce, alludes to Piedmontese invasion.
Leo XIII.   Lumen in Coelo, alludes to arms.
Pius X.   Ignis Ardens, alludes to religious arms.
* * *   Religio Depopulata.
* * *   Fides Intrepida.
* * *   Pastor Angelicus.
* * *   Pastor et Nauta.
* * *   Flos Florum.
* * *   De Medietate Lumae.
* * *   De Labore Solis.
 * * *   Gloria Olivae.

In Persecuzione extrema sacrae Romanae ecclesiae
  sedebit Petrus Romanus,
Qui pascet suis (? oues) in multis tribulationibus
  quibus trasactis civitas
Septicollis diruetur et iudex tremendus iudicabit
  populum.

Taking the average of the Popes' reigns in modern
days, the eight future Popes would come to an end
about the middle of the first half of the twenty-first
century, which would once more exemplify the fact
that religious sovereignties are the most lasting of all.

The accession of King Humbert to the throne of
Italy gave rise to no changes in the first instance.
Though the young King had not the imposing physique
of his father or the same vitality and energy, he had
many qualities which endeared him to those who
knew him well. At dinners and suppers or balls,
where he never danced, not even as Crown Prince, I
often had long conversations with him, and the straight-
ness and simplicity of his character inspired me with
respect, whilst his affectionate nature won all my
sympathies. Shy and distant in manner, his sterling
qualities were not at once appreciated, and it was
only later that his sense of duty, and almost too great
conscientiousness, won for him a popularity which
at first was all the Queen's. The King had the
physical courage of the House of Savoy, and he was
a faithful and generous friend. In religion tolerant,
he was outwardly correct, though personally probably

an agnostic. Eminently reasonable, and by nature unambitious, he discharged his duties as a constitutional Sovereign without taking much, or I might say, any, pleasure or pride in his kingly position. His longing for a quiet, unobtrusive life was pathetic, and he often said to me : ' Je suis profondément triste ' ; and then added, half in fun, ' J'aurais été un excellent sergent de ville, c'eût été ma vocation ! '

He too, like his father, clung to Piedmontese traditions and surrounded himself with a Piedmontese Court. I remember his once asking one of Queen Margherita's Roman ladies, who was talking to some friends : ' What are you doing there ? ' and she answered : ' Speaking Italian, Sir ' ; for the King and Queen always spoke in dialect to their immediate *entourage.* King Humbert's charming consort was in many things her husband's opposite. She loved splendour and was born to be a Queen. She liked it, and attracted about herself all the glamour which ought to be a Queen's patrimony. Always gorgeously attired at all festivities, covered with precious laces and priceless jewels, she used, on entering or leaving a room, to sweep a long and gracious curtsy in a semicircle, including everybody, such as we are told Marie Antoinette had the art of making. Indeed, Queen Margaret was in many ways not unlike the martyred Queen of France ; for from her Austrian ancestors she inherited the same full underlip, the bright blue eyes, the fair complexion, and the wealth of shining blonde hair. She is a woman of many parts, speaks four or five languages in perfection, is very musical, highly cultured, and well read. Her charities are proverbial, and now, after bitter trials and living long in partial seclusion, she still holds the popular imagination; and the day her much-beloved figure and beneficent influence are seen and felt no more will be a sad one for Italy.

A few months after King Humbert's accession a man named Passanante made an attempt on his life at Naples. It was when he was driving through the streets with the Queen. When shortly afterwards the Royal couple made a solemn entry into Rome, the streets were packed, and they had a great ovation. They drove at a foot's pace almost from the station to the Quirinal; they were in an open carriage with the little Prince, and the mob swaying and screaming all around them, with no attempt to keep it in bounds. Only a number of police in plain clothes were hanging on to the carriage and were mistaken, by many, as part of the mob. The King held his hat, as was his habit when acknowledging a salute, almost at arm's length from his head; the Queen showed no symptoms of fear and bowed with gracious smile on every side, but I think the fact of her disguising her apprehensions, following upon the shock which the attempt must have given her, caused the nervous illness from which she suffered for several years, and from which it took her so long to recover.

The little Prince of Naples was a most engaging child. Intelligent and bright to a degree, he spoke English perfectly, and told me how, when he went to England, the thing that interested him most was his visit to Woolwich, about which he gave me details far beyond my comprehension. One day I happened to mention before him that a Miss Fox had come to see me. 'What!' he said, in his quick way, 'anything to do with the Prime Minister?' He was very quick and sharp at repartee, and when his English nurse complained that her colds were so terrible that she had to use towels instead of handkerchiefs, 'Why don't you say sheets at once, it would be nearer the truth?' mocked her royal charge of eight.

Even at that age his principles were clearly formulated and unbending, and it was only with the greatest trouble that he was persuaded to shake hands with one of the Ambassadors whose country was at war with another country for which he had conceived a sympathy.

He is now a most exemplary and conscientious Sovereign, but what scope is there for a constitutional King in a democratic country in which he and his Government have often to conciliate millions of utterly uneducated electors, who frequently decree their own misfortunes? Still, the Italian has one great safeguard, and that is—a pleasure and a pride in his own country. We see it now in their present Tripolitan war. The menace of Socialism was imminent, but

all quarrels and ill-will between the different parties
and factions are sunk in the overwhelming feeling of
patriotism. It is the same feeling which has made them
pay their heavy taxes for so long without a murmur,
which makes them bear the expenses of their army
and navy cheerfully, and which, poor as the nation is,
allows their King a Civil List far more generous than
any of our Sovereigns ever had.

The other members of the Royal family hardly
ever appeared in Rome. They were scattered about
at Turin, Florence, and Naples. The Roman Court
was an eminently young one. All the gentlemen and
ladies in attendance on the Sovereigns were young,
some of the women very beautiful. It was rather
like a brilliant picture without a background ; which
was natural, as it was all the growth of a few years.

Roman society was like a tidal river flowing backwards and forwards, for every winter brought back
well-known faces, and yet there were every day new
additions, and this it was which gave it so much unrest and instability, for people were all the time on
the alert as to ' Who is that ? ' and ' Who is coming ? '
and they had adopted the English fashion of continually moving about at parties and never sitting
down.

The enormous influx of strangers from all countries
increased from year to year, more and more engulfing
the Roman element, and it was this ever-moving,
ever-changing, and elusive atmosphere which makes

it so impossible to describe the Rome of that day. The society was composed of Romans proper, and, quite distinct from them, the other Italians, brought to the Capital by their avocations, such as the Government, the Senators and deputies, and the army; though the military element, except at balls, was conspicuous by its absence. Then there were the two sets of diplomats, artists, scientists, writers, and the masses of foreigners.

Owing probably to the very enthusiastic and also practical sympathy which England had ever shown to the cause of United Italy, our house was, in Rome as it had been in Florence, a gathering place for many of the men who played a conspicuous part in the *Risorgimento* of their country. They have all vanished except one or two. They were a short-lived generation. Cavour and the King were the first to go. Those we saw most of were Minghetti, Quintino Sella, la Marmora, Ubaldino Peruzzi, Ricasoli, Bonghi, Massari, Visconti Venosta, Count Corti, Guerrieri Gonzaga, Giovanni Baracco, Lacaita, and many others who had tasted the bitter bread of exile. I often wonder whether any of them foresaw the troubles which prosperity was to bring to the country they loved so well.

One of our intimates was Mario, thirty years before the idol of London. He was very poor, having dissipated the enormous sums which his and Grisi's divine voices had brought them. Mario was, on and off the stage, always the great gentleman. With snow-white hair and beard and the complexion of a girl of sixteen, he also retained the fire of his dark eyes. His dress was superlatively neat and fresh-looking, and even when he dined with us quite alone he wore white waistcoat and gloves, things unknown to his countrymen of that day. He was a hermit; and the only other house he visited was that of his kind and devoted friend Prince Ladis Odescalchi, who once persuaded the great singer to come to one of our balls, and it was delightful to see how his friends of ancient days crowded around him, and the greatest lady in the land called to him gaily with threatening finger: 'Ah! I have to come to the English Embassy to find you!'

Giovanni Costa, so much admired in English art-circles as the greatest painter of that day, but in his native country only appreciated as a patriot, was another hermit who often darkened our doors, and I blush to say that he lost many hours, when not approving of something I had painted, rubbing it over with soft soap and holding it for half an hour under a tap until the texture which he so much liked was obtained. He used to treat his own pictures in that way—a fact which may interest those who possess some of his treasures. Lenbach, the great Bavarian painter, was also much in our house. He was very generous to me in giving away what he called his tricks in painting. He retained much of his peasant origin in his rough-and-ready speech. He told me how, when he was young, he used to wander about on foot and paint portraits for six or seven shillings. One day in his studio, in which were assembled the portraits of most of the famous men of that day, he pointed to that of Mr. Gladstone, a splendid likeness, saying: ' Ist er nicht wie ein fanatischer Bauer ? ' This remark became very interesting to me when, many years later, I heard of the contention of Theosophists that Mr. Gladstone was a reincarnation of Jack Cade.

Mr. W. W. Story's studio was at the end of our garden, and I often sat with him whilst he was working. As a man he was even more interesting than as an artist, for he was full of information, fun, and original thought, with a very kindly disposition. He was a delightful and witty companion, and I often think of the summer evenings when he accompanied me to the Correa, the open-air theatre in the tumulus of Augustus, where, when the bells of the neighbouring churches began to ring, the actors had to leave off speaking ; and when a summer shower came on, all the audience, which sat on chairs on the gravel, rushed into a semicircle of booths at the back, which did duty for boxes.

One hot afternoon in May, I went with Mr. Story to the celebration of Metastasio's centenary in the gardens of the Arcadia. This is a literary society dating from the Renaissance, which still exists. On a small stage in the open air men and women, boys and girls, recited poetry. Around them in a semicircle were seated many Cardinals and Roman Princes and great ladies of the Papal camp. A little farther back were those that belonged to the Arcadia, with their friends and relations.

Above the trees of the garden rose the cupola of San Pietro in Montorio, the roofs of the Spanish Academy, and in the background the Acqua Paula. Below lay extended the whole of Rome—mellow, brown, and mysterious in the waning sunlight. Beyond, a strip of the Campagna vanishing in the vapour which bathed the base of the Sabine and Latin hills.

I had unusual opportunities of knowing many artists and scientists, as they did me the honour of electing me a member of the ' Insigne Accademia of San Luca,' the oldest academy of the world, I believe. Only one other lady belonged to it, the learned Countess Ersilia Lovatelli, daughter of the artistic and scientific blind Duke of Sermoneta, the cleverest and most cultured man in Roman society. The sittings of the Academy were most solemn and dignified, and it was difficult to remember that one was in the nineteenth century.

Another typical Roman scene lingers in my mind. One day my old and valued friend Princess Corsini Scotti came to see me. I was her only link with the white society of Rome, for she was ultra-black, had frequent audiences with the Holy Father, and received chiefly Cardinals. She came to ask me whether I would come to her *matinée*, the first one she had

given since her husband's death. ' Only,' she begged,
 could you come as your own private self and not as
English Ambassadress ? and please bring your daughter.'
I readily agreed, and on the appointed day, escorted
by the Duke of Ripalda, also a most pronounced
Papalino, and, as possessor of the Farnesina Palace,
Princess Corsini's nearest neighbour, we mounted the
wide stairs leading to the splendid apartment on
the first floor of the palace.

On the first row of arm-chairs, disposed in a semicircle, sat the Cardinals, and behind them on chairs
the black society of Rome. Against the wall stood
a kind of altar raised upon a daïs, and upon it burned
wax tapers in tall candlesticks, though it was the
middle of the day. The Cardinals and the bright
spring *toilettes* of the ladies made a rich harmony
against the splendid gold and velvet hangings
of the palatial room. We came purposely late,
so as not to embarrass our kind hostess while she
was receiving ; but if a bomb had burst in the middle
of the room the consternation could hardly have
been greater, for a good many of those who
were present knew me by sight, and some of
them to speak to. We sat down very quietly, and
the Duke of Ripalda stood near us. The recitals
began, all of them by pupils of Seminaries. They
were eulogies of different Popes in verse. There was
a good deal about heretics in them, but we did
not take this to ourselves. One phrase, however,

proved too much for my daughter's youthful gravity; it was piped out in a high treble by a little fellow nine years old :—

Il nostro buon Papa, il sesto Alessandro,

and then followed a panegyric of the Borgias. The whole thing had a wonderful *cachet*; it was like one of the receptions the President de Brosses describes in his lively diaries. Then followed a collation set out as they were in the time of Louis XIV; but we went away, fearing that our remaining might make difficulties for the old Princess.

Soon after this we left Rome. It was a sad leave-taking, for the charm and glamour of the sunny skies, the atmosphere of art and intellect, had cast a powerful fascination over me. I thought that life in the North would appear grey and dull, and I remembered the words Lord Lytton had said to me many years ago : ' When you have once lived in Italy it takes the colour out of everything else.'

When I saw the crowd of friends who had come to see us off, words failed me and it was with tears only that I could bid adieu to the ' Città Eterna.'

CHAPTER IX

VANISHING VIENNA: A RETROSPECT

THESE notes, made some fifteen years ago, have hardly more than a historical interest now, for Viennese society has since then undergone great changes. The ensnaring old-world aroma, elusive and intangible though it was, is now barely more than a memory, and I dare say the generation which has replaced the one I knew will declare that my account in many ways is incorrect. This, however, is not the case, as those who knew Vienna in the eighties can aver, and these notes were made soon after my departure from that city, when my impressions were quite vivid, and the sorrow at the parting from so many loved friends still fresh. I will, therefore, give them as they were made, without any changes, as I fear to trust the correctness of my memory after a lapse of fifteen years.

It is not possible, I think, to give a just and adequate idea of Viennese society without showing out of what roots it sprung, and this I propose to do in a few words. When Francis I renounced in 1806 the title of Emperor of the Holy Roman Empire, and assumed the one of Emperor of Austria, he severed himself completely from German interests, and many of the highest German aristocracy who had hitherto flocked to Vienna withdrew to their respective countries, leaving only a small nucleus of society, formed of the richest and most powerful families belonging to the different parts of the Austrian Empire. The diaries of Frederic Gentz, the well-known and celebrated diplomatic agent, give a very good idea of this transformation. This society was composed of some families belonging to Austria proper, a fair proportion of great Bohemian names, a few Hungarians, and a sprinkling of Poles. They all had splendid palaces in Vienna, and some of these families live in them unto this day. The principal and ever-recurring names in Gentz's diaries are Liechtenstein, Auersperg, Dietrichstein, Harrach, Metternich, Esterhazy, Schönborn, Rasomoffsky, Pallavicini, Palffy, &c. Such was the composition of society at the time of the Congress in 1815, and it is not very much changed now. Vienna had, through the best part of the nineteenth century, the reputation of being the gayest capital of Europe. Relieved from the strain and agitation of Napoleonic days, the Austrian aristocracy gave itself up with its natural *insouciance* to its love of sport, pleasure, and display, living a life of continual social intercourse, whiling time away in its own *gemüthlich* fashion, and never caring what

the future might have in store of good or evil.   Vienna
was always pre-eminent for the facilities it affords of
spending money, and together with Paris it set for
the Continent the fashions in dress, furniture, and
carriages.   Many foreigners of high degree came there,
and were always received with cordial hospitality
whatever the season of the year might be ; for, until
the existence of railways, many of the great families
lived in their villas and country-houses close to the
town, or even in the suburbs or in summer resorts on
the green and smiling slopes of the ' Wiener Wald,'
a chain of wooded hills which encircles Vienna on the
south and west.   The waters of Carlsbad, so fashionable
up to the beginning of the sixties, were a favourite
meeting-place for aristocratic Europe.   Princes, statesmen, and diplomats went there, and many members
of great Austrian families, also some of the bankers
and rich merchants came from the capital; but
these latter formed a completely different society, for
then, as now, the line was clearly and firmly drawn,
and when Viennese society is spoken of, it must be
understood that it means the score or two of noble
families, some of which have been mentioned, and that
no exception is made to this rule.

A second society does exist ; it is wealthy and
very fashionable, and said to be amusing, and some
of the young men belonging to the first society frequent
it.   It consists of bankers, artists, merchants, architects, engineers, actors, employés, and officers, with

their families. The only occasions on which the two societies meet are the great public charity balls; but even then they have hardly any intercourse.

The predecessor of the Emperor Francis Joseph was the Emperor Ferdinand—a Prince of weak intellect, during whose reign a regular and unvaried routine had been maintained at Court. The year was portioned out between Vienna, Schönbrunn, and Laxenburg, the three Imperial palaces, all of them only a few miles distant from each other. All the Archdukes followed this example, spending their winters in old-fashioned stateliness in Vienna, and the summers in the extremest simplicity in their country-houses. This curious combination is very distinctive of Austrian life, even to this day. When the young Emperor at the age of eighteen came to the throne, through an understanding between his mother and his aunt the Empress, his eyes opened on troubled waters, for it was in the midst of the Hungarian revolution; but he was full of hope and courage, and to youth everything seems possible. His chivalrous manners, his kindness and great charm, won every heart; and under his impulse the troubles were soon forgotten, and Vienna became gayer than ever. The Emperor loved dancing and acquitted himself of it with supreme grace and elegance. Through many cold winter nights the windows of the old 'Burg' shone with a thousand candles, and the strains of the graceful *trois-temps* and mazurkas filtered out into the frozen air, and the faithful Viennese rejoiced at the thought that their young Emperor was enjoying himself.

In 1854, six years after his accession, the Emperor married the Duchess Elizabeth in Bavaria, his first cousin. The slight pale girl, barely seventeen, with the marvellous crown of chestnut hair, did not then give the promise of the incomparable loveliness which dazzled Europe for so many years. She had been brought up with Spartan simplicity amongst the mountains and the woods of her native country, and she came with diffidence to take the place of the first lady of a society which was known to be the proudest and the most exclusive of the whole world. It has been said that the great ladies of that day discovered a flaw in the pedigree of the young Princess, and, conceiving themselves to be better born than her, made her feel it. This circumstance, many think, accounts for the dislike the Empress has always shown for Vienna and its society. The political events of the Emperor Francis Joseph's reign are too well known to require repetition ; but it is not to be wondered at that a Sovereign who ascended his throne during the terrible Hungarian episode—who, ten years later, was compelled to sign the disastrous Peace of Villafranca ; who, in 1866, ended a seven days' war with Sadowa and the cession of Venice, and the year after was doomed to see his brother Maximilian perish in the most tragic and humiliating way, and for whom the utmost limits of grief and shame were reached in the mysterious, incomprehensible, and shocking death of his only son—should bear upon his brow the impress of these storms. (When these lines were written, the cruel, wanton assassination of the Empress had not yet been committed; nor could in these pages allusion be made to the many minor family misfortunes which have at times befallen one of the best of men and most conscientious of monarchs.) The lines about the Emperor's forehead and mouth are very sad, but courage and, above all, resignation look out of his blue eyes, and now and then, when talking to his children and grandchildren, flashes of gaiety light them up. The highest and the most rigorous sense of duty is the mainspring of the Emperor's character. At his writing-table every morning by five o'clock, he dispatches all his business himself, and when the press of work is very great his meals are brought in to him on a tray, and eaten in a perfunctory fashion. I have heard it said that at times the food is not very good; but the Emperor, instead of scolding, simply remarks to his A.D.C. : ' You are a lucky man ; you can go to the club and get another dinner.'

After the Crown Prince Rudolph's death, the Empress, who until then had made short appearances at the Court balls, and also assisted at a few dinners given at the ' Burg,' retired altogether from the world, and the Emperor had alone to bear the brunt of these receptions. He did so from the first with unflinching courage, his slight, straight figure as erect as ever, and addressing all those present with his usual courtesy and *bonhomie*. The Empress, whose transcendent beauty and great love of solitude have made her such an object of romantic curiosity to all strangers who visit Vienna, used for many years to give herself up entirely to riding and hunting. So fond was she of this latter pastime, that it was reported that a visit to Ireland was the promise held out to her if she would consent to assist at the Court festivities given in honour of some foreign Sovereign. Later on, when she lost her nerve, she carried on fencing with the same keenness, and at last it was mountaineering which claimed her energies. She could walk from sunrise to sundown over the Styrian Alps, refreshing herself only with a glass of milk and sleeping on the fragrant hay in the loft of a mountain hut. The Hungarians were always the preferred of the Empress ; she learnt to speak their language, and resided much at Budapest, where, after Count Beust had created the dual system, nearly all the rich and brilliant Magyars had withdrawn. This naturally dealt a great blow to Viennese society, for many of the Bohemian nobles followed suit and went to live at Prague, loudly declaring that their country also ought to be recognised as a separate monarchy.

Viennese society therefore now consists mainly of families belonging to the German provinces and a very few from the other parts of the Empire who have remained attached to the old order. Its numbers fluctuate from two to three hundred. This does not include the diplomatic corps or many high officials, civil and military, who, though bidden to Court festivities, never appear at the smaller social *réunions* at private houses.

Every winter during the carnival, two Court balls are given. The first one, which is styled ' ball by Hof,' includes from 1500 to 2000 persons. No invitations are issued for it ; a simple announcement that the ball will take place is sent to all those who are entitled to go to Court. The second ball is called ' Hofball,' and to it only the *élite* of society and the *corps diplomatique* are convened by a formal invitation. It ends with a supper at small tables, at each of which a member of the Imperial family presides, the ladies of highest rank being told off to the Emperor's table, the corresponding gentlemen to that of the Empress or the Archduchess who represented her. These small Court balls were very brilliant indeed, but quite informal, and no *cercle* preceded them. The young ladies (*Contessen*) were generally there in good time, standing in a compact phalanx in front of their mothers, seated on the benches to the right of the throne. *Contess* is the term by which any young lady of rank is designated at Vienna, be she a Princess or a Countess. On these occasions they were all dressed more or less alike, in very fresh and well-fitting tulle dresses, with little plush capes identical in shape, but differing in colour. Around them, walking or standing, were the dancing-men, all of them officers, with a card and pencil in hand making up their books. Involuntarily one was reminded of a saddling-paddock. When the ' fanfare ' announced the approach of the Court, the capes all flew off like a flash of lightning, and were stuffed away under the sofas, on the knees of the mammas—anywhere in fact—all the *Contessen* faced round in a row and stood ready for the race, which began at once with a spirited waltz.

These balls were given in the large room added on to the Burg for the Congress of 1815. The walls are of white stucco, and a row of fine yellow scagliola columns runs right around the room. The space between the walls and the columns is filled with hundreds of blossoming shrubs, and though the room is not beautiful, it looked very brilliant with its many crystal chandeliers, studded with hundreds of wax candles, and the assemblage I saw before me justified its reputation of being the most aristocratic society in Europe. They certainly all looked gentlemen and ladies, with a great air and good manners, and they moved and stood naturally and with grace. The ladies were covered with fine family jewels in old settings, to which the well-developed expanse of their persons afforded ample room. The men were in uniform, and those in Hungarian costume looked particularly well, and outvied their wives in the gorgeousness and size of the precious stones they wore. The Empress took her seat on a raised sofa, the Austrian ladies sitting on the benches on one side of her, and on the other side were the Archduchesses, Ambassadresses, and any foreign Princess who might happen to be at Vienna. About ten o'clock tea was taken by the Empress at a large round table to which a dozen ladies were convened, and on the return from this we found the cotillon had already begun. It is danced standing, and lasts two hours. The *Contessen* never show the slightest sign of fatigue. The figures of the cotillon were the prettiest and the best executed I have ever seen, and they were danced with the precision of a military manœuvre. A score of *Contessen* tear to the other end of the room like a charge of cavalry, and then get back to their places through the most intricate mazes in the nick of time, without ever making a mistake. Strauss's band played with the greatest spirit and *entrain*, whilst the patient and exemplary mothers on the benches never took their eyes off their sprightly daughters. These balls begin precisely at eight o'clock and end at midnight.

Viennese society is almost one vast family, and there are few belonging to it who are not related to nearly all the others. Putting official rank on one side, their respective positions would come in this order : The Liechtensteins, being a still reigning family, come first. After them the mediatised Princes, i.e. those who at one time exercised sovereign rights directly under the Holy Roman Empire. These have the privilege of intermarrying with Royal houses on an equal footing. Thus the daughter of the Duke of Croy has become an Archduchess. The next in rank are the Austrian Princes created after 1806. Then there are mediatised counts and also counts of the Holy Roman Empire. The title of baron is almost unknown in this society ; it is reserved for the *haute finance*, and is considered specially Semitic.

In order to be received at Court it does not suffice to belong to a noble family, it is absolutely necessary to have irreproachable quarterings. The most curious complications sometimes ensue. A young lady who had always gone to Court, as she belonged to one of the best families, married Count R——, who, though belonging to the aristocracy, was not *hoffähig*—that is, he could not go to Court, his mother not having been of noble birth, and his wife had to share his fate. A few years after their marriage, Count R—— accepted some official position, and received from the Emperor what is termed a *Handbillet*—a letter making him *hoffähig*, allowing him to go to Court. His wife, who had the right by her birth, was not, however, permitted to accompany him. These Imperial *Handbillets*, called so because they are written by the Emperor himself, sometimes grant the right to go to Court for life, but often only during official tenure. Many of the ministers and high functionaries spring from the middle class, and though they go to Court they never mix otherwise in society. The one brilliant exception to this rule is that of the late Count Hübner, once Ambassador in Paris during the second Empire, and later on to the Vatican, who, though being of humble birth, managed, with the protection of Prince Metternich and infinite patience, tact, and good fortune, to penetrate into the inmost circles.

It is natural that, in a society thus composed, mere wealth counts for nothing, and that the introduction of new elements on this basis would be quite impossible. Daughters of great houses, however numerous, plain, or poor they may be, never dream of marrying outside their order to secure a rich husband. Even if they had the wish to do so, the opportunity would be lacking, as they only meet the men belonging to their set. In some very rare cases the younger sons of impoverished families have been constrained by debt and extravagance to seek salvation in a money marriage; but then they retire into the country or live abroad, as their wives would not be received. Nearly all the great families who compose Viennese society have large means to keep up a good style of living. Those who cannot keep pace with the others retire to the country. Thus a few years ago the head of one princely house was completely ruined by racing, betting, and gambling, and he, together with his wife and children, left their fine town palace and retired to their château in the country, never to be heard of or seen again. Gambling and betting are a great scourge in Viennese society, and nearly all the young men get hit hard at one time or another. The

Emperor has been most desirous of stopping it ; but in vain, for this passion is deeply ingrained in the blood of the Teutonic race. I am told the gambling in Austria and Germany is much higher than in any other country. It is, however, only fair to say that, whenever the crash comes, all the friends and relations rush to the rescue to help to the best of their ability. The feeling of solidarity is very great.

Vienna is probably the most expensive capital in Europe for people of high rank, as you pay there according to position. Nobody belonging to society, however badly off, could think of going in anything but a two-horse *fiacre*, the shortest fare being a florin. Most men, whether married or single, keep a *fiacre* (a matter of three or four hundred a year), irrespective of their own stables. Many ladies use *fiacres* in the evening to save their horses from standing in the bitter cold winds and blinding sleet of a Viennese winter's night. Most new-comers who enter a Viennese drawing-room would probably be struck by the extreme simplicity in the dress of the ladies, and it would not occur to them that, to secure these garments, prices are paid in excess of anything in Paris or London. These clothes are remarkable for their extraordinary good fit and their exceeding freshness. The girls especially always look as if they had come out of bandboxes, and as if their dresses had grown upon them.

Large dinner-parties are confined to the diplomatic

and official circles, but the Austrians dine out a good deal amongst themselves in a quiet, unostentatious way. At some houses a large circle of relations flocks in almost daily, without any particular invitation. The way of living is eminently patriarchal; the large retinue of servants, badly paid, but well cared for, generally all come from their masters' estates.

After all dinner-parties, even the great official ones, everybody, ladies included, retires to the smoking-room. One's æsthetic sense is rather shocked, by seeing a beautiful young woman, with bare shoulders and blazing tiara, lighting a big cigar over a lamp. The first thing a man does when he gets engaged is to request leave from his future mother-in-law for his *fiancée* to smoke. Many girls, however, do not wait for this moment, and anticipate; and there are evening parties of nothing but *Contessen*, where the fumes of havanas have been seen hovering in the air. Until quite lately the usual dinner hours were from four to six o'clock, this latter being quite the latest and most fashionable time, for everybody had boxes at the Burg and the Opera, and these begin at seven and have to be over by ten, as that is the charmed moment at which all who do not live in a house of their own have to be back, unless they wish to be mulcted of the sum of ten kreutzers. Every porter closes his door punctually at ten, and the ten kreutzers are his perquisite. When, some years ago, the question was mooted of putting back the closing time to eleven o'clock, there was a revolt amongst the porters, and the authorities had to give in.

In spite of the pleasure-loving reputation of the Viennese, there are few theatres, and it is only the large subsidies the Emperor gives to the Burg Theatre and the Opera which makes it possible for them to exist. A new ballet or an opera of Wagner's always commands a full attendance, but at a classical play or an opera of Gluck's or Mozart's the house is nearly empty, though the acting and singing are first-rate. The most prominent actors of the Burg are Messrs. Levinsky and Sonnenthal, who to their own individual talent unite a thorough knowledge of the stage. At the opera such representations as Massenet's *Manon* with Vandyke and Mlle. Rénard in the principal parts can hardly be rivalled anywhere. The younger sporting generation do not, however, care for the theatre. They like dining late, and then meet in small sets and play bézique or less innocent games. The men go a good deal to the club, where their conversation is entirely of racing and shooting. The Austrian shoots nearly all the year round, and all his faculties are devoted to this pursuit. He does not mind how much he roughs it or what weather he is exposed to. He is nearly always a good shot, and so are some of the ladies, who often accompany their husbands on their expeditions. Princess Pauline Metternich is a great proficient in this line. The chamois shooting begins in August, and is succeeded by stag and roe-deer, partridge and pheasant, with ground game, all through the autumn and early winter. Then comes the bear and wild boar season, and in February, amongst mountains of snow, the arduous shooting of the hinds. When this is barely over the stalking of the capercailzies begins. In order to secure this wily bird at the moment at which he sings his lovesong to his mate at the break of day, whilst she is sitting on her nest, it is necessary to get up between one and two A.M., and to scramble for hours uphill in the dark. Many men do this for the six weeks during which the ' Balzing ' season lasts. They live in the most elementary log-huts, existing on the coarsest food, and return to their homes perfectly attenuated.

The only time during which it is possible to count with any certainty on the presence of young men in Vienna is at the time of the races, which begin in April and go on with short intervals all through May till the end of June. This is the really brilliant time of the Vienna season, when the young sporting world comes to the capital for a short spell of amusement. Sport of every kind is what really hypnotises the Austrians, and they are also fond of games, but they are not nearly so adroit or athletic as the English. They are devoted to horses and dogs, and are good and judicious riders ; but the hunting which had been started at the Empress's instigation came to an end when the Emperor withdrew his support, and there is only one private pack of harriers in the monarchy, and this belongs to Count Larisch Moennich. If an Austrian travels, which is a very rare occurrence, it is sure to be in order to shoot lions or tigers, but otherwise they are the most stay-at-home people of the whole world. The Austrian loves to be in the open air. The first thing that strikes the foreigner are the numbers of *cafés* in the Prater. They are crowded all the summer through. There the Viennese shopkeepers breakfast, dine, and sup, imbibing the most fabulous quantities of beer and *café au lait*, and smoking all the time whilst a band plays a waltz, a *czardash*, or a march.

There is one aristocratic restaurant in the Prater which goes under the name of ' Constantin Huegel,' and as long as anybody in society is left it is much frequented in spite of the plague of mosquitoes that infests it. There is no other capital which becomes as thoroughly empty and deserted as Vienna does in the summer. Even the smallest tradesman goes with his family to the country, and the aspect of the broad two-mile-long Prater Avenue under a sweltering August sun, with the accompanying clouds of huge mosquitoes, is the most desolate thing one can imagine. The climate of Vienna is neither healthy nor agreeable, and, for those who live there always, rather exhausting. Whether it be owing to this or the too frequent inter-marriages amongst the Austrian aristocracy or the very small circle of interests bred by the extreme exclusiveness in which they live, it must be conceded that charming, amiable, and kind though they be, Viennese society is pervaded by a great moral indolence and a want of energy and initiative.

Politics, religion, literature, art, and science are hardly ever alluded to in general talk. The Viennese ' Salon ' (annual exhibition) is far below that of Munich, both in number of pictures and excellence of merit. There are exquisite concerts, but none but the middle-class frequent them. Most Austrians are musical, but they do not cultivate their talent. Occasionally you hear a young man, after a small and *intime* dinner, strumming, among clouds of smoke, a waltz or galop on the piano. The ladies hardly ever play or sing, and seem to care less for music than the men.

Referring to the constant intermarriages, there is no doubt that they often have most injurious effects, and they ought to be prohibited, especially those of uncles to their nieces, of which there are some examples. Somehow these marriages seem to be less deteriorating to the mind than to the physique, as some of the most intelligent, agreeable, and gifted couples of the Austrian nobility belong to historical families which have con-stantly intermarried for more than two hundred years. Love marriages are the only unions known at Vienna and admitted. The daughters of great families have small fortunes, for everything is entailed on the eldest son. Beauty, charm, and goodness are the only dower these young ladies bring their husbands. It sometimes happens that a young Austrian chooses a bride in the German Empire or even a foreigner. If the young lady is well-born, well-bred, and simple, she is at once received with open arms. The one thing Viennese society most heartily detests are airs of affectation; and if anybody is suspected of indulging in them it is hopeless for that person to think of getting on. In this peculiarity lies the whole secret of the popularity of some people. Diplomats often do not like Vienna. They have a difficult part to play, and, especially those who represent Republican Governments, are looked upon with coldness and distrust.

Exceptions to this rule are, however, every now and then made in favour of those endowed with good manners, distinguished appearance, and a modest, retiring behaviour. In a society so closely united by the bonds of relationship, where rank is so clearly defined, every member knows its own place, and there can be no unseemly struggling or pushing, as takes place too often in more mixed communities. Snobbishness is also a thing unknown; for the reverence which Austrians have for good birth can hardly be designated as such. To them it is a law—nay, almost a religion—which if taken from them would make them feel as if they were landed on a quicksand.

Another thing which makes it sometimes difficult for foreigners to get into Viennese society is the language, as German is now almost universally spoken, and the younger generation is not at all proficient in French. The ladies as a rule acquire a smattering of

English from their *promeneuses*, a kind of daily governess, only engaged to take the *Contessen* out walking. Things were very different fifty years ago, when Princess Lory Schwarzenberg was the queen of society. All conversation was then carried on in French. The ladies who do so now belong to a former generation, and the type was mainly represented by three sisters, daughters of a princely house who were a power in Vienna. The youngest of them, Countess Clam Gallas, held for many years, by dint of her grace, intelligence, and kindness, the sceptre laid down by Princess Lory. The *salon* of her eldest sister is accounted the most exclusive one of the capital. A score of habitués resort there every other evening, and this illustrious conclave has been nicknamed the ' Olympus.' To be one of the elect implies that you are at least a demigod. Another clique goes by the name of the *Cousinage*, and is formed mainly by the members and relations of the powerful Liechtenstein family. If one of them dies the whole of society is paralysed for the time being, and to obviate this all mournings are shortened considerably. It does not, however, prevent their tears from flowing, for kindness of heart is the fundamental virtue of this society. It is quite enough for anybody to be in trouble that all their faults and shortcomings should be forgotten, and everybody flock around them with proffered help and sympathy.

The one form of amusement dear to every Viennese

heart is dancing. The young ladies think and talk of nothing else during the season, and everything is sacrificed to the amusement and wishes of the *Contessen*. They are quite the dominant party, though of late a few of the young married women have shown signs of revolt, for they not only come to town, but they actually have the hardihood to dance!

At every ball and party the *Contessen* have a room set apart for them, into which no married man or woman may penetrate. They go to this room the moment they arrive, and if it be a party they are not seen again until they leave. At balls the *Contessen* always move about in bands of six or seven, linking arms. They never sit about with men as other girls do, but the moment the music begins they stand up in rows, three or four deep, for the dancers to choose from. As the *Contessen* are very numerous, their partners are not allowed to take more than one turn with them, so as to give the less popular girls a chance. After every dance there is a stampede for refreshments, which stand about on different tables in nearly every room. At supper the young ladies develop appetites only to be compared to their endurance in the dance. Quite different is the fate of the devoted mother. If once she succeeds in capturing a chair in the ball-room, no blandishments of any kind, no hopes of whist or pangs of hunger, will ever move her again. She would rather die than miss seeing how many turns her Finny takes with Sepperl T——, and how

many more bouquets Fannèrl S—— gets than
Mimi L——.

The *Contessen* have an enchanting time of it
before they marry. They dance, they ride, they
smoke, they shoot, they go to races, they have expensive hats and frocks, they eat as many sweetmeats
as they like every afternoon at Demmel's shop ; in
fact, there is nothing that they wish for which is
refused to them. They sometimes have the appearance
of being very fast, but the moment they marry they
become the best and the most devoted wives. Without
a regret they follow their husbands into the country,
and often only reappear again when they have a
daughter to bring out.

It strikes strangers as very curious that girls
brought up in severely religious and strictly moral
households should be allowed to go to every race for
weeks together. Such, however, is the case. In fresh-
est dresses of latest fashion the *Contessen* crowd
together in the passages and on the steps of the
grand stand or walk about in bevies in the enclosure.

Society flocks to these races in great numbers.
The weather is generally fine in May, and the race-
course, which lies between the greater and the lesser
Danube, is a pretty one. Most of the men and some
of the ladies bet very heavily. For those who wish
to be moderate the *totalisateur* is an easy solution.
Many of the great bankers and merchants go to these
races, accompanied by their wives ; but there, as

everywhere else, the separation from the society of which we treat here is absolute. The return from the races is one of the sights of Vienna. The long Prater Avenue is filled with carriages, three or four abreast, most of them horsed with very fast Hungarian *yukkers*, tearing and careering along as fast as they can lay legs to the ground. The coachmen hold the reins in two hands at arms' length, shouting, laughing, and splashed from head to foot, which is supposed to be the acme of *chic*. In the evening the racing set meets again at drums and dances, given at some hotel, but here young ladies are excluded.

Though nearly every great family has its palace at Vienna, few of them entertain, but picnic balls are very much in the fashion. They are so popular because everybody can do as they like, and that is what suits the temper of Viennese society. The finest private balls are those of the Marquis Pallavicini, a rich Hungarian magnate, whose handsome wife, wreathed in priceless jewels, receives the Court and society in spacious and profusely gilt halls. The Harrach and Schönborn palaces are renowned for their beautiful and costly appointments, dating from the days of Maria Theresa, whose prosperous reign gave a great impulse to architecture, and there is little that is good in Vienna left of an earlier date. People who do not possess houses of their own live in flats. As they never receive, it is difficult to penetrate into these apartments, unless you are a relation or an intimate friend. No casual visitor is ever admitted, which, I imagine, accounts a good deal for the strict morality of society. The excuse always given by the servant who opens the door, no matter at what hour of the day, is that the lady is at her toilet. The Ambassadresses, the Mistress of the Robes, and the wives of one or two high officials, have days; but if anybody else presumes to take one they are considered forward. Amongst themselves the Viennese are in and out of each other's houses all day long. However occupied a married daughter may be, she is supposed to find time to visit her mother during the day. Whenever they meet, even at a dinner-party or a ball, the daughter respectfully kisses her mother's hand. This holds good in the case of aunts and nieces, and indeed nearly all the girls would kiss the hand of the lady to whose house they go, if she were a relation or an intimate friend of their mother.

All the women, of all ages, address each other with ' thou,' and for the men the rule is the same. In the army it is even made obligatory. A girl writing to an older woman would begin her letter thus : ' Honoured Princess—Mamma hopes thou wilt,' &c. If there is a shadow of relationship, men and women always use the ' thou ' in speaking to each other as well as Christian names. If a lady of a certain age and rank shakes hands with a man, he always kisses it as a sign of respect. Everybody is called and addressed by a diminutive or nickname which is utterly bewildering to a stranger, and the general topics of conversation being family affairs and purely local gossip, carried on in Viennese jargon, it is utterly incomprehensible to the uninitiated.

The Austrians bring up their children at home. The sons have tutors till they go to the University or into the army. This latter profession, diplomacy, and internal administration are the only careers open to young men of good family. Abbés are not, as in France, tutors in families, and the clergy play no part in social life. Except occasionally some cardinal of high degree at a dinner-party, no Church dignitary ever appears in society. The Austrian ladies are strictly religious and severe in the observance of Church rites. It would be impossible to give dinners on Fridays, as is done in Italy, for all the women fast. The men, though less bound by forms, are extremely respectful in their attitude towards religion. This example is set by the Emperor, who at Easter, before the assembled Court, washes on his knees the feet of twelve old men, and at Corpus Domini walks bareheaded through the streets of Vienna accompanied by all the great dignitaries of the realm, and devoutly kneels before the many altars erected on the way. In former days the Empress and all her ladies joined in the procession, in full Court dress, with their diamonds glittering in their hair, and bare shoulders and arms; and those who remember this say it was a sight worth seeing.

A great deal is done in Vienna for the poor. There are many practical and widespread organisations, headed by all the great ladies. The number of charity balls during the carnival is something appalling. At these festivities the lady patronesses sit on a raised daïs, and one or two of the Archdukes grace the entertainment. The dancing public consists entirely of the middle class. The prettiest ball of this kind is the artists' ball, which is always in fancy dress. The walls of the spacious rooms are every year decorated in a new way with great talent and skill. Sometimes they represent Alpine scenery, at others the bottom of the sea, a tropical region, or a medieval town. Painters, sculptors, musicians, poets, actors, architects, and engineers are to be seen there with their families in picturesque or comic disguises. The week after this ball has taken place a public sale of all the decorations, ornaments, furniture, &c., takes place, and often the things go for fabulous prices. They are all clever imitations of real objects, and are called in Viennese dialect *gehnaas*.

Princess Metternich, a lady of extraordinary wit, prodigious energy and resource, sets every year some charitable scheme on foot when the spring approaches. Sometimes it is a *fête* in the Prater, sometimes an exhibition, or *tableaux vivants*. The proceeds go to the hospitals and the poor.

The inclination to remain at their country seats gains ground very much with the Austrian nobility.

In spite of this, few of them are good administrators, as their native indolence and easy-going disposition prevent them looking into their affairs. Sport fills up all their time. They are not great readers, nor do they take the slightest interest in what happens in the world at large. Even the affairs of the Empire sit very lightly on their consciousness. They live contentedly in the midst of their large family circle, in comfortable but unpretending affluence. Intimate friends are always welcome, but invitations are seldom extended to mere acquaintances, an exception being, however, made for those English who come to Austria in search of sport which their own country does not offer. They are always most hospitably received. It is difficult for anybody who has not lived in it to imagine a society of this stamp, and those who only see the outside of it are apt to form a wrong estimate. The extraordinary exclusiveness of the Austrian aristocracy is not a matter of pride : it is one of habit. The people who compose the second society would not wish to enter the first, as they would not feel at home in it, and the rare artists and literary men who sometimes are asked to great houses are more bored than flattered by these attentions, as it obliges them to don evening clothes and tears them away from their beloved pipes and Pilsen beer.

Prejudiced as many may be in these go-ahead times against a society so narrowly restricted, there is nobody who, once having passed the charmed boundary, does not appreciate the lovable qualities of those that form it ; and whatever changes years may have wrought in its outward forms, the intrinsic qualities must remain, and they are most attaching, for they consist of kindness of heart, purity of life, frankness, and extreme simplicity.

CHAPTER X

I MET the other day a friend whom I had not seen for a year or two. She had then looked out of tired eyes, her face was drawn, and her languid movements seemed more those of an aged invalid than of a woman on the right side of forty.

I now saw before me a creature *svelte* and strong, who seemed to tread on air like a goddess. Her eyes had the fire of youth, and her shining hair framed a face like a rose.

' What have you done ? ' I exclaimed. ' You don't look twenty ! '

' Oh, Brixen,' she said.

' What is Brixen ? ' I asked.

' The water and air cure, you know. Dr. Guggenberg's ! His is by far the best, since Father Kneipp is dead.'

I am interested in the regeneration of humanity, so I treasured this information, determining to go, if only for a few days, and judge for myself at my first leisure moment : not as a patient, for, having studied the philosophy of life, I do not, thank God, require cures, but as an anxious and intelligent amateur, with the hope of improving my knowledge of hygiene for the benefit of a world suffering through its own indolence, carelessness, stupidity, greed, or vanity.

One morning early in January I tore myself away from my beautiful southern home, with its garden still full of roses and the violets beginning to peep out of sheltered nooks, to face the battlefield of an Italian railway station. The one I am alluding to is a most dangerous place, as blows are freely dealt, right and left, while the more able-bodied passengers take the carriages by assault as the trains come in. They swarm up their sides like bees, and it is a real case of the survival of the fittest. The weaker vessels have to content themselves with departing standing up on their feet in the corridors of the cars. This time, however, after a few weeks' correspondence with the railway authorities and the help of some tall and open-handed young men, I secured a place in a *coupé* and never emerged from it till midnight, when I stepped out on the frozen snow at the little station of Brixen. Long before my arrival, I had noticed that the great mountains were swathed in spotless white down to their feet and that their frigid garments trailed over the whole valley ; also I saw the frost embroidering transparent flowerets on the windows of the compartment. Paracelsus or Ennemoser or Reichenbach or another of the older occultists says that these ice flowerets are the spirits of the flower-seeds lying about the earth, which manifest themselves thus in the winter. The bright northern stars were twinkling overhead, and I was prepared for cold, yet as I left the overheated railway carriage, the almost solid crystal atmosphere was a shock to me after the soft and mobile air of the South. I write as if I had been landed in Siberia, yet this was only a valley in the southern part of the Tyrol, miles below the Brenner Pass, and looked upon by North Germans and even Austrians as a mild winter resort.

In a few minutes I arrived at the *Wasser-heilanstalt* (*anglice,* hydropathic establishment), and was ushered from the snowy road almost directly into a simple but well-warmed room by a silent attendant, who whispered with finger on lips that no noise must be made, for the curfew had been rung three hours ago, as nine is the fated moment when every properly educated patient ought to be in bed. As I drew the sheets of roughish Kneipp linen over me, I listened to the splash and rush of the mountain stream which came through the open window and breathed the liquid crystal of the air in long delighted gasps.

On the door of the large, bare, but scrupulously clean dining-room a notice is posted that after nine o'clock no breakfast can be served and that those who come late to meals must begin at the point at which the others have arrived. I was in ample time for breakfast, and as I gazed at these injunctions over my cocoa and bread-and-butter (honey also being allowed), I reflected upon the profound wisdom and knowledge of human nature they displayed; for, as many or most of the patients go to this water-cure for what they are pleased to term nerves, but which is generally only the result of their own misunderstood way of living, it is well to enforce two of the most important conditions for the health of the body and the soul—namely, early rising and punctuality.

Somebody has said that the English were being left behind in the race of peoples because the whole nation rose an hour too late. I should almost feel inclined to make it two hours, instead of one !

> *Morgenstunde* [morning hour]
> *Hat Gold im Munde* [has gold in its mouth]

is a German and most true adage. Early risers alone know the delightful peace and vigour the first hours of the morning impart to work or exercise; also to them is given the luxury of having time for everything. The true hygienist is persuaded that there is nothing so fatiguing as getting up late. As to having breakfast in bed, we will not mention it in the same breath with Brixen !

As far as punctuality is concerned (to which the placard on the door also alluded) there is no better remedy for nerve troubles than thinking of others—and is this not the essence of punctuality ?

Though only an amateur, I thought a bit of a cure

R

would be interesting ; I therefore sought out Dr. von Guggenberg, the head and director of the establishment. He is a man much beloved by his patients for his ready sympathy, his almost unfailing diagnosis, and his cheerful upright and deeply religious character—no small factor in so many diseases in which body and soul are inextricably interlaced. It is much to be regretted from the hygienic point of view that the confidence which Dr. von Guggenberg inspires also in other respects has caused the Province of South Tyrol to elect him as their member into the Reichsrath, which forces him to make much lamented absences at Innspruck and Vienna.

During our colloquy, the doctor told me that the most serious cases generally come to him in the depth of the winter, as then it appears the reaction is strongest. I cannot help thinking that the extreme purity of the almost always windless air at that season must also have a most beneficent effect.

With a smile at my assertion that there was absolutely nothing the matter with me except rare and very transitory reminders of a fall I had had years ago, the doctor said he would write out a little treatment that would meet my case. Every patient is given a small book into which these treatments are inscribed for the whole week. Every patient's treatment differs from the other patients', and no two days the treatments are alike. Mine consisted in being wrapped, at six in the morning, into a sheet dipped into a decoction of hay-seeds (cold of course), after which I remained an hour in bed. Then at half-past ten, after half an hour's very brisk walk, cold water was poured out of a common watering-can over my arms, beginning from my hands to the shoulder and down again. After this, another even quicker walk. During the afternoon, between two more walks, my feet and knees were treated in the same way. Some days I had large pine-needle baths, and after them cold water was dashed all over me. It is impossible to exaggerate the invigorating effect of these treatments and the perfectly delicious glow that follows. One afternoon I neglected my walk before the treatment, and I got no reaction and felt shivery for the rest of the day.

The bath cabins are all open at the top and only separated by wooden partitions; and while undergoing one's treatment one hears the shrieks and wails of the weak-minded and the self-indulgent under the cold jet and the voice of the active and intelligent bathing-woman commending the courageous ones, who bear the streams poured over them with befitting dignity.

A favourite remedy for a cold is the so-called Spanish mantle. This ample garment is dipped into cold water, wrung out, and placed on the sufferer's bed. The shivering patient is laid upon it and tightly rolled up in it, from chin to toes, just like a mummy. Several blankets are now spread over the utterly helpless victim and energetically tucked in. Thus he remains for an hour and a half, not able even to drive a fly away if it settles on his nose. When he is delivered from his bonds he arises cured. Influenza and too ample proportions are treated in the same way.

One is, of course, always dressing and undressing all day long, therefore the simplest garments are recommended, especially to those patients who have complicated sitz and electric baths with massage. Many are also made to saw wood and lie for hours on deck-chairs in the sun, with the snow all around them, in a large wooden shed called the *Liegehalle*.

Such abominations of civilisation as stays, tight shoes, high heels, and stiff collars have to be discarded at once, and are not replaced at all, or only in a very modified form. Thus sandals are all the fashion; and I used to see a stately and dignified princess taking her morning walk in heelless sandals with only small caps to them to protect her stockingless feet; while a pretty young Polish girl, with nothing but a pair of leather soles held on by straps, bravely scattered the frozen snow with her bare pink toes. Nobody at Brixen would dream of taking any notice of such things, and it is this great simplicity of life which rests and rejuvenates exhausted constitutions, and makes those who have ruined them by absurd indulgences understand that there still exists such a thing as health in the world and that it is in the grasp of almost anybody.

Perhaps the greatest trial for spoilt society beauties, who go there to regain their looks even more than their health, is the wearing of the Kneipp linen undergarments. This linen is of very open and rather coarse texture, and the friction it sets up produces a most wholesome action of the skin especially useful to those who have deteriorated and blocked it by warm baths or noxious unguents containing poisonous matter.

As all those who appear at meals have every time to pass through the open air, this by itself constitutes a hardening cure. At first I wrapped up my head and put on a cloak, but in a day or two I constantly neglected these precautions, as one gets so accustomed to the many changes that one hardly feels the bite of the dry and icy air.

Quite half the patients, I was told, were so ill that they never appeared at all. At the end of our passage lived the Mother Superior of a convent of Sisters of Charity. She is renowned at Vienna for the great good she does in the hospitals. I used to hear the sweet-faced little nuns murmur prayers at frequent intervals; and on Sundays and feast-days Mass was celebrated in their rooms, and a delicious and purifying odour of incense pervaded the passage and made me regret for the hundredth time that the burning of incense, instituted by wise pagans, at first I imagine solely as a hygienic measure, should be banished from our Protestant churches.

This saintly lady had arrived completely paralysed, but she was already much better, and was daily taken for quite long walks in her Bath chair. She was a large woman, with a gentle and serene face under her great white coif, and the bevy of five or six little nuns around her, with their winged headdresses, looked like a flight of white pigeons settling on the snow. There were invalids in such pain that they never showed, poor children with St. Vitus's dance who never left their beds; but the little company assembled in the dining-room was always cheerful and gay. The excellent breeding which generally distinguishes Austrians of all ranks asserts itself here. Each person on entering acknowledged those who were seated already by a bow and a smile, and if a new man appeared on the scene, he was formally presented to the rest of the company by the amiable and able young assistant physician who sat at the end of the table. This young doctor lives in the house and attends to the wants of the patients with inexhaustible patience and good humour.

The cultured and interesting Prince and the kind and amiable Princess at the head of the table were not really patients. They pay a yearly visit to Brixen to stave off, like sensible people, advancing years and all that hangs thereon. The Princess, like all great Austrian ladies, is very pious, and in spite of her cure she attended Mass in the town every morning at half-past six, and so did the shy and silent *chanoinesse*, though suffering from nervous exhaustion. The discipline the Roman Catholic Church enjoins is most admirable.

Then there was a witty and what schoolboys would call an extremely jolly Anglo-German lady, fluent in both her native tongues, who kept her neighbours in fits of laughter, and a very charming young one quite English, who with admirable pluck and patience was persevering in a cure of many months, keeping up all the time her fresh enthusiasm for her surroundings and loving the beauty of the little town and of the mountains above it.

Opposite to me sat the very young-looking Polish mamma of a pretty daughter and a little boy dressed in a Russian semi-uniform. He told us he had gone through all the horrors of Odessa, and his sister said that they had been bereft of all their estates and that her uncle had had a hundred Arab horses *coupé en morceaux* by the people. She added, with a resigned smile : ' The peasants did not want to do it, as they loved my uncle, but the agitators insisted, and they had to obey or they would have been killed themselves.' They had been shut up for months in their house. No wonder mother and children looked anæmic.

There were more Poles and Russians—men, all of them, and Austrian officers, come, I suppose, to heal the smart of some old wound. The whole of the little company was quiet, contented, and extremely well-mannered.

The food, which is in great part vegetarian, is quite good and very nourishing, as it is cooked to retain all the salts and phosphates in the vegetables. Nothing but clear icy water stands on the table.

Brixen is a bishopric and stands on many waters. At the end of every tortuous street a bridge spans a rushing stream. The ancient houses have an architecture quite their own, with the fantastic German element much accentuated, especially in some flat bow windows, which look as if the wall had been pressed out after it was built.

One evening, walking quickly along a narrow street, I nearly stumbled over the end of a bier set half-way out of a small doorway. On the black cotton-velvet pall, which was thrown over the coffin, a wreath of artificial pink roses with crudely green leaves and some gilt Christmas-tree paper was placed around a little lamp with a transparency of the Virgin upon it. It must, I think, have been the coffin of a child, it was so very short. Some women in black stood around it.

The bishop's palace is built in a bold uncommon German Rococo style, with an interesting doorway, flanked by two windows which form part of it ; but the most unique and enchanting feature of the town are the ancient Romanesque cloisters entirely frescoed, which possess the mysterious charm and attraction produced by the union of the Byzantine and the earliest Gothic. I had not time to learn their history, and the frost nipped too fiercely to stand for long under those sunless vaults ; but on a summer's day one might pass a few delightful hours communing with the quaint figures on those walls. Around the town, among trees, or in the middle of white fields, which in summer would be green, stand little houses, each one by itself, dotted about rather like the houses out of Nuremberg toy-boxes. They are verv square and all of them rather high, and their surroundings are often perfectly bare. Upon entering, you are astonished to find in them apartments not spacious, but the acme of comfort, beautifully warmed, thickly carpeted, and replete with good furniture, plate, and pictures. These flats are often inhabited by ladies, highly cultured, who come to Brixen in search of health and then have stayed from affection for the place or gratitude for the cure achieved. One of them told me that she had been sixteen years on her back in agonising pain, she could not even bear to be touched. She is now straight and lithe, and walks with quick elastic steps. A miracle to look at, when one knows what she has gone through.

One afternoon late I was sitting in one of these pretty retreats, to which the French term *calfeutré* applies so well. It had been snowing all day, but now the moon was beginning to struggle out. All round the square house lay a spotless, pathless shroud of snow, and the great white mountains loomed up into the sky, with the serried ranks of dark firs straggling up their flanks. On one side of the house a few hundred yards away, just on the edge of its own particular snow-field, stood quite by itself a grey Franciscan church. It was Gothic in style and very plain, but right down its façade, from the roof to the portal, ran a wide and vividly frescoed band upon a gold ground. It stood out when the rays of the moon touched it in a curious and unreal way, like the leaf of a missal in limelight. As I walked home, the absolute stillness of the air, the utter solitude, and the absence of sound gave me the idea of being in a dream.

The sunsets in that valley are stupendous in colour and effect. The clouds and mists that hang about the mountain sides take most fantastic shapes and shades. In the daytime the pointed peaks of the Pusterthal gleam like frosted silver on a dark and stormy horizon, and at sunset they glow on a background of serene and translucent blue in every scale of gold and apricot to the flaming of live coal and then fade back into the ghostly green which sends a shiver of regret through all those who know and love the mountains well. I left Brixen as I came, silently in the dead of night. I was sorry, even after so short a time, to lose sight of the kind faces that had surrounded me, no more to feel the icy kiss of the pure air upon my cheek, to miss the well-filled, reposeful life which braces one up till one feels one cannot be ill. I reflected as I leant back in my railway compartment upon the problem why so many live out their day without ever grasping what health really is, without ever trying to arrive at it or finding how easy it is to attain. That it is positively wicked to be ill when one might be a joy to oneself and a pleasure to others many will even not own. When one considers how simple and safe the means, how delicious the feeling of vigour and exultation, and, most important of all, how lasting the effect of this knowledge of a healthier, simpler, better life must be on those who have any character and intelligence, one cannot help wondering how few there are who can muster the courage to root themselves up out of their sluggard ways and try the experiment !

CHAPTER XI

A MODEL REPUBLICAN

I was turning over some old papers in an idle hour. They had been labelled ' Useless ' by one who had looked them through for a more serious work than would ever come within my scope. I am, however, curious of historical oddities, and my eyes were arrested by some folds of thick yellowish paper, on the top of which were inscribed, in the flourishing, aggressive, and yet sentimental calligraphy which distinguished the patriots of 1789, the magic words :—

LIBERTÉ   ÉGALITÉ
        FRATERNITÉ

Magic words they must indeed have been, as so many believed in them as a panacea for every evil ; and yet, when was there less liberty in any country than in poor handcuffed France during the ten years which followed the ' Serment du jeu de paume,' on the 20th of June 1789 ?

The ' Égalité ' consisted in ignorant and brutal ruffians trampling on the conscientious, the weak, the timid, and educated; and the 'Fraternité,' in murdering every brother who was not of the same opinion as themselves.

Just as I was handling the paper, a French diplomat was announced. I knew him for a man whose knowledge and learning was only equalled by the charm of his manners. He had for twenty years presided over the inner economy of the Quai d'Orsay, and ended his distinguished career as Ambassador at one of France's most important and difficult missions.

He was, I knew, acquainted with most of the eminent men of his country, and innumerable papers of every kind, historical as well as political, had passed through his hands, whilst his pure and vigorous diction and refined taste made him an excellent judge in literary matters.

Delighted with my *trouvaille*, which I had hastily scanned, I gave him the paper, asking him whether he thought it had ever been published. He read it through twice, once to himself, and the second time aloud, giving the proper emphasis to the salient parts, and he declared that seldom, if ever, had he come across a document with so much local colour and such extraordinary savour; nor did he think it had ever been printed.

It may be well to preface the document with some short historical notes. The paper is a denunciation to the French nation, and in especial to the 'Directeur

Leveillère Lépaux,' against the 'Citoyen Bonnier,' plenipotentiary of the French Republic at Rastadt. It is signed by one General Barein, a personage of whom it has been impossible to discover anything— a meet punishment for his arrogance, bloodthirstiness, and egregious vanity.

The accused Bonnier was a *ci-devant* Marquis d'Arco, and his name became celebrated because he, together with his two colleagues, the renegade priest Roubergeat and the *citoyen* Jean de Bry, were the victims of the great political murder which electrified the whole of Europe in April 1799. These were the events which led to this climax. Immediately after the signature of the Peace of Campo Formio, a congress was called to promote the general peace. It met at Rastadt in the autumn of 1797, and lasted till the spring of 1799. All the Powers sent their delegates to this congress.

Sir Arthur Paget, who at that time was accredited as Minister Plenipotentiary and Envoy Extraordinary to the Court of Munich and the Diet of Ratisbon, was in constant communication with the delegates at Rastadt, and it was thus probably that the unique document I referred to got into his possession. These facts also speak for its authenticity.

The French envoys propagated revolutionary ideas amongst the German populations, and tried to detach the southern States, especially Bavaria and Wirtemberg, from Austria. This was bitterly resented by the latter Power, and it was determined to get hold of documents which should prove these facts.

The three French envoys received notice from Austria to leave Rastadt within twenty-four hours, and after having been detained during the day by various reasons, they left the town just as darkness was setting in and in pouring rain. They were accompanied by their wives, daughters, and servants ; there were four or five carriages.

They had hardly proceeded a mile when they were surprised by a detachment of Czeckler Hussars, who, without parley, at once put the delegates to the sword in the presence of their wives and suite.

Jean de Bry, one of the envoys, was, however, not mortally wounded, and, favoured by the darkness, managed to creep behind a bush, where he lay in hiding until towards morning a market-gardener came by and took him in his cart to the neighbouring Strasburg.

There, though wounded in many places, he wrote a letter to one of his relations giving an account of the tragedy. This letter is still in the possession of one of his descendants, who twice within the last ten years directed France's foreign affairs, and from whose lips I hold the foregoing details.

Thugut was at that time Foreign Secretary at Vienna, and the Archduke Charles commanded the troops in Southern Germany. He was horrified at the crime, and at once made profuse excuses.

It never transpired, however, whether the officer who commanded the detachment which perpetrated the deed was punished.

The Czeckler Hussars are Hungarian troops, formed from a tribe or clan descended from the Huns, from whom they have inherited all the distinguishing attributes. They have straight coal-black hair and small gleaming black eyes. Their faces are round and flat ; they are short, with lithe figures, and have an inimitable seat on horseback.

They hardly speak German, and it is probable that the moral qualities of their ancestors have descended to them as unalloyed as those of their physique.

The accusation against the envoy Bonnier was penned about a year before these tragic events, and was addressed to Leveillère Lépaux, one of the Directoire, a well-meaning, absolutely incapable theorist. Botany was his favourite occupation, and he was everybody's laughing-stock.

He had invented the ' Theolantropy,' and nourished a violent hatred for religion, on account of which he was loathed by Royalists and Churchmen.

In the diaries of M. de Bray, a Frenchman who was by no means a reactionary and on a good footing with many of the foremost Republicans, we find some curious notes on the society which produced such people as ' General Barein.'

Bray had returned to France in 1797, after ten

years' exile, and he was immensely astonished and shocked by the things he saw.

He says that:—

The theatres, which formerly were filled by a select audience, well educated and with charming manners, are now crammed with a dirty and disorderly crowd and women of disreputable and common appearance. Men and women seemed to be coarse and brutal.

Formerly one entered into conversation with one's neighbours about art, literature, or the plays that were being acted, but the present ignorant public knows nothing of these topics or has the most absurd ideas about them.

The men are attired in short jackets and long breeches, and the women appear in *juste au corps* and gigantic caps. Everybody looked gloomy and cross. Talent, grace, and beauty [he continues] have disappeared from society, which can hardly be said to still exist.

The *salons* have become the arena for indiscreet champions, who hurl coarse abuse at each other for differences in political opinions.

After the theatre the crowd adjourns to Valloni, the great confectioner of ices. He has his shop in the Pavillon de Hanovre, which formerly belonged to the Duc de Richelieu and stood in his garden. The garden has been turned into a street, and only one corner of it is used for a café.

Here the Incroyables, with their huge cravats and hats and their straight hair, and clothes hanging on them like sacks, lead their ladies, who, with a shawl hanging over one shoulder and their unbecoming *coiffures*, look more like victims being led to the scaffold than the Roman matrons whom they are

s

striving to imitate. With one hand they hold up their draperies, which, made of transparent fabrics, model their forms in no very attractive way, and they justify M. de Talleyrand's biting remark ' Habillées comme on ne se déshabille pas.'

Of conversation there is no trace, and when all have bored themselves sufficiently for their money they go home.

The Republic created an enormous mass of officials, many more than were wanted. These men, belonging to the dregs of the population, uneducated and greedy, separate their personal interests entirely from those of the Republic, and only live to make money. The entire absence of morals and religion makes them absolutely indifferent to right and wrong.

The decay of all educational establishments and the licence of manners have brutalised the French nation, and a generation is growing up which may become the disgrace of humanity. The young men of seventeen to twenty-four are insolent beyond description, and their insolence is only equalled by their crass ignorance.

They have grown up without any guidance in the midst of revolutionary corruption, and unite the most ridiculous and extravagant manners to spiritual decadence.

These arrogant young dunces believe themselves to be philosophers, and their code of morals is to despise all that is good and useful. The abolished religion is replaced by the chatter of philanthropists, which stands in lieu of Christianity, and the criminal code is such that it invites evil deeds.

Lepelletier St. Fargeau, who indited this code, seems to have made it for angels, and not to have believed in sin. He was, of course, murdered by a man who, in obedience to these laws, was allowed to go scot-free. With such laws it is almost impossible to convict anybody, as the most ghastly crimes are only punished according to the intentions the perpetrator acknowledges to have had.

It is impossible to give in detail the terrible picture M. de Bray delineates of the state of France in those days, and one can only look upon Napoleon's murderous wars, which entirely wiped out this criminal and debased generation, as the greatest blessing for France.

Though wounded and curtailed in many ways, she was able to rise once more, if not for long, to be the leading nation of continental Europe. We can at present afford to smile at the mixture of pomposity, false sentimentality and tigerish ferocity displayed by the ' honest and pure Republican Barein '; but if we reflect that more than four years had passed since the ' Terreur ' was ended by the death of Robespierre, and that it is generally considered that France had by that time returned to a more normal state, it gives one rather the cold shivers to think in what an atmosphere of fear, suspicion, delation, and hatred that unfortunate country must have been enveloped for many more years than is generally supposed.

The relations of the accused Bonnier with his servant, who is also his friend and brother-in-law, are extremely funny and subversive; and still more astounding are the apostrophes of the writer to the shades of the ' bon Marat and brave Carrier,' and his satisfaction at his own rectitude and the extreme humanity of the French nation, whilst it was engaged in sweeping away at one fell stroke 10,000 priests, murdering the wretched prisoners of the Abbaye, and drowning in hundreds monks and nuns and other quiet and helpless people for no other offence than that of having a religion.

Most humorous, too, is the condescension towards the *Être suprême*, which he deigns to recognise because *l'état civil* has been conferred upon it. What sorrows, what misfortunes, what injustices, one asks oneself, must a soul that has sunk so low have gone through, and what an abyss of ferocious madness unfolds itself in the following document!

I give it with the original spelling.

LIBERTÉ ÉGALITÉ
FRATERNITÉ

Denociation au peuple français et au *Directeur* Reveillère Lépaux Contre le Citoyen *Bonnier* ministre plenipotentiaire de la République française a Rastatt.

Un Citoyen vraiment zèlé pour le bonheur et la prospérité de la grande nation, croirait manquer a ce que l'honneur et les sermens lui prescrivent s'il ne mettait au jour la Conduite que vient de tenir a Rastatt le Citoyen *Bonnier*.

Guidé par l'amour de la patrie et la vérité, le dénonciateur exposera les faits purement et Simplement ; il abandonne aux Republicains *probes et sévères*, le droit de pronocer sur le compte d'un des premiers fonctionnaires de la république.

Un patriote de 89, agent du Directoire et chargé Specialement de surveiller les agens diplomatiques a l'Exterieur, est passé hier a dijon, revenant de Rastatt, ou il a été témoin du scandale occasionné par le Citoyen *Bonnier*. Le Recit qu'il m'a fait de cet acte vraimedt incivique, m'a paru d'une telle importance, que j'ai jugé a propos d'y donner la plus grande publicité.

FAITS

Le Citoyen *Bonnier* avait un valet de chambre, vrai républicain, et qui depuis le commencement de la Révolution a donné des preuves d'un Civisme aussi ardent qu'eclairé. habitant un pays ou le peuple n'est pas encore a la hauteur des principes, il s'occuppait dans les momens de loisir, a propagér Ceux de la liberté. tantot il haranguait avec chaleur ses confrères domestiques de differens aristocrates de Congrès ; tantôt se mêlant parmi le peuple, il lui demontrait combien la révolution est avantageuse a l'humanité en general et au peuple français en particulier. il retançait avec une audace etonnante ces imbéciles imbus de préjugés et vils flagorneurs des despotes. en vain le Citoyen *Bonnier* cherchait sous différens pretextes a diminuer le zèle patriotique dont Son serviteur etait enflâmé :

injonctions, menaces, prières, rien ne pouvait l'Empêcher de dire hautement des vérités utiles : aucun danger ne l'intimidait, c'est ce qu'il vient de prouve en périssant froidement pour *la liberté et l'Egalité*.

depuis qu'il est mort les infâmes suppots de l'aritocratie, entassent sur Son Compte, Calomnies, Sur Calomnies :

suivant eux, cette victime intéressante ne fut autre chose qu'un taquin, un insolent, un jacobin forcené, mals j'oppose a leurs déclamations qu'il fut *patriote pur* et a ce titre sacré, ennemi juré des abus de l'ancien régime.

Le hazard l'ayant conduit dernièrement dans un Cabaret, ou étaient réunis quelques vils esclaves, il s'approcha D'eux avec douceur et chercha a les amener par degré a une conversation toute patriotique : Ces Brutaux échauffés par le Vin, firent a peine attention aux discours du républicain, Cependant rien ne le decouragea et multipliant les bons argumens il parvint enfin a se faire entendre : Les yeux rayonnant de joye, il croyait avoir operé dans ses auditeurs, un changement salutaire, lorsque profitant d'une circonstance locale, il ôta son chapeau et presenta au baiser fratérnel le signe sacré de la liberté, la cocarde nationale.

Mais Ô Crime ! Ô Vengeance ! les scélerats loin de se rendre a son invitation, l'insultent, le frappent et le chassent du Cabaret : transporté de fureur, hors de lui, le malheureux jeune homme ne voit de resource que la Mort. il vécut republicain, il veut mourir digne de ce beau titre.

en vain le Citoyen Rippaille Cuisinier du Citoyen jean debry, veut le détourner de ses projets sinistres, il s'échappe de ses mains, courre et se précipite dans la rivère . . . a l'instant même il est englouti sous l'épaisseur des glaces ! ! ! ! ! ! ! ! ! ! ! ! ! ' ! ! ! ! ! ! ! ! ! ! ! ! ! ! ! jettons quelques fleurs sur sa tombe et venons aux torts que la posterité toujours juste, imputera au Citoyen *Bonnier*.

En vain tu te flattes, ministre hipocryte d'en imposer au public par des regrèts simulés ; la Conduite que tu viens de tenir, prouve invinciblement, combien tu étais indigne d'avoir dans la maison, un aussi Vertueux républicain.

Ton cagotime et ta bigoterie ont outragé la mémore de ce martyr de la liberté, que tu devais chérir sous le double rapport, d'ami fidèle et de beaufrère.

que repondras tu a sa sœur l'objet de tes affections

les plus tendres, lorsqu'elle te reprochera d'avoir assimilé son frère a un capucin décédé ?

Monstre, lis ton acte d'accusation.

Le Cadavre de ton malheureux serviteur ayant été retrouvé, les patriotes de la Legation française se flattaient que tu ordonnerais en son honneur, une cerémonie simple, touchante et républicaine ; mais non, au lieu de te conformer a nos lois et nos usages, tu as livré les restes inanimés d'un républicain a un clergé refractaire et fanatique.

aux hymnes patriotiques, au Drapeau tricolore qui devait couvrir le cerceuil de ton Concitoyen, tu as fait substituer un drap mortuaire et les psaumes d'une secte que nous exterminons depuis dix ans. Quoi donc le peuple français te paye-t-il pour faire revivre cette superstition, dont les effets ont été si funestes, a une foule de bons patriotes ? et ces cloches que tu as fait sonner avec tant de fracas, ne rappellent elles pas les declamations ridicules de ce *Camille jordan* qui étourdissait le Conseil des 800, avec la religion de ses pères ! ton procédé anticivique insulte a la république, a la morale et a la philosophie.

as tu donc oublié les beaux jours de 7bre 1792 ! ce moment regenateur ou le peuple purgea la france de plus de 10,000 prêtres séditieux et fantiques ? je presidais alors le tribunal établi dans la prison de l'abbaye *et je fus juste.*

Les fondateurs de la république, respectables membres de la Convention nationale firent égorger cette secte de pertubarteurs, et six ans après toi, *plenipotentiare* de notre république, tu as l'effronterie et la bassesse de te servir du ministère de prêtres Catholiques ?

j'étais membre de la commission militaire de Saumur, a l'Epoque ou la Convention nationale *toujours grande et toujours juste,* fit noyer a nantes et a angers, prêtres, moines, religieuses, ainsi que tous leurs partisans : tu siegeais au sénat et tu approuvas ces mesures salutaires, par quel inconcevable travers d'ésprit, as tu donc fait celebrer un service funebre par des prêtres refractaires, aux lois de la république ?

ô temps ! ô mœurs ! ô patrie !

C'est donc inutilement, que lorsque je dirigeais la commission temporaire de lyon, je faisais foudroyer les ministres d'une religion proscrite puisque *bonnier* au milieu de nos ennemis, fait par sa conduite la satyre de nos institutions sages et républicaines.

puisqu'il fallait un Curé au Citoyen Bonnier, que ne s'addressait-il a son Collègue Rouberjeat ? ce dernier n'avait-il pas toutes les qualites requises ? il fut jadis curé de macon, jura, preta dix sermens civiques pour un et secoua gaiement tous les préjugés dans lesquels nos ancêtres étaient encroutés.

O vertueux ami du peuple, bon marat ! ô incorruptible Robespierre ! ô Brave Carrier ! vrais et sincères républicains, qui accellerates au prix de votre sang la régéneration du peuple français, Braves montagnards qui fites noÿer, fusiller et deporter les prêtres, aux grandes acclamations du corps législatif, l'action de *Bonnier* ne vous fait elle pas tresaillir d'horreur dans vos tombeaux ? *Bonnier* partagea vos honorables travaux, *Bonnier* vota la mort du tyran, *Bonnier* proscrivit le Catholicism, *Bonnier* fut associé a votre gloire, et aujourd'hui ce même *Bonnier* se met en contradiction avec sa conduite antérieure et avec nos principes de philantropie.

Que dis-je ? Bonnier a agi d'après l'impulsion de sa conscience, car jamais Bonnier ne fut républicain. la peur seule, l'associa aux enfans de la montagne, mais il conserva toujours au fond du cœur les habitudes aristocratiques.

Sans culotte a l'extérieur, il fut toujours chez lui le magistrat de l'ancien régime, le president de la cour des aides de montpellier, en un mot le ce-devant impudent Marquis d'arco.

il repousse avec une insolente fierté les républicains qui s'adressent a lui et si il faut que je dise ici toute ma pensée, je le soupsonne fortement de trahir les plus chers interêts de la république.

je denonce Bonnier au peuple souverain et je l'accuse d'avoir fait enterrer par un clergé Catholique, un Cityen qui n'était plus Catholique a datter du jour ou la Convention nationale accorda l'Etat civil a l'Être suprême et décrèta qu'elle reconnaissait son existence.

j'accuse Bonnier d'avoir fait dire trois messes a rastatt, d'avoir forcé ses valets d'y assister et par conséquent d'avoir provoqué le retour du Culte Catholique, dans l'interieur de la République.

je te denonce *Bonnier*, sensible Reveillere L'épaux il appartient au fondateur et au propagateur du Culte théophilantropique de prononcer solennellement sur un délit aussi grave que celui dont l'infâme *Bonnier* s'est rendu coupable.

Le directeur éxécutif chargé spécialement *de désoler la patience des prêtres*, ne manquera pas de punir l'incivisme de son délégué au Congrès de Rastatt.

fasse le ciel que le tartuffe Bonnier cesse Bientôt de représenter, la plus grande, la plus juste et surtout la plus humaine des nations ! Si le Directoire n'est pas sourd a la voix d'un de ses plus fideles appuis, il exaucera mes vœux et fera remplacer le Catholique-fanatique Bonnier par quelque bon sans culotte, ennemi des despotes et des tyrans coalisés, C'est a dire par un républicain placé entre le succès et l'Echaffaud, tel que le tyrannicide jean de bry.

A Dijon le 1er nivose de l'an 7 de la République,

une et indivisible, démocratique et impérissable et la cinquieme de la mort du tyran.

Le General de brigade Barein vainqueur de la Bastille, ex-président de la commission temporaire de lyon et depuis le 18 fructidor, nommé par le Directoire Commandant miltaire a Dijon.

CHAPTER XII

THE MYSTERIOUS CITY

I SEE a town set in a cup of green jasper. Its towers and palaces, its domes and spires glitter like jewels in the southern sun.

The rich and verdant plain, and the majestic sapphire mountains which hem it in, are studded with many thousands of shimmering villas and castles, convents and churches, and opalescent little burghs, and villages half hidden under their silver veils of olive, or watched over by dark and stately cypress groves.

Wild windstorms sweep down over the plains in winter, and lurid thunderclouds often lower amongst the snow-capped mountain-peaks; and those who are left in the beautiful valley to watch the pomegranate unfold its flaming petals, or the oleander flood with its sea-spray blossom the gardens of the ancient palaces, pray that the benignant showers may descend from the hills to refresh the riches which in this favoured spot spring in every season from the bosom of the earth.

A writer and great art-critic, walking the other day upon the terrace of an ancient villa, which stands aloof above the town, said, looking down upon it :—

Es ruht ein Glueck auf dieser Stadt !'
[' Happiness reposes upon this citv ! ']

And this is true, for the sparkling air acts upon one's vitality like a glass of champagne. The atmosphere is of a transparency equalled only by the Isles of Greece; and the gracefulness of its buildings, and the graciousness of its setting, its wealth of flowers, and its glittering life, inspire the superficial observer with a feeling of gaiety and romance unknown in any other place.

For some months in the year, lighthearted thousands and hundreds of thousands rush at breathless speed through the frescoed and monumental churches ; they give a cursory look at the priceless pictures of the unequalled galleries, and thev pace quicklv through the rich museums of the town.· They ransack for treasure the ever-renewed stock of attractive brie-à-brac shops. They turn over the picturesque trinkets on the Jeweller's Bridge; and the most venturous or wealthy embark in ropes of pearls which they always maintain to have got at half-price.

The less energetic ones wander up and down the sunny quays which border the waters which Shelley sung and which his words reflect almost poignantly into our souls.

Within the surface of the fleeting river
The wrinkled image of the city lay
Immoveably quiet, and for ever
It trembles, but it does not fade away.
You, being changed, will find it then as now!

In the golden afternoon, merry crowds can be seen driving in the wide avenues of the fairy woods, planted by a long-exiled line of Princes. When the sun paints in rose-colour and violet the mountain ranges, the ladies draw about them their costly furs and order the coachman to drive to some great palace where they join a friend's select ' five-o'clock,' or they go to the fashionable confectioner to devour cakes in company of the native garrison. In the evening they play, sing, and dance in the spacious halls of the amply gilt, largest, and newest hotels.

To these visitors of a fleeting hour the mysterious city is a place of distraction, excitement, and amusement—and nothing else. They never even suspect what lies beneath the polished surface of ' Quella citta pulita come un gioello,' as that exceedingly clever, but absolutely immoral rascal, Benvenuto Cellini, called it.

This town was once the capital of a most happy and thriving little land. A country, which by its beauty, the *gentilezza* and culture of its inhabitants, and the security and liberty which were enjoyed within its limits, attracted all art-loving foreigners: not in the great masses of our modern days, but still in larger quantities than any other city. Society there was, a hundred years ago, just as cosmopolitan, peculiar, and vague as it is now.

A witty woman called the mysterious city ' la ville du pardon,' because whatever sins against society made people impossible in other places, they are sure, as soon as their foot treads its charméd soil, to be at once engulfed into its moral chiaroscuro, where none suffers an eclipse unless they wish to do so.

But there are many who do wish to disappear, and for them there is no surer refuge.

The other day, one of those ubiquitous men whom everybody knows and who seems to be in every place at once and who call every man and woman in smart society by their Christian names, always claiming them as intimate friends, and often as cousins, said :—

' I met **X——** last night, as I was walking back from my club ' (he named the well-known bearer of a great historical English name). ' He is a relation of mine, you know, and I used to be very intimate with him. I was so astonished, and asked him when he arrived, and he answered :—

' " My dear fellow, I have lived here for seven years, but I don't go anywhere, and do not wish to know anybody." '

I said I would go and see him, and questioned him as to where he lived, and he only vaguely mentioned one of the least attractive outskirts of the town. I was, however, determined to find out, and I discovered, hidden amongst bays and oleanders, what must have been a wing of some ancient summer-palace of the former dukes. A broken fountain stands near the house and some moss-grown statues border a grassy avenue that leads into the open country.

There X—— has lived for seven years with a lady I did not see. The husband I am told comes and goes and seems quite satisfied !

There are hundreds of such unsuspected existences within and without the walls of the mysterious city, and if in summer you wander along the white moonlit lanes or walk on misty winter afternoons in the deserted woods, figures emerge before you which give you a sudden shock, because for years they had completely faded from your memory.

There is no Court in this town, no official life, no social centre. People come to it as to any other winter resort. Everybody does what they like ; nobody knows or asks.

Those who for years have lived next door to each other often do not know their neighbour's name, and people who for fifty years have dwelt in a villa on one side of the town have never been to a villa on the other side.

In the days when a brilliant and hospitable Court was at the head of society, many clever and art-loving men and beautiful and charming women of every nation and every reputation flocked to the city. The famous ' Dame aux perles ' had her palace on the banks of the river, and to hers I could add a string of equally well-known names. These ladies had the strange habit of only beginning their life at midnight—that is, their doors only opened then to their acquaintances. Even some decades ago, and long after the gay and benign Princes had fled, and a few years of an ephemeral official life had quite changed the face of the city, a few of these ladies still remained, and were termed by a younger and more matutinal generation *les dames d'après minuit.* At balls they never appeared till long past one in the morning, and if they gave balls they thought themselves disgraced unless their guests remained to breakfast. Let us glance into the houses of the most typical ones.

We enter a very splendid palace and ascend a wide staircase lined with huge mirrors in profusely gilt frames. In the ante-room several well-styled servants receive our wraps and furs. The doors are thrown open and a long vista of luxuriously furnished *salons* stretches out before us. The walls are hung with the crude and expensive brocades of the early sixties, and all the sumptuous furniture is covered with the same silk, thickly *capitonéed* within frames of elaborately carved gilt wood.

Candles burn in bronze chandeliers, and ormulu carcel lamps stand on boule consoles.

The mistress of the house, a distinguished-looking woman of uncertain age, advances to meet us. About half a dozen men arise as we enter. A lady sitting down, with a gilt chiavari chair in front of her, takes one foot off the cross-bar on which its companion still reposes, and feebly moves her fan. A slight perfume of cigarette astonishes our, in those days, unaccustomed nostrils, and we perceive the master of the house, young and very dapper, in a small *fumoir* some rooms off, surrounded by another half-dozen men. These are the *fine fluer* of the sporting circles, and most of them are almost boys; whilst those who listen to the lady's animated and amusing conversation are nearly all deputies and senators and other persons of mark, brought to the mysterious city by the evolutions and exigencies of the new government.

We sink down into the luxurious ' Poltrone ' and one of the men at once puts the inevitable chiavari chair in front of us; for though the carpets are thick, the icy marble floor strikes chillily through our satin shoes. The friend, simply attired in black silk, had once been fast and fair. She wears a string of huge and faultless pearls, and in her ears single diamonds the size of cherries. She intersperses our hostess's brilliant talk with little grunts, whilst the men sit around in admiring silence. A servant appears with some iced lemonade, and after three-quarters of an hour we retire, and get to bed about two in the morning, knowing that our hosts will sit up a good hour more, as they do night after night.

Another night, at twelve-fifteen, our carriage stops

in a forlorn and narrow street near the great city walls, which in those days still encircled the town with a magic ring of beauty. The house, or rather villa, looks, in the parlance of the country, ' *decaduto.*' Wreaths of wistaria curtain the tall garden wall.

The door is opened by a scrubby and very sleepy porter. The steep and rather narrow staircase, covered by the common carpet made in the prisons from rags, takes us into a neglected lobby. As we enter a long, high, but rather narrow room, the stifling smoke of many strong cigars nearly arrests our progress.

The room is badly lit ; but we notice that an indiscriminating taste has furnished it from second-rate bric-à-brac shops.

At one end of the room, before a long dresser, a score of men are crowded together. Nearly all of them wear uniform. They are busily employed in devouring ham sandwiches and lobster salads. A long row of Marsala bottles and flagons of Chianti wine reveal that these gentlemen are not teetotallers. A tall and portly lady, with a mass of very fair hair and some remains of good looks, stands on the hearthrug at the farther end of the room puffing at a large cigar. She receives us with expansion and makes us feel that our advent is a real pleasure to her. Her manner at once betrays that her earlier years were spent in a society very different from the rather mixed and rough one which seems to be her present choice. She is an Englishwoman, the bearer of a great name, but none would know from her speech that she is a foreigner, for she formulates the *lingua Toscana* with as much airy grace as any native. She landed the barque of her life in the mysterious city years ago, after having tossed rudderless on the ocean of misfortune. However, the sins which she may have committed towards herself have been redeemed a hundredfold by her wide charities and her unbounded kindness. Her wit and her powers of conversation are second to none.

The pretty, sad, and refined-looking little woman who now enters, belongs to the same aristocratic society from which our hostess seceded by her own free-will; but Lady Gueraldia had not the same metal in her. She fades away under the ostracism of her friends and family, and within a few months her dying request will be to be laid in a pauper's grave without name or sign, with only a number upon it, on the sunny hill where stands the white-and-gold basilica, the most ancient and pathetic church of the city

It is now nearly one o'clock and the door opens again and displays a vision of *sémillante* beauty and brightness, followed by a short, stout man. Our hostess folds the vision into capacious arms, and the men at the other end leave their sandwiches and gather around the little whirlpool of pink tulle, diamonds, and tea-roses, her *piquante frimousse* crowned with essentially artificial golden curls, so oddly contrasting with the large childlike trusting blue eyes. She too is a exile from the Island beyond the silver riband,

and had she only lived twenty years later, her naughty little ways and means would have been considered, if not quite correct, at least allowable, and she would not have been obliged to seek sanctuary in the mysterious city.

We now take leave of the *dames d'après minuit* to make the acquaintance of some of the other inhabitants of ' years ago.'

It is the reception day of the greatest lady in the town. She lives in the largest and most beautiful palace. Wide double stairways—such as are rarely seen but in royal precincts—lead to an immense hall of which all the entrances are hung with rich embroideries representing the arms of the family. A copper *brasero*, as large as a table for eight, stands in the middle of the marble floor, and round it huddle a number of footmen in ill-fitting light-blue liveries.

A white-haired Major Domo flings open a door and our eyes rove through a suite of ten or twelve rooms, all hung with priceless velvets and silks, and filled with objects of virtu ; but nowhere, though we are in January, is there a trace of a fire.

We walk briskly to keep ourselves warm, watching our breath as it becomes visible in the icy air ; but suddenly we come to a standstill at the door of a very small and narrow room with one window only.

The walls are sumptuously hung and decorated, and the shape of the room is so peculiar that we think we are in a chapel, until a feeble and rather high-pitched voice addresses us from the dark and narrow end opposite the window, and we perceive something small and fantastic, seated on a red-and-golden throne on each side of which are set six equally red-and-golden chairs closely ranged together against the walls. There is no other furniture in the room.

I seat myself on the chair nearest the throne, and consider the little bundle which addresses me in excellent and formal French, with great inflections of dignity.

Some very precious lace, yellow with age, covers the sparse white hair which lies in flat bandeaus over the waxen forehead. Bright, intelligent, kind little eyes blink at me out of the small wizened face, to which a peaked but firmly moulded nose lends character. An ermine tippet hangs down far below the waist, and the gloved hands are hidden in an ermine muff. Two very small satin-clad feet protrude from under a skirt of black Genoese velvet and are set on a silver *scaldino*.

Other ladies appear; they are all past middle age; they curtsy to the great One and arrange themselves according to rank on the chairs.

When the Princess addresses them they sway forward and respond in respectful undertones. When the thirteenth lady appeared, we got up and resigned our chairs and, flying down the wide staircase, ran along the sunny quays to warm our feet and raise our spirits again.

It was carnival, and I had staved later than was my wont at a ball. The rooms were hot and I longed for a breath of fresh air. Taking the arm of an old friend, I ordered my carriage to follow at a distance. We walked along the quays that border the river. A large cold winter moon flooded the white pavement. The street-lamps of those days would be taken by a younger generation for glow-worms. Not a living creature was to be seen except two velvet-footed pussies—the animal of predilection of the inhabitants of the mysterious city.

Then suddenly, at some little distance, I perceived a dark figure flitting along under the shadow of the palaces; it stopped for a moment, and then crossed over into the moonlight and leant over the stone parapet under which the river swirls and rushes dark and sinister.

' Look! who is that ? ' I said, my attention aroused by the slim grace of the outline.

My companion walked faster. He is short and thickset, a senator from the South, a man much versed in politics, and as much at home in Paris as in his native *dolce Napoli*.

' I think I know ! It must be she,' he says to me as we approach, and putting his hand on the lady's arm he adds :—

'Nini! since when are you here?'

She turns and reveals in the white light of the moon that face which for ten years had drawn crowds around her in every capital of Europe.

She moved her arm as if she wished to keep my companion at a distance, and as her long black cloak fell back I saw beneath it, covering her from throat to waist, the famous necklace of white-and-black pearls which I knew could only belong to the celebrated Countess C——

'What are you doing here alone at this hour and with all those pearls on? What new folly is this?' exclaimed my friend impatiently. But instead of answering, the Countess only drew a stiletto from her bosom. 'Much good that will do you, my child; and now go home; do not risk your life and pearls any more, and to-morrow I will go and see you. Where do you live?'

She named a house in an obscure street, and my friend told me some days later that he had found this adulated beauty, who a few years before had not shrunk from gratifying her maddest caprices, who had had Emperors and Kings at her feet, who had been entrusted with political missions by the greatest statesman of her country, in a miserable lodging, with no other servant but an old woman who cooked for her, whilst her son, a handsome lad of fifteen, swept the floor and did the most menial offices.

She had disappeared from the scene of her triumphs

because she thought she perceived that her beauty was waning, and had lived for months in the town which was her birthplace and full of her friends and relations without anybody having a suspicion of it.

One of the *dames d'après minuit*, who had been her intimate friend, told me, that from the age of ten the beautiful Nini had only one thought, which was to lay by every penny to buy pearls for herself. On the day of her marriage she had to be dragged to the altar, as she did not think Count C—— good enough for her. It was she who said : 'What a fool my mother was not to take me to Paris, for I now should be Empress of the French !' Of other women she said :—

> Par ma naissance je les égale,
> Par ma beauté je les surpasse,
> Par mon esprit je les jugé.

It is night, and we stand before a dark and frowning palace—one of the oldest in the town. It looks like a fortress, and great iron-barred doors shut out the curious from a view of a small but very beautiful court.

Open stairs, with balustrades supported on slender pillars, go up to the third and fourth story ; but we stop before a door on the first landing and flit unseen through rooms frescoed or hung with arras, and furnished stiffly with high-backed settees and chairs. Not a sound is heard. We traverse the long gallery, at the end of which we reach a locked door ; but we have the spirit password which dissolves matter, and we stand in a large room decorated in more modern taste. Its walls are covered with Empire silk of creamy pink, with embroidered wreaths of myrtle sprinkled all over it.

One solitary candle is burning before a small shrine of the Madonna. The bed of satinwood, with finely chiselled bronze ornaments, stands on a raised step. A young lady, very pale, but beautiful, half hides her face amongst the laces which border her pillows. As she turns for a moment to whisper something to a motherly looking woman who is leaning over her, we see that her brow is wrung with pain and moist with great drops of perspiration; for it is June and yet all the windows are tightly closed and shuttered, and the thick silk curtains are carefully drawn across the door. An agony of terror is depicted in the lady's large and liquid eyes, and the elder woman whispers:—

'Courage, courage, Carina! it will soon be over and nobody will know, only do not moan'; and she hands a large silk kerchief to the lady, who stuffs it between her teeth.

In another moment an infant's wail echoes through the vaulted chamber, and something like a muttered oath resounds on the other side of the door. But the women do not hear: they are only thinking of the child born; not to the joy, but to the mother's woe.

The old woman deftly wraps the child into some sheets, and throwing a dark shawl over the little bundle, she opens the window and softly calls out ' Barnabo ! '

A peculiar low whistle is the answer, and firmly tying a silken cord around the child, she lowers it into the street.

' It is all right, Signora Contessa; do not fret; Barnabo is a good man, and my daughter, his wife, is kind ; they will take care of the poor lamb.' Then she busies herself with tidying up the room and effacing every trace of what had happened.

' See, Signora ! I got these Spanish jessamines yesterday, and will put them before the image of the blessed Virgin. Everybody knows that their scent is mortal to a woman in childbed, but they shall not hurt you, dear, for I will stand the bowl in a saucer of water with some drops of oil on it, and you will be safe. This is a secret my grandmother told me and which nobody knows.'

The lady wearily closed her eyes, and the waiting-woman withdrew after carefully unlocking the only door of the chamber and drawing the silk curtains aside.

The day had not long dawned when an unusual noise and clatter was heard in the courtyard. Horses stamped and neighed and stablemen ran to and fro. Doors banged and messengers seemed to be dispatched in every direction. Soon after the sun had risen into the bluest and serenest of skies a heavy step was heard approaching from the gallery. A sharp knock, and the door opened quickly, and a tall burly man walked into the room. His type of features was material—almost brutal—though not without some good looks. He had the prominent eyes of the first Cosimo, so well depicted in the bust of coloured marbles by Benvenuto Cellini. You saw at once that his was a will not to be gainsaid. A cruel and sarcastic smile parted the thick lips over the long and pointed teeth.

He stopped short for a second, sniffing the overpowering scent of the jessamine, and, perceiving the bowl with the flowers, said :—

' How good and pious you are, Fiametta, to put these strong-scented flowers before the Holy Mother in your bedroom ! for they must give you a headache.'

' Yes, you are right, Cesare; I could not shut an eye all night, and I feel very tired.'

' I have prepared a surprise for you this morning—a little *festa* to celebrate my return after the many months I have been away; and that is why I came so early to wake you; and you must get up at once and prepare to come with me.'

' Oh, Cesare, what is it ? Can you not put it off to another day ? I am not fit for much exertion in this great heat. It was too stupid of Caterina to put those flowers there ! '

' This plan of mine will cure your headache at once ! ' and a flash of hatred flamed up in his hard eyes. ' You have never seen my villa of Belcrudele with its great tanks, high up in the hills. It is quite

unique, and a charming ride of only twenty miles—and
you used to be so fond of riding.   Some of our friends
will accompany us and others follow in carriages.   I
have ordered a banquet to be ready, and we will have
a dance afterwards and ride back by moonlight.   There
is nothing like tiring oneself out when one has nerves
like you ! '

' Need I tell you,' said Prince P——, who told
me the story, ' that the programme was literally
executed.   I know the lady, she is alive now.   It
happened a good many years ago ; the child was a girl
and she is married.   The man is dead.'

None in the town suspected the tragedy in those
days.

As I was driving past Santa Maria del Fiore one
day, a small crowd pressing round the base of Giotto's
tower attracted my attention.

' Do not look ! ' said the friend who was with me,
' somebody has again thrown themselves off the
tower ! '

There is between the great church, clothed in its
rich marbles, and the marvellous campanile which
rises up like a flower, a little space—perhaps thirty
feet square—into which those who are sick of life
always throw themselves down.

' Have you ever heard the touching story attached
to that spot ? ' asked my friend ; for it was my first
winter in the mysterious city.

' I will tell it you ' ; and we sat down on the stones where Dante used to sit when he spoke to the people.

' It was the last day of Carnival late in the afternoon. The sky was a tender grey, and a warm south wind was blowing. The great bells of the Duomo were ringing in Lent.

' That little space across there, but which is now hidden by the tower, was in the Middle Ages the burial place of one of the greatest families of this town. It was there that Ginevra degli Adhemari was laid when she was thought to be dead, and it were those selfsame marble flags upon which that poor wretch crushed himself to death an hour ago, that she lifted up to escape from her grave. The little street behind us is still called " Via della morte," for it was there that she met a man who, seeing her, screamed out " Oh la morte ! ecco la morte ! " as she was trying to reach the house of the man she had always loved.'

' Oh, tell me all you know about it ! ' I cried, thrilled by the feeling that all this had happened on the very spot where we stood.

' Ginevra degli Adhemari lived five hundred years ago. She was the daughter of a great house, and lovely. She had from her childhood been attached to a young noble, brave and handsome, but poor, and her parents decreed that she must marry a man twice her age, but very rich, whom she hated.

' Young Folco, who had always worshipped the ground on which Ginevra trod, could not bear to see her misery, and went to Pisa, taking service with the Signory there.

'After he had been there three years, he heard that the great plague had come to his native town, and he returned to take care of his old mother, who was in deep distress at his absence.

'The first thing he heard was, that Ginevra, who had pined and sickened since her marriage, had just died of the dread disease, and had been buried at once by her terrified husband in the family vault.

'He was sitting up the first night of his return, thinking of her whom he had loved so deeply and so long, and hoping that he too might die soon.

'Suddenly he was startled by a faint whisper creeping through his open casement. It was like the rustle of dead leaves driven by the wind forming faintly his name. He rushed to the window and beheld just beneath him leaning against the closed door, white in the moonlight, Ginevra's wraith wrapped in grave-clothes.

'"Oh, beloved and adored spirit!" he called out. "Wait for me!" and flying downstairs he tore open the door to receive the real but fainting Ginevra in his arms.

'He and his mother nursed and tended her till she got well and strong again. She told them that when she lay as dead in the vault the rays of the moon which trickled through the chinks of the ill-joined stones had aroused her from her faintness. She had crept off her bier—for in those days of panic the dead were never properly buried—and with infinite trouble she lifted a flag and hoisted herself up on the pavement. She dragged herself to her husband's house which was near S. Lorenzo, calling upon him to open the door. He heard, and answered from a window, showing every sign of terror: "Go back to your grave, you troubled spirit! I will have a Mass said for your repose, but do not come near me any more." Sick, fainting, and despairing, Ginevra had then turned her steps towards the house of her early and faithful lover. The only man she met on her way fled from her in terror, and, abandoned and repulsed by all, she sought refuge in Folco's protecting arms.

'When Ginevra had recovered her health and beauty, she and Folco sought out the Archbishop of the town, who had once been a Pope under the name of John the Twenty-second, and he declared that she, having been dead and buried, existed no more, and that the resuscitated Ginevra was free to marry the man who had loved her so faithfully.

'The Archbishop himself pronounced the Benediction.'

Who is this strange little bent figure which we perceive ambling along the sunny side of the street on a warm and windless day? A velvet skull-cap is set over his straggling white hair. A long grey beard covers the lower part of his face, and a shabby black cloth coat, lined with a ragged, reddish fur, descends to his feet.

This man, whose name is now almost forgotten, was a painter, an archæologist, and a scholar of no mean reputation. In pre-Victorian days he painted every young Court beauty, and was the friend of the best artists of the later Georgian era. It was he who discovered one of the finest and most pathetic frescoes in the chapel of the great public palace. It was the figure of the great seer and poet attired in the white, red, and green of young Italy—the colours so dreaded by the Princes who reigned at that time, and therefore chocolate was the hue substituted, until ten years later, after the revolution, it was submerged again by the tricolour.

In the days when Mr. K—— discovered this fresco, it was not even allowed to tie up sweetmeats with red and green ribbons or ever to bring these tints into a lady's dress.

We follow our tottering friend into an ancient house overhanging the river and close to the corner formed by the bridge with the jewellers' booths. We enter a very large room, square, except for one sharp and irregular corner—a habit indulged in by the builders of this country who believe it to be a protection against bad spirits. It has a raftered ceiling covered with cobwebs. The pattern of the tiled floor is indistinguishable, so thickly is it overlaid with dirt and dust. Grey furry things shoot over it in the dusk. A pussy, velvet footed, rubs itself against the old man's legs. In one corner two large tortoises are having their tea on lettuce-leaves, and a dozen pigeons descend from the rafters to peck at the yellow maize which is liberally distributed all over the place.

The walls are entirely lined with books in musty old bindings, and as we read the titles we note, with astonishment, that nearly all of them are cabalistic or spiritualistic works on necromancy, magic black and white—especially the former—records of wizards and witches, and volumes filled with secret recipes for poisoning or beautifying, for love philtres and life elixirs, or the creating of homunculi, and suchlike.

One of these books, I remember, was full of recipes composed by a monk—a certain Giovanni di Medici —and given as a wedding present to his cousin, Catherine di Medici. Among others there was the following recipe for turning the hair golden, far preferable to any of the known methods as it makes the hair grow thick and tinges it with an aureole, as if the setting sun were at its back. Here it is :—

R. Mele rosato le mettelo dentro una storta che sia grande e accomodela dentro al fornello e dalli fuoco lento e si stillera aqua bianca e quando commincia a stillare aqua gialla muta recipiente e aumenta il fuoco fino a che non stilli piu e quest'ultima stillazione sara di color di rubino e bagnando i capelli con essa gli tinge in color di oro e gli fa crescere bellissimi e

U

lunghi. La prima acqua biaca lavandosi la faccia con essa la fa lustra e bella e conserva la carne che non si 'inneschie mai.

I fear even these recipes could not win back poor Catherine's truant Lord from the fascinating Diane.

These occult books, perhaps the most precious collection of the kind ever made, were dispersed ten years later in a public sale and went for next to nothing. The world had forgotten their owner and had not yet taken the metaphysical and supersensuous turn of our latter days.

In the deep embrasure of the window hangs a delicate pencil drawing of the head of the great Tuscan poet with his signature beneath it. The expression of the mouth especially has a sweetness so striking and peculiar that it at once arrests our attention.

'It was drawn by the spirits one night when I had left paper and pencil on the table,' we are informed, 'and I only added the wreath of bays. I left it out another night, praying for the signature, and it came also.' The signature was beautifully written in clear gothic letters: 'Dante Allighieri.' Opposite this drawing hung a small sketch in oils—Paolo and Francesca, blown about in a whirlwind of clouds. The tones were all in tender greys and blues; Francesca's slender and misty figure lay half fainting in Paolo's protecting arms, but the feeling of the 'eternally driven ' made it into one of the most poignantly pathetic records of that pathetic couple.

The tinkle of the doorbell brings us back to this sublunary world; and, ushered in by the solitary servant, two young and beautiful women enter, whose appearance seems singularly out of place within these precincts. They are dressed in the height of Parisian fashion, and a practised eye at once recognises on their graceful heads the creations of Virot, and appreciates that their light summer dresses are the masterpieces of Worth—those two famous artists of the last years of the second Empire.

As they advance towards the table which stands in the middle of the room, one of them gives a little shriek as a rabbit skipping across her feet gets entangled in the laces of her dress, and the other one quickly ducks her head as a pigeon and a parrot nearly meet on her pretty feathered hat. These ladies are evidently foreigners and belong to the official circle which, during the short years that the mysterious city was the capital of a great country, lent it an ephemeral brilliancy. They are searchers of the occult and interested in the new phenomena, known by so few in those days. They have unearthed the forgotten old painter whose little adopted daughter, Gioia, is supposed to have great mediumnistic powers.

Some weak tea in dusty cracked earthenware cups is set before the ladies and they are asked to drink in order to encourage the spirits. When this ceremony has been reluctantly performed Gioia, a child of twelve, draws near the table, and the maid-servant is called and sits down near the child.

The maid is a most peculiar-looking woman, with a long oval face, deadly pale, and squinting eyes that are hardly ever raised. Her long yellow fingers are twisted in a ghastly way, and form a strange contrast to the lovely hands of the ladies as they lie side by side on the table.

The room is nearly dark, and only the reflection of the afterglow on the river plays on the jewelled fingers of the ladies.

We are told that Ursula, the maid, is an ex-nun from the 'Sepolte vive' (buried alive); that ill-treatment is the cause of her deformed hands, and that she was turned out of the convent in the revolution. The ladies shrewdly guess that some close tie unites the old wizard, the woman, and the child.

The swish of the water against the basement of the house and the faint hum of the city alone break the silence.

The jewellers put up the shutters before their booths below; and a large white moon rises over the wooded ridges of Vallombrosa.

'See the fluffy white rabbit in the moonlight!' the older lady says. 'Oh, look!' whispers the other one; and out of the floor arises a filmy mist like a piece of white gauze held up by an invisible hand.

And then another and another one rise like the flowers' ghosts in a marshy meadow at eventide. On every side the floor seems to open, and waves of mist grow out of every fissure.

They sway to and fro and shape themselves into figures and wave their arms in slow cadence. They are unstable and intangible, only their eyes shine with the passions and sorrows of past lives.

One stately presence floats towards the old man. It stands with folded arms, and its tender and melancholy gaze recalls the pencil drawing of the poet which hangs in the window.

The misty figures multiply and press nearer to the table.

The ladies shrink back, but the old man, the nun, and the child remain unmoved. The wizard points with his wizen finger to the darkest corner of the room, and there, floating and circling in mid air, faintly delineated, pressed in each other's arms, the ladies saw, or thought they saw, the figures of a man and woman.

As the two ladies drive across the Jeweller's Bridge, one of them says :—

' Is this the new science—the sixth sense which we are now to develop—or is it the old magicians' lore and the revival of long-forgotten secrets ? '

' It is both,' said the other one; 'and in future and not too distant days, the two will be united, not as black magic and a power for evil, but as white magic and for the good of the world.'

A score of years later than the days I have been speaking of, I was back in the mysterious city.

It was a capital no more, and had taken upon itself the quiet and reserved aspect of an old beauty that had given up the pleasures of the world.

It was towards the end of May, and I was wandering with a friend—a writer of delightful stories—in the fields not distant from the villa where he spends some months in happy work each year.

We were walking along wide grass-paths which, bordered by vine-draped trees, intersect the fields of corn and maize and the olive-yards, in the midst of which the villas with their gardens stand.

We could see above the high box-hedges the crenellated tower and the roof of the long grey house.

It had been a watch-tower in the days of the Goths and the Lombards, and the most imaginative of the new-world writers had composed his most fantastic and romantic novel under its shadow.

The green corn stood high all around us, and the warm scent of the blossoming vine was upon the air.

We saw coming to meet us along the path which led to the peasant's house a little old woman with a bright purple kerchief tied over her white hair.

It was Sunday, and she was dressed in her best, and held a Mass Book in her hand.

' You read without spectacles ! I congratulate you ! ' my friend said.

' Si Signore ! ' she answered, ' I used to have some glasses, and when I was ninety I broke them, and that is six or seven years ago, and I find I do not want them now.'

And then she told us that she was the mother of the old man, who tilled all the land around with his children and grandchildren—a numerous clan. She had always lived in the white house with the cool arches and paved threshing-ground in front of it. She remembered the terrible wars when she was a child, and how the tyrant with his legions perished in the northern snows, and then at last after more horrors and terrors the world was ridded of him and he was shut up on an island.

She was well and happy, but had only been twice to the beautiful city, which lay but a mile away on the other side of the little medieval piazza which crowns the olive-shaded heights.

As she was talking, the sound of young voices came to our ears ; and out of another grassy avenue about fifty paces ahead a little procession appeared amidst the green and sturdy corn.

First, walked a lady, tall, long-limbed, and slim— almost a girl. In her crown of copper-coloured hair scintillated a large butterfly of precious many-coloured stones. Her small head was poised on a wide and statuesque throat, her arms and shoulders were bare, and a flashing gem on her breast held together a shimmering silvery scarf over a trailing rose-coloured dress, which appeared rosier still in the level rays of the setting sun. Rose-coloured slippers, embroidered in gold and pale-green stones, pressed lightly on the carpet of daisies, and the folds of her long satin dress brushed against the buttercups and ragged robins in the grass. She holds by one hand a fair clear-eyed boy dressed all in white. He chatters in a northern language to his young mother.

A little space behind them walks a tall man in the irreproachable garb of the upper British servant of a great house, carrying a large key, and by his side a handsome dark-eyed woman, in white cap and apron, holds in her arms a smaller child and coos to it in the dulcet accent of the country.

We watch them walking on to a small postern door in the high grey wall which encircles the *podere*.

The servant unlocks it and we perceive that it leads into a lane bordered on the other side by a convent ending in a small chapel. The convent has no windows below the first story, and these are barred and shuttered in such a way that the nuns can only look heavenward and never by any chance catch a glimpse of who passes in the country lane.

Beyond the convent, already wrapt in the evening shade, lay the towers and palaces, the churches and campaniles of the mysterious city.

The young mother turns at the door and stoops

to kiss her children.   The little boy clings to her dress
and wants to come with her to protect her, he says ;
but she tells him gently that this is impossible, as she
dines at some neighbouring villa.   She draws together
her shimmering garments and steps out into the
darkling lane followed by the solemn servant.   The
old woman was still standing beside us, and I asked
her who the lady was, but she said she knew not her
name, but that she was the wife of some great *milordo*
who had taken the villa with the watch-tower for a
month or two, because when the lady was a child she
had lived in the mysterious city, and whenever the
month of May came round she longed for the flowers
and the sun.

'What a strange and lovely vision!' said the
novelist ; ' and this is the only spot in the world where
one could come across it in such surroundings.'

The western declivities of the hill, upon which
the villa with the watch-tower stands, are in the spring
curtained with a wealth of blossom, white and red,
amongst which the silver olive almost disappears.

Many smaller villas nestle there in rural solitude as
if they were a hundred miles away from any town.

In one of these villas lived an artist with his family,
his wife and married sons and daughters with their
children.   They were all of them highly educated,
refined, and gentle people, devoted to music and
painting, and keeping much to themselves.   I knew,

however, that humble and pious as they were, they had independent and liberal ideas in religion and were befriended with some of the most eminent thinkers and pioneers of a more spiritual faith.

One cold winter, the artist's wife, the mother and grandmother, a woman bright, intelligent and energetic though almost eighty, went to sleep peacefully. I heard that a Mass was to be said for her at a village church not far from the house where she had passed her happy and peaceful life.

It was on a bright and crisp January morning, quite early, that I bent my steps through the olive-groves, down the narrow steep lane where in March the scarlet poppies nod over the high walls, down to the sunlit plain, and again a narrow path which leads to the steps that encircle a quaint fountain and land us on the great sunny grassplot where stands the little church on the summit of a knoll.

Some young peasants were sitting on the low wall which borders the smooth lawn around the church, and I stopped a moment to gaze down the wide valley closed in the distance by the great marble alps which glistened in the morning sun.

Unwillingly, I turned from the bright landscape to enter the church, which I thought, according to the habit of the country, would be all draped in black.

I held my breath for an instant as I pushed aside the leather curtain, as a flood of soft and brilliant light, a glory of colour, and the scent of many flowers met my senses.

The church was almost empty; only a few peasant women knelt on the bay-strewn floor, and a little nearer the altar I saw a small group of persons clad in black.

The high altar appeared to me like a flight of lights and flowers towards heaven. Every one of the many white and crimson wax candles was surrounded with what seemed bunches of growing narcissi, and higher still great sprays of pink roses crept up to the gold and crimson draperies which fell from the ceiling.

The side altars also were full of light and flowers, and the great candelabras in the nave were shrouded in tall olive-branches which mingled picturesquely with the chains of glittering crystals which hung around them.

The marble balustrade around the altar was a bed of violets and daffodils with the morning dew still on them.

At the altar a tall young priest, in gold and crimson, officiated in a simple and dignified way, and four other priests in red and white assisted him. A feeling of peace and happiness stole over me, and I felt respect and admiration for these humble law-abiding people, who had the courage to go against all usages and traditions of their country and gave expression to their own feelings and beliefs.

As I stepped out into the golden sunlight again, the daughter followed me, and said :—

'You understand, do you not, that for our dear mother who was so góod, so strong, so pure, we cannot mourn sadly? A festival of light and flowers is what must accompany her dear soul to heaven.'

One fresh and sunny morning I knock at my friend's door. He lives in the villa where Owen Meredith wrote his 'Good Night in the Porch,' when he was scarcely more than a boy.

'Would you like to go and see the villa which Mrs. Browning describes in "Aurora Leigh"? It is close by here, but you would never guess at its existence. Ten years ago, I remember Clare Claremont living there in two rooms all by herself. She was a daily governess then, and none of her pupils knew that she was the mother of Allegra.'

We went along a winding road and entered by an old iron gate on to a vast grass-covered piazzale, and so suddenly and steeply does the ground fall off that one almost has the feeling of floating in the air.

The house stands fantastically aloof from everything, and from its terraces the eye roves over mountains and valleys a hundred miles apart.

The mysterious city lies spread out below like a preciously woven carpet, and all the riches of that beauteous land enthrall the soul and eyes. A great square tower rears itself up out of tangles of lilies and roses into the serene blues of the summer skies and in winter disappears in sun-tinted mists, which rise white and chill from the river-shore.

Many pathetic figures have paced up and down beneath this tower. It was owned by a patriot and poet, exiled by the popular faction, and he stood here conversing with his best and most trusted friend, the mystic singer whose glory will never fade.

Out of that window in the tower chamber, a girl— almost a child—gazes anxiously. Her great black eyes contrast curiously with the masses of very fair hair which frames her small white face. She is to be married shortly to the son of the powerful noble who owns the greatest and the most splendid palace in the town. But this man is vicious, a bore, and almost an idiot; and she loves a boy tall and strong, of high bearing with flashing blue eyes and a ring of courage in his voice; but, alas! he is poor and a nameless offshoot of the family she is to enter.

' I must go, my beloved one,' he whispers to the girl as he stands on a dark night below her barred and grated window. ' I must go to the wars; but let Padre Anselmo bless us before I go. You can resist the wishes of your parents till I return covered with glory, and then you can divulge to them that you are my wife and we shall be happy.'

In the white and chilly dawn these two stood before the altar of the little church among the cypresses, and in the midday sun she saw him caracoling on his white charger, with the crimson trappings, down the walled road which led to the gate of the town.

It was the bonny month of May, and battles were won and lost ; but the blue-eyed boy never returned.

It is Christmas-time when we enter the tower chamber. Low and uneven arches support the vaulted ceiling. A double oaken door with heavy locks alone gives access to this prisonlike room.

The girl, who was a rose in May, now lies like a broken lily on a pallet bed, and in her arms is clasped a wailing babe.

A handsome dark-browed woman enters the room locking the door after her. ' We must put an end to this,' she says ; ' your father returns to-night and he could never keep the secret ; besides, the child's cry might be heard by the serving-men he brings ; the danger is too great.'

With this she snatches the whimpering babe from her daughter's arms, and with strong deft hands she draws a silken cord around its throat and twists it tightly upwards. Only a slight gurgling sound is heard, and the young mother groans.

In the garden court, under a stone flag overhung by a bush of blue rosemary, the babe is laid, and to this day it is called ' the grave of the child with the golden locks.'

A hundred years later we view another scene.

A lady sits trembling in the great withdrawing-room

hung with red and gold *sopra riso*. Everything around her is rich and splendid. She is the daughter of an ancient house, but her hunchback husband is allied to the reigning Princes, which makes him powerful and his influence great. She trembles, because she knows that the man she loves has been bidden that very day to a great banquet by the wily Pietro de Rossi, and she is certain that he will attempt her lover's life.

The hunchback, clad in black velvet and white satin, is at that moment arranging and rearranging the flasks of sparkling wine which stand upon the festive board which has been set surrounded by orange- and lemon-trees within the garden *loggia*. He shakes a white powder into the golden cup which stands at the place of honour and then rinses it out again, first with water and then with wine, so that nothing can be seen. But poisons in those days were subtle and strong, and that evening the young and handsome Prior of the great Badia of F——, who entered Orders because the fair hostess of that evening was refused to him by a grasping father, lies on the white road which leads up to the Abbey with his still pale face bathed by the July moon.

Though not so rich as Pietro de Rossi, he was a Prince of the reigning family, and the murder was not forgiven.

Before the moon was full again the hunchback lay

stabbed in the back, one stormy night in the long and narrow street of the ' Discontented Ones.'

Carina, carina ! ' called out the old nurse to the lady as she announced the husband's death. ' You need not live on raw eggs any more.'

Outside the southern and eastern walls of the town, wooded knolls alternate with lovely green valleys. Two score years ago, only half a dozen neglected villas and two or three convents occupied those sites.

Charles Lever lived in one of those villas and wrote some of his inimitable Irish stories there.

At the present time, one of the most beautiful drives of the world has been created on this site by the exertions of one of the city's most prominent patriots. Hundreds of houses nestle on those gentle slopes amongst thickets of oleander and *Oleas fragrans*. Green-shuttered and jealously fenced in from the gaze of passers-by, these villas, though new or comparatively so, give an impression of extreme mystery. Nobody knows who lives in them, or, indeed, whether they are inhabited or not. Vaguely, you will hear it mentioned that a Russian Princess, very rich and past fifty, lives in one of them because she has run away with a barber. In another, a famous political character is supposed to hide himself from anarchists, whom he deserted after having been their leader for a long time. A little farther on is the deserted studio of a famous sculptor, long since dead, who electrified the world by the first tinted statue. Then at the end of one of the most withdrawn valleys in the midst of grass-fields and overshadowed by large limes, a young couple, but lately very well known in the most brilliant circles of a great capital, are supposed to live. She was the fair-haired and lovely wife of some northern Prince, and he the scion of a noble family of southern origin. The Prince, alas! will not divorce, and the mysterious city draws its veil over the unpardonably happy pair.

Let us intrude into one of the smallest and most neglected-looking of these houses, merely to see what surprises they offer.

A shabby man-servant reluctantly opens the gate after much ringing. The usual expanse of rough shingle planted with conifers and oleanders faces the house. Some raised voices and the fumes of food fried in oil inform us that the kitchen lies to the left. To the right, in an arbour, we see two little boys—one of them a mere baby—having their evening meal under the auspices of a very prim-looking nursery governess. Only bread and milk is set before the children, although they are Princes of a royal house and a crown may one day rest upon the younger one's head. At the back of the house the ground rises steep and unexpectedly, and great flights of wide and stately steps lead up to what appears to be a dead wall with a closed porch in its centre. The indolent man-servant motions us to proceed, and we begin the ascent; he follows at a distance dangling a key.

The sun is setting and gilds the tips of the cypresses which stand on each side of the steps, whilst their lower part is already in deep shade. The man slowly inserts the great key into the rusty lock and pushes the door open with his shoulder. We pass and he bangs it to after us. We stand upon the rocky ledge of a stream and look across it far out into the country. A group of cypresses and some half-ruined masonry, the remains of some stately gatehouse, betray that this must once have formed a part of some princely domain. The scene is so surprising and unexpected that we do not at first notice the slender figure of a lady dressed all in white, sitting in the shadow of the rocks. Had she been hewn in stone and covered with lichens I should have thought her a meet statue for this *mise en scène*. She might have been the goddess of repose or a dryad watching the murmuring waters; but her velvet brown eyes are not of stone, and her abundant *cendré* hair lies soft and silky on her shoulders. A large star sapphire fastens her soft and spotless draperies on her breast. A book of sonnets rests open on her knee, and a guitar lies on the grass beside her.

She is the mother of the boys, and is seeking consolation and oblivion in the territory of the city ' where none inquires.'

A great villa, almost a fortress, stands on the slopes of the mountains only three miles from the city, on the road where Romola met Savonarola on that sultry summer's day. In the Middle Ages this castle frowned down with its battlements as a perpetual menace on the mysterious city, for it held one of the northern mountain passes and could at any time have flooded the emerald cup of the valley with enemies from the vast plains which stretch to the foothills of the Alps.

Less than three centuries ago a gay young noble, the head of an illustrious race, lived within these gigantic walls. He was handsome and skilled in all courtly arts. His consort was the daughter of a powerful and reigning house. She was much older than her husband and her masculine features marked the difference still more.

This great lady had a soul of fire and a will of iron. Jealousy preyed upon her spirit like a vulture.

Her young husband whiled away his time with the chase and masquerades. He instructed his falcons and ordered himself fine clothes, to which latter pursuit the *jeunesse dorée* of the mysterious city are very partial even now.

About a decade after their marriage, the Duchess Veronica, who was now nearing forty, heard through one of her spies that her young spouse was in the habit of visiting a house in the street of the almonds—a lonely district surrounded by gardens and vineyards—

and that in this house lived a beautiful girl called Caterina, a weaver of fine laces. The lady's resolution was soon taken. She instructed her confidential tiring-woman to get at once as many yards of the finest holland linen as would make twelve shirts, and to buy from Caterina all the lace she had and trim the shirts with it. The work must be done within the next ten days for the Duke's birthday, as she wished to present the shirts to him. He should have a birthday gift so beautiful as he had never had before. The morning of the auspicious day dawned and a page entered the Duke's room obedient to his call.

The boy bore in his arms a basket covered with a cloth of blood-red Genoese velvet, and, setting it down by the Duke's bed, said :—

'Greetings from her Excellency the Duchess ; and knowing how much her noble spouse values fine laces, she sends this dozen of fine holland shirts trimmed with the best laces she could find as a birthday present, and hopes that this year may continue as happily for your Excellency as it has begun.'

The Duke, pleased and astonished at so infrequent a mark of attention, threw back the velvet cover and looked admiringly at the fine linen and precious laces it had hidden.

Daintily he lifted up one of the shirts, intending to wear it that very day in recognition of his wife's kindness ; but as he did so, a long wisp of soft golden hair curled round his fingers. He looked down astonished, and his eyes assumed a stare of horror as he noticed a spot of crimson blood filtering through the laces.

His mind, paralysed by terror, had lost all control over his movements, and violently with both hands he tore away the contents of the basket, scattering them through the whole room.

At the bottom of the basket lay the beautiful head of Caterina! The Duke had loved her not only for her surpassing loveliness, but for her gentle and affectionate nature, which had been his solace from the stern and imperious society of his Duchess.

A wreath of golden curls lay around the small pale face like a halo, and the transparent lids were only half closed over the dark blue eyes. Turned to stone with grief and horror, history says that the Duke never saw his wife again.

Gayer thoughts are, however, conjured up by the remembrance of this stately villa some forty years ago.

During the short years when the mysterious city was a capital, two artists of world-wide renown dwelt there.

The gayest of the gay went in and out of the wide-open portals and were hospitably feasted within the great hall.

The walls were covered with pictures and huge mirrors framed in brightest gold. The costly furniture recalled the most brilliant days of the second Empire.

The master of this sumptuous home had been

worshipped throughout Europe not only for his matchless voice, but also for his charm, his good looks, his great air, for he was a scion of an impoverished but noble family. He had been a young and impecunious soldier when the impresario of a great opera heard him by chance singing, as he was bathing in a river in northern Italy, and called out to him, saying :—

' Throw up the army and come with me ; every note in your throat is worth a piece of gold.'

And mountains of gold he had amassed together with the lady of the house.

She looked as if Norma's wreath of oak-leaves must always crown her classic brow ; and her splendid, full, and yet so mellow, voice will still be remembered by some.

In those days only the three pretty little daughters —nicknamed by the ever-wagging sharp tongues of the mysterious city, sometimes ' marionettes ' and sometimes ' grisettes,' in allusion to their respective parents —used to warble songs like so many birds, for the delectation of their mother's guests.

Every night they could be seen sitting all three in a row on two chairs in their mother's opera-box.

In the morning, Norma used regularly to shop on the Jeweller's Bridge and regally dispense her money and the presents she had bought with it.

Sometimes when guests bidden to a sumptuous feast arrived, they were amused to find that, except

their hosts, not a soul was within the walls of the great
villa, as every single servant had departed an hour
before, scared by the tragic anger of the great *prima
donna*.

Such little contretemps, however, did not affect
the souls of great artists, and life went well and merrily
at the great house until the sad day when all was broken
up by the sudden death of the lady, and the luxurious
furniture, the plate, the jewels, were hastily sold for
a mere song and the villa stood lonely and forgotten
through many decades, passing from hand to hand,
till the great earthquake almost gutted it, and its
owner, a very old lady, whose husband had served
in foreign capitals under a legitimist, Orleanist, and
Imperial Government, and who had withdrawn after
the *anée terrible*, scared by what appeared to him
the monster republic, had settled in the peaceful
shadow of the great eaves.

The earthquake, however, appeared even more full
of terrors than the Republic, and so the lady fled back
to Paris, never to return.

A lovely walk through a green valley and along
a pine-clad hillside takes us to another great villa
where, at the time I have been speaking of, the favourite
daughter of an Emperor lived with the man she loved,
or had loved, and the child she adored.

This Princess was still very handsome, and she
had always been witty and original.

The southern slope upon which her house stood

was the last spur of the great mountain which stands out so imposingly over the long green valley. The house was absolutely lined with gobelins and heated up to the temperature of an orchid-house.

In the daytime the Princess walked in faultlessly fitting dust-coloured garments along the white roads on the sunny mountain side, followed by a splendidly horsed English carriage and servants in Imperial liveries. At night she drove through dark and lonely lanes to the mysterious city to gamble and sup with some of her brother's subjects.

The little daughter led a lonely life, for her father was not royal, and her Imperial cousins looked askance at her. A kind but circumscribed English nurse was her only companion.

This child's greatest happiness consisted in being allowed to drive to a neighbouring villa, a real Medicean one, in which a dear old fairy lived who tried to make everybody happy.

The little girl brought a silver *batterie de cuisine* with her and cooked her dinner on the fairy's kitchen range.

This range was never used at other times, for the fairy being a fairy did not live as we humans do. She did not sleep in a bed, but simply on a kind of big portfolio laid on the floor, and she averred that in the morning she and her big dog jumped into the fountain together and then shook themselves, and then they had some bread and figs and that was quite enough.

One fine morning, the little countess—for it was thus that she was styled—visited the fairy, and said to her :—

' I will tell you a secret if you promise not to repeat it.'

The fairy of course promised, and also kept it many years till it mattered no more.

' To-day is mamma's birthday, and so she permits me to open her telegrams, and there was one from the Emperor Napoleon congratulating her, and it ended by saying : " Cette année nous aurons la guerre ! " '

This was on the seventh of January 1870 !

Another story the fairy told me was this one.

We were looking down from the terrace upon the roof of a fine square villa now a convent, and she said :—

That is the villa where Bianca Capello lived, and it belonged to Count S—— in the beginning of the century. His daughter Augusta was a great friend of mine and told me that when she was a child she was playing at ball with some other children and that when they threw the ball against a certain part of the wall it sounded hollow.

' Count S—— had that part of the wall knocked down, and in a recess they found a large red velvet dressing-case all lined with white satin, absolutely fresh, and furnished with beautiful white-and-gold Venetian glass, with Bianca Capello's cypher upon it.'

My old fairy lives now—for fairies never die—and

she is as bright, lively, and amusing as ever. She still adheres to the fashions of the novels of Thackeray and Dickens, and wears a crinoline, the amplitude of which now strikes us as something oddly romantic, in some of the early Rossetti's and Burne Jones's, and arrests our imaginations as exotic and uncannily seductive in the decadent pen-and-inks of Aubrey Beardsley.

Whatever happens this fairy of ours will always keep her place in the hearts of her many friends, and will ever be alive and present to them.

On our way back from the fairy, we passed many ancient houses and towers and *loggias*, every one of which might have been the scene of one of Boccaccio's tales. They lie within high walls, and only a half-open gate now and then allows us a glance along grass-paths between vines, ending in the deep shade of secular trees. The ground in winter here is almost marshy, and in summer the white dust lies many inches deep, and that is why that district is called ' In via polverosa.'

Very suddenly, we stand in a dark and narrow lane before a long low house with many cupolas. It is backed by tall trees. The whole building on this side seems to consist of a dead wall, but whichever side we tried to enter on, it always seemed to be the wrong one, and the object of our search retired before us like a mirage.

We had vaguely heard that the eccentric lady who now owns the palace and inhabits it for seven days every two or three years, never during her stay leaves her couch, which she shares with several giant wolf-hounds. She terrifies the neighbourhood, who look upon her as a witch and a magician to be feared, but not loved.

Somewhat more than half a century ago, the sound of revelry never ceased within these now so empty and forsaken halls.

A Prince, who drew his fabulous wealth from the mines of a savage and quite unexhausted country, had collected here everything that art and luxury could yield and that money could buy. His wife, the beautiful and witty descendant of a new but Imperial house, attracted around her whatever the international society of that day could offer of its best. Men and women of the smartest and also the most intellectual set of several capitals met there. Statesmen, artists, writers, poets, and wits were all received with equal graciousness by the mistress of the house.

Great winter-gardens—a novelty almost unknown in those days—extended from both wings of the palace. The floors of all the rooms were of precious marbles and covered with carpets of velvet pile as thick as moss. The tables were of jasper, malachite, and amethyst, and rich embroideries and brocades, half hidden by a mass of priceless pictures, covered the walls.

One of these pictures, which used to strike the

imagination of the young, was Delaroche's execution of Mary, Queen of Scots. It was, I believe, painted for a wager, to show that it was possible to produce an impressive picture without a single eye in it.

The Queen's eyes are bandaged, and the executioner is stooping down with his eyes averted. The priest, who has just pronounced his blessing, has both his eyes closed, and the two women in the background are weeping on each other's shoulders.

A small pink saucer was one day thrust into my hand as I was looking at some rare china the house contained. It was quite plain except for a little white medallion representing two little cupids in sepia. I could see no particular merit in it, but I was told that it was Rose Dubarry and had just been valued at a thousand pounds !

The nabob Prince was followed in the villa by his son or his nephew. He had a pale and beautiful young wife; she was very delicate and only every now and then people caught sight of her large glowing eyes and a sombre *parure* of magnificent sapphires, behind the red silk curtains of her opera-box. The Prince, her husband, used on the contrary to lean forward holding in his straw-coloured irreproachably gloved hands—the fashion of the day—a black opera-glass set with one huge yellow diamond.

In little more than a year the young wife had faded away, and for the last forty years the grass has sprouted upon the gravel paths. The trees have grown up with a wilderness of underwood beneath them, the rooms of the palace are empty, and through the broken windows the summer sun shines, and winter rains sweep across the marble floors. A casual passer-by does not even suspect where the stately gates once opened to the élite of European society, so thickly are they overgrown with brushwood and rampant creepers. ' Sic transit gloria mundi ! '

One day in early spring, as I was wandering with my friend in that fruitful plain which extends like a garden of blossoms along the southern margin of the river, we came to an ancient stone portal over which two cypresses stood sentinel with their feet in the earth and their heads in the clouds.

' Here,' my friend said, ' lived during the days of the Capital, one of the most charming, the most distinguished and clever men I ever met. Let us go in, and you will see how picturesque his retreat was.'

As we approached the house—I should almost call it the hold—it appeared to me to be quite a ruin covered with ivy and roses ; but on turning the corner, I noticed that one wing was still inhabited. It was an old and hoary fortress with two low square towers, and its birth must date back to the dark and tumultuous days of northern invasions into these sunny climes.

At present the grounds in the vicinity of the house are planted with exotic shrubs and flowers, as the owner is an enthusiast and an expert on sub-tropical vegetation.

'I often used to walk out here in those days,' my friend said, 'to see Sir J. H——. He was a most remarkable man, and it was impossible to know him without loving him. Nobody really knew exactly who he was, and I have heard it said that he came of semi-royal descent. He was certainly one of the handsomest and most dignified-looking men, and his features re-called those of the first gentlemen of Europe, at the time he was at his very best. He soon rose in his career to the highest honours, and was the trusted friend of kings and statesmen, and this country owes to him in a large degree its present unity. Then, suddenly, at the most brilliant moment of his career, some misunderstanding, which has never been cleared up, arose between him and his chief, and he resigned and came to live here at this lonely villa. His many friends were deeply hurt at what they considered this unjust treatment; but he had so many resources in himself that time never hung heavy on his hands. He was a poet, a writer, and a painter, and interested in all he saw. Though hardly even his most intimate friends suspected it, he did not live quite alone at the villa. In the days of his official life he had admired a very beautiful and cultured woman who was linked to a man, cruel and ferocious, as this country still sometimes produces.

'When H—— resigned his position, the lady fled

from her husband and put herself under his protection, but never by word or sign did he make allusion to her presence. Once only, when I entered his room unannounced, did I detect a symptom of a lady's presence in the house. It was a small work-basket, forgotten, on the table.

'Do you see how absolutely a brilliant public life can be hidden and buried in this loneliest of places? Though barely a few miles from town, only the neighbouring peasants know how to thread this maze of narrow country lanes. So there he lived, a man who for twenty years more might have swayed the fortunes of nations.'

On our way back to town we passed Lever's house. My friend had known him also, and all his jolly household, and said that one day when he was staying with him at San Terenzio they went for a sail on the gulf of Spezia, and as they got to about the middle of the bay one of the daughters casually remarked, 'Can you swim? for we are going to swamp the boat!' No sooner said than done, and the whole party had to swim home.

Arising amongst the low hills which give the country its richest and choicest vintage, the green and silent waters of the Greve gently circle around the cypress-clothed rock which is crowned by the great Carthusian monastery. They then wander for a couple of miles through a green and sheltered valley before uniting themselves to the great river, to flow with it into the blue waters of the Tyrrhenean sea.

The gentle declivities of the narrow valley, which takes its name from the Greve, are covered on one side with copses of young oaks and knots of cypresses. In these woods, under bushes of tall Mediterranean heath, we find the slender star of Bethlehem, the pink orchis, the cuckoo-flower, and the dark-blue burridge.

On the other side of the stream the hills face straight to the south and are swathed in blossom from February to May. Below the fruit-trees, the ground is spread first with a cloth of golden aconite, then little by little it is embroidered by the delicate wind-flower and the great anemones in their triumphant scarlet, violet, and purple, their flashing pink and soft grey-blue. These are in their turn displaced by tulips of every hue, the tall crimson ones, the frail lemon-coloured, and those white and red striped, which put one in mind of the pari-coloured hose of the gilded youths in the old masters' pictures; indeed, those flower-fields in the spring recall Ghirlandajo's and Piero di Cosimo's brightest creations. A few rather decayed-looking villas and farm-houses, with buttress and tower, are set on these slopes, where no breath of winter ever blows. They are surrounded by overgrown and tangled gardens of rosemary, lavender, and myrtle. The roses which creep over their walls are never checked by frost or cold. No carriage-road leads up to them, and they can only be

reached by steep and narrow paths which serpentine
between high walls and olive-yards. Those who
could gain an entrance to the jealously closed gates
would be astonished to find in some of them
beauty, art, and refinement—even luxury—and men
and women whose names were once in everybody's
mouth and who held brilliant places in society. They
have carried with them to this hidden nook the great
woes and sometimes the great happinesses which have
driven them away from mankind.

As I was musing over the strangeness of destiny—
for I had known some of these self-made outlaws in
former days—my friend recalled me to the present
time.

'Do you see that great villa at the end of the valley?
That is where Ouida lived for fourteen years.'

I followed the direction indicated with my eyes,
along the stream bordered by slender pollard poplars
exactly like those in Corot's masterpieces. I saw,
almost hidden by a *bouquet* of tall trees, the roof of
a large house.

'I knew Ouida intimately, and for many years.
She was always surrounded by a great troop of yap-
ping dogs. They were nearly all of them white,
but she would pick up any mongrel in the street.
She was generally dressed in trailing white silks and
laces, though in her younger days she spent great sums
upon " confections " she ordered from Worth, who was
then at his best. Her old mother she always clothed

in rich black garments as a contrast. Her father was a Frenchman, and I think he taught at the young ladies' school in England where her mother was a teacher. Ouida never knew whether he was dead or alive, as he belonged to many secret societies, and the last she saw of him was when one day, shortly after having published her first novel, "Idalia," she was sitting on a bench in Kensington Gardens, he suddenly appeared out of the bushes and congratulated her on her achievement.

'She said she was sixteen then, and she never saw him afterwards.

It was here she wrote many of her novels and the "Village Commune," which are those houses you see there beyond the stream.

'Ouida certainly was a genius; she had a power of language, a love of nature, and, above all, a *flair* for *couleur locale* almost unequalled.

'If you consider that she wrote "Pascarel" when she had been but three weeks in Italy, you must confess that the achievement is only second to Byron's lines on the Dying Gladiator, after having seen it for the first time. Ouida was extravagant, generous, insolent, ungrateful, unreasonable, and revengeful, but she was tender to animals and to the poor. I think that the secret of her bitterness lay in her exceeding lack of charm and her plainness, which a woman with her intense love of beauty must have felt very deeply. She had not even the compensating quality of a lovely voice. She was very proud of her small hands and feet, but they were small in excess, and made her face look heavy. Her only good feature were large dark blue eyes. She used to wear her hair hanging down her back long after she was quite middle aged. Her conversation was not witty, as she was so often aggrieved or sentimental. She did not like women as a rule and only made very few exceptions, either on account of their beauty, position, or cleverness. She had no sense of proportion or any knowledge of the world, except in her books. She has described the mysterious city as no writer has ever done, for she loved the very stones of it and understood their language.'

As my friend finished speaking, we stood before the iron gates of the villa. It has been uninhabited ever since Ouida left it, and the owner appears to continue her system, which was never to allow even a branch to be lopped off. The sleeping beauty could not have slept in a more unapproachable palace. I sighed, for one always feels sad in a place orphaned of great or lovely thoughts.

If anybody were for a whole year to wander around the mysterious city and visit a villa every day, there would still be just as many left which they had not seen, and about which they could discover nothing, and they are sure to have stories just as strange and thrilling as their walls are picturesque and suggestive.

The *contadinis*, whom you may question, will generally say that they do not know the names of the people who live within those silent houses, but that they believe that they are *forestieri*, and they are not sure they are Christians.

Sometimes in our peregrinations I wished that the little owls which nestled under the wide eaves and the rubbish which had accumulated before the entrance door had been left undisturbed, for modern taste backed by easily acquired money is often violent and subversive.

Old villas are turned into houses that look like a Riviera hotel, or the suburban residence of a semitic magnate. Ancient grass-clad terraces, overshadowed by semicircles of secular cypresses, are desecrated by banal conceits in stone, out of keeping with the mellow harmony of the past ; but, on the whole, the ephemeral and mysterious society offers a harvest of beauty, originality, and especially of *imprévu*, to the mind as well as to the eye, unattained by any other place.

Those whose names have been wiped off the register of the great world and who have sunk into the golden misty oblivion of the mysterious city, can be counted by hundreds and thousands ; but even were their numbers doubled, they still would find countless portals open within which they can create for themselves a paradise of surpassing beauty, and a life of work or contemplation in which they can find the peace and forgetfulness which, to storm-tossed wounded souls, means the nearest approach to happiness they can hope for on this side of the stream which divides them from the fields of pink asphodel.

THE END

PRINTED BY
SPOTTISWOODE AND CO. LTD , COLCHESTER
LONDON AND ETON

Recent Publications

Large Post 8vo.   7s. 6d. net.

Recollections, Grave and Gay.

By Mrs. BURTON HARRISON.

Times.—' Mrs. Burton Harrison's recollections of the many celebrities in various fields whom she has met will be of considerable interest.'

Daily Chronicle.—' Her book throughout is full of good companionship and good reading.'

Second Edition.   With 2 Portraits.   Crown 8vo.   3s. 6d. net.

Murphy : A Message to Dog Lovers.

By Major GAMBIER-PARRY.

Author of "Annals of an Eton House," "The Pageant of my Day," &c.

Punch.—' It is a simple history of an Irish terrier, a beautiful and supremely intelligent animal, who devoted to the service and joy of his master an unsurpassable genius for love and friendship. Let dog lovers all the world over read this book. They will be as grateful for it as I am.'

Plays and Players in Modern Italy.

With 14 Illustrations.
Small Demy 8vo.
7s. 6d. net.

By ADDISON McLEOD.

Daily Telegraph.—' Mr. Addison McLeod's agreeable book grows upon the reader in interest and significance the further the study proceeds. The author is genuinely interested in his subject and ends by making us as interested as himself.'

Men and Measures.   Large Post 8vo. 7s. 6d. net.

A History of Weights and Measures, Ancient and Modern.

By EDWARD NICHOLSON, F.I.C., F.C.S.

The Standard.—' The most exhaustive and interesting work on this subject we have ever seen.'

Spectator.—' This highly interesting history. Not the least interesting part of the book is to be found in the curious differences brought about by local customs and other causes.'

With 5 Maps.   Large Post 8vo.   6s. net.

Morocco in Diplomacy.

By E. D. MOREL.

Author of "Affairs of West Africa," " Great Britain and the Congo,"
" Nigeria : its People and its Probl— ," &c.

` *Daily News.*—' Written with the lucidity and force   ~ne of the most skilful publicists in this country. It presents a reading which is not the official or the vulgar reading. The orthodox view is about as false as any version can be.'

London : Smith, Elder & Co., 15 Waterloo Place, S.W.

Recent Publications

The Child of the Dawn.
Large Post 8vo, 7s. 6d. net.

By ARTHUR C. BENSON.
Author of 'From a College Window,' 'Beside Still Waters,' &c.

Times.—'In this, more than in any of his books, the singular charm of a sweet and gracious mind is opened out to us, and the old truth is told with new beauty.'

With a Portrait. Crown 8vo. 2s. net.

The Robert Browning Centenary
Celebration at Westminster Abbey, May 7th, 1912.
Edited with an Introduction and Appendices by Professor KNIGHT.

Glasgow Herald.—'A neat little volume, forming an interesting souvenir of the occasion, which will appeal to all lovers of Browning.'

Crown 8vo. 3s. 6d. net.

The Brain of the Nation, and other Verses.
By CHARLES L. GRAVES.
Author of 'The Hawarden Horace,' 'Humours of the Fray,' &c.

Spectator.—'Mr. Graves's new volume possesses all the qualities with which his former work has made us familiar. His social and political satire is as witty as ever, and his rhythms and rhymes as neat.'

In Cloth, Red Edges. Demy 8vo. 2s. 6d. net.

The Epistles of St. Paul.
The Text prepared by The Right Hon.
Sir EDWARD CLARKE, P.C., K.C., Solicitor-General, 1886-92.
Author of 'Selected Speeches, with Introductory Notes,' &c.

Times.—'The alterations mean errors corrected and the meaning made clearer.'
Daily News.—'Sir Edward's Version is successful in combining the dignified and stately language of the Authorised Version with the greater accuracy and lucidity of the Revised, and it deserves careful attention.'

The Church in the Pages of "Punch."
With 6 Illustrations. Small Demy 8vo 6s. net.

By the Rev. D. WALLACE DUTHIE.
Author of 'A Bishop in the Rough,' &c.

** Including the parsons of the Church of England—the Roman Catholic priest —the dissenting minister—the Jew—the Spiritualist—and the Salvationist, &c.

Oxford Chronicle.—'Glancing through these lively pages we get a great deal of sheer amusement from Mr. Punch's keen-edged but rarely savage or cynical jests.'

London : Smith, Elder & Co., 15 Waterloo Place, S.W.

CPSIA information can be obtained
at www.ICGtesting.com
Printed in the USA
LVOW04s1149090117

520292LV00032B/926/P

9 781330 519226